COLLIER NUCLEUS SCIENCE FICTION

Consulting Editor: James Frankel

The Compleat Traveller in Black by John Brunner
Eye in the Sky by Philip K. Dick
Darker Than You Think by Jack Williamson
Star Bridge by Jack Williamson and James E. Gunn

Science Fiction and Fantasy by John Brunner

THE
Compleat
Traveller in Black

JOHN BRUNNER

COLLIER BOOKS
Macmillan Publishing Company
New York

Copyright © 1986 by Brunner Fact & Fiction Ltd.

Published by arrangement with Bluejay Books

Collier Books
Macmillan Publishing Company
866 Third Avenue, New York, NY 10022
Collier Macmillan Canada, Inc.

Library of Congress Cataloging-in-Publication Data
Brunner, John, 1934–
    The compleat traveller in black/John Brunner.—1st
Collier Books ed.
        p.   cm.
    ISBN 0-02-030720-9
    I. Title.
PR6052.R8C6   1989   89-9829   CIP
823'.914—dc20

First Collier Books Edition 1989

10 9 8 7 6 5 4 3 2 1

Printed in the United States of America

Contents

ONE

Imprint of Chaos

Ante mare et terras et quod tegit omnia coelum
unus erat toto naturae vultus in orbe
quen dixere Chaos: rudis indigestaque moles.

—Ovid: *Metamorphoses* I, 5

I

HE HAD MANY NAMES, but one nature, and this unique nature made him subject to certain laws not binding upon ordinary persons. In a compensatory fashion, he was also free from certain other laws more commonly in force.

Still, there was nothing to choose as regards rigidity between his particular set of laws and those others. And one rule by which he had very strictly to abide was that at set seasons he should overlook that portion of the All which had been allotted to him as his individual responsibility.

Accordingly, on the day after the conjunction of four significant planets in that vicinity, he set forth on a journey which was to be at once the same as and yet different from those uncountable which had preceded it.

It had been ordained that at this time, unless there were some pressing reason to the contrary, he should tramp along commonplace roads, and with goodwill enough—it was not a constituent of his nature that he should rail against necessity—he so arranged his route that it wound and turned and curved through all those zones where he might be made answerable for events, and ended within a short distance of where it had begun. It ended, to be precise, at the city called Ryovora: that place of all places in his domain where people had their heads screwed on the right way.

He did this for an excellent reason. It was an assurance to him that when he subsequently reviewed his findings the memory of one spot where he might justly feel pleased with his work would be uppermost in recollection.

* * *

Therefore, on a sunny morning when birds were singing and there were few clouds in a sky filled with the scent of flowers, garbed in a cloak of black like any wayfarer's, save that its blackness was exceptional, he began to trudge along a dusty road towards his first destination.

That was a great louring city upreared around a high tower, which was called by its inhabitants Acromel, the place where honey itself was bitter. It was sometimes a cause of mild astonishment—even to him of the many names and the single nature—that this most contrary of cities should be located within a few hours' walk of Ryovora. Nonetheless, it was so.

And to be able to state without risk of contradiction that anything whatsoever *was so* was a gage and earnest of his achievement.

Before him the road began to zigzag on the slope of a hill dotted with grey-leaved bushes. A local wind raised dust devils among the bushes and erased the footprints of those who passed by. It was under this hill that the traveller had incarcerated Laprivan of the Yellow Eyes, to whom memories of yesterday were hateful. Some small power remained to this elemental, and he perforce employed it to wipe yesterday's traces away.

He took his staff in hand—it was made of light, curdled with a number of interesting forces—and rapped once on an outcrop of bare rock at the side of the pathway.

"Laprivan!" he cried. "Laprivan of the Yellow Eyes!"

At his call the dust devils ceased their whirling. Resentfully, they sank back to the earth, so that the dust of which they were composed again covered the exposed roots of the bushes. Most folk in the district assumed that the leaves were grey from the dust of passage, or from their nature; it was not so.

Laprivan heaved in his underground prison, and the road shook. Cracks wide enough to swallow a farm cart appeared in its surface. From them, a great voice boomed.

"What do you want with me, today of all days? Have you not had enough, even now, of tormenting me?"

"I do not torment you," was the calm reply. "It is memory of your past dreadful acts that brings the pain."

"Leave me be, then," said the great voice sullenly. "Let me go on wiping away that memory."

"As you wish, so be it," the traveller answered, and gestured with his staff. The cracks in the road closed click; the dust devils re-formed; and when he looked back from the crest of the hill his footsteps had already been expunged.

The road wound on, empty, towards Acromel. For some distance before it actually reached there, it ran contiguous with the river called Metamorphia, a fact known to rather few, because although it seemed that this was the same river which poured in under the high black battlements of the city, it was not the same—for good and sufficient cause. It was the nature of the river Metamorphia to change the nature of things, and consequently it changed its own after flowing a prescribed number of leagues.

The traveller paused by a wall of stone and mud overlooking the dark stream, and meditatively regarded objects drifting past. Some had been fishes, perhaps; others were detritus of the banks—leaves, branches, rocks. Those which had been rocks continued to float, of course; those which had been of a flotatory nature sank.

He broke a cobble from the crumbling parapet of the wall, and cast it down. The alteration it underwent was not altogether pleasant to witness.

He raised his eyes after a while, and descried a girl on the opposite bank, who had come forward out of a clump of trees while he was lost in contemplation. She was extremely beautiful. Moreover, she had been at no pains to hide the fact, for she was dressed exclusively in her long, lovely hair.

"You also are aware of the nature of this river," she said after gazing at him for a little.

"I have been advised," the traveller conceded, "that the nature of this river is to change the nature of things, and consequently it changes its own nature also."

"Come down with me, then, and bathe in it!"

"Why should you wish your nature changed?" was the reply. "Are you not beautiful?"

"Beautiful I may be!" the girl cried passionately. "But I am without sense!"

"Then you are Lorega of Acromel, and your fame has spread far."

"I am Lorega, as you say." She fixed him with honey-colored eyes and shrugged the garb of her hair more closely around her. "And how do men call you?"

"I have many names, but one nature. You may call me Mazda, or anything you please."

"Do you not even know your own name, then? Do you not have a name that you prefer?"

"The name matters little if the nature does not change."

She laughed scornfully. "You speak in resounding but empty phrases, Mazda or whoever you may be! If your nature is unchangeable, give demonstration! Let me see you descend into the water!"

"I did not say that," murmured the traveller peaceably. "I did not say my nature is unchangeable."

"Then your nature is that of a deceiver, for you made me imagine that you did. Nonetheless, come down and bathe with me!"

"I shall not. And it would be well for you to think on this, Lorega of Acromel: that if you are without sense, your intention to bathe in Metamorphia is also without sense."

"That is too deep for me," said Lorega unhappily, and a tear stole down her satiny cheek. "I cannot reason as wise persons do. Therefore let my nature be changed!"

"As you wish, so be it," said the traveller in a heavy tone, and motioned with his staff. A great lump of the bank detached itself and slumped into the water. Its monstrous splashing doused Lorega, head to foot, and she underwent, as did the earth of the bank the moment it broke the surface, changes.

Thoughtfully and a mite sadly, the traveller turned to continue his journey towards Acromel. Behind him the welkin rang with the miserable cries of what had been Lorega. But he was bound by certain laws. He did not look back.

Before the vast black gate of the city, which was a hundred feet high and a hundred feet wide, two tall and brawny men in shabby clothes were fighting with quarterstaves. The traveller leaned on his own staff and watched them batter at one another until they both found themselves too weak to continue, and had to stand panting and glaring while they recovered breath.

"What is the quarrel between you?" asked the traveller then.

"Little man in black, it concerns not you," grunted the nearer of the pair. "Go your way and leave us be."

"Wait!" said the other. "Inquire first whether he likewise is bent on the same errand!"

"A good point!" conceded the first, and raised his cudgel menacingly. "Speak, you!"

"First I must know what your errand is," the traveller pointed out. "How else can I say whether mine is the same or not?"

"A good point!" admitted the second, who had now also approached to threaten him. "Know that I am Ripil of the village called Masergon—"

"And I," interrupted the first, "am Tolex of the village called Wyve. Last week I set forth from my father's house, he having six other sons older than I—"

"As did I!" Ripil broke in. "Exactly as did I! Stranger, you've registered my name, I trust? You'll have good cause to remember it one day!"

"All men will!" snapped Tolex with contempt. "They will recall your name to laugh at it, and when mocking boys scrawl it on a wall with charcoal old women will spit on the ground as they hobble past!"

Ripil scowled at him. "Booby! Possessed of unbelievable effrontery! Go your way before it is too late, and the people of this city hang you in chains before the altar!"

"Your errand, though!" cried the traveller, just in time to forestall a renewal of their conflict.

Tolex gave him a huge but humorless grin. "Why, it's all so simple! This idiot called Ripil came hither thinking to make his fortune, dethrone Duke Vaul, and claim the hand of the beauteous Lorega! As though a dunderheaded lout like him could do more than *dream* of such glories!"

"And your own ambition?"

"Why, I have come to make my fortune and be chosen heir

to the duke, whereupon naturally *I* shall be assigned Lorega's hand!"

On hearing this the traveller laughed aloud. Thinking it was Ripil's foolishness alone which afforded cause for amusement, Tolex too guffawed, whereat Ripil, his face as dark as storm clouds, caught up his quarterstaff and began to belabor him anew.

The traveller left them to it and went onward through the gate.

II

AT THE MIDPOINT OF ACROMEL there stood a temple, crowning the black tower round which its buildings clustered like a single onyx on a pillar of agate. In the said temple, before the red idol of the god Lacrovas-Pellidin-Agshad-Agshad, Duke Vaul yawned behind his hand.

"Take *her*," he said to the chief priest, nodding his large black-bearded head to his left. The priest bowed to the hard slippery floor and beckoned his minions. In a moment the consort who had shared Vaul's life for fifteen years, and until that moment had also shared his throne, was hanging from the gallows in front of the altar, her heart's blood trickling into Agshad's hands.

And still that was not enough.

Duke Vaul knitted his brows until his forehead creased like a field trenched to grow vegetables, and his thick fingers drummed on the arm of his ebony chair. He stared at the idol.

From the vantage point where he sat, he saw Agshad in the attitude of accepting sacrifice: mouth open, eyes closed, hands outstretched and cupped to receive the victims' blood. On the left Pellidin, who shared Agshad's body but not his head or limbs, was portrayed in the act of exercising justice: to wit, wringing the life from three persons of indeterminate sex—indeterminate, because Pellidin's cruel grasp had compressed their bodies into a gelatinous mess and left only their arms and legs sticking out between his carven fingers, much as a child might crush a captured beetle. On the right, Lacrovas was depicted in the mode of obliterating enemies, with a sword in one hand and a morning-star in the other. And finally, facing away from the spot where by preference Duke Vaul had his throne located, there was the second Agshad in the posture of devotion, with hands clasped together and beseeching eyes cast heavenward. That was the aspect of the Quadruple God with which Duke Vaul was least concerned.

Below the dais on which he presided, priests and acolytes by the hundred—predominantly sacrificers, expert in every art of human butchery—wove their lines of movement into traditional magical patterns. Their chanting ascended eerily towards the domed roof, along with the stench of candles made from the fat of those who had earlier hung in the clanking chains before the altar. There was no point in letting their mortal remains go to waste: so held the duke.

But on the other hand there was no point—so far—in any of this ritual. At least, the desired effect had not been accomplished. If even his own consort had not provoked the sought-after reaction, what would? Duke Vaul cast around in his mind.

On impulse, he signalled the deputy chief priest and pointed a hairy-backed finger at the chief priest himself. "Take *him*," he directed.

And that was no good, either.

Accordingly, half an hour past noon, he dispatched the temple guard into the city under orders to drive all idle citizens into a courtyard adjacent to the fane. If it wasn't a matter of quality, reasoned the duke, it might perhaps be a matter of quantity. The second priest—now the chief priest by right of succession—had been consulted, and given as his considered opinion that a hundred all at once might have the desired effect. Duke Vaul, to err on the safe side, had ordained that a thousand should be brought, and had set carpenters and metalsmiths to work on extra chain-jangling gallows to accommodate them.

The guardsmen carried out their duties with a will, all the better because they feared the lot might fall on them when Duke Vaul had used up his supply of ordinary townsfolk. They brought in everyone they could catch, and among the crowd was a small man in a black cloak, who seemed to be consumed with uncontrollable merriment.

His hilarity, in fact, was so extreme that it became infectious. The duke, noticing the fact, bellowed across the temple floor in a fit of fury.

"What idiot is that who dares to laugh in such a sacred spot?" his bull voice demanded. "Does the fellow not realize that these are serious matters and may be disturbed by the least misconduct in our actions? Drag him forth and make him stand before me!"

After some delay, because the throng was so dense, the black-clad traveller was escorted to the foot of the dais. He bowed compliantly enough when the rough hand of a guardsman clouted him behind the head, but the cheerful twinkle did not depart from his eyes, and this peculiarity struck Duke Vaul at once.

He began to muse about the consequences of sacrificing one who did not take the Quadruple God seriously, and eventually spoke through the tangle of his beard.

"How do men call you, foolish one?" he boomed.

"I have many names, but one nature."

"You claim so? Well, we'll see about *that*! Why are you laughing at these holy matters?"

"But I am not!"

"Then are you laughing at me?" thundered the duke, heaving himself forward on his throne so that the boards of the dais creaked and squealed. His eyes flashed terribly.

"No, I laugh at the foolishness of humankind," replied the traveller.

"Do you indeed? Hmm! Pray, then, explain in what impressively mirthful manner this foolishness is manifest!"

"Why, thus," the traveller murmured, and told the story of Tolex and Ripil.

But Duke Vaul did not find the anecdote in the least degree amusing. He commanded that the temple guard should at once search out these two, and fumed while they were hunted down. When they arrived, however, it was as corpses they were laid upon the stone-flagged floor.

"Your Mightiness!" the guardsmen cried respectfully, bowing their heads as one, then let their captain continue.

"Sire, we found these two clasped dying in each other's arms. Each bore one bloody cudgel; each has a broken skull."

"Throw them in the river," snapped Duke Vaul, and resumed his converse with the traveller.

"You arrogate to yourself the right to laugh at human foolishness," he said, and gave a wicked grin. "Then tell me this: are you yourself entirely wise?"

"Alas, yes," was the answer. "I have but one nature."

"If so, you can succeed where all my so-called wise men have failed. See you this idol?"

"I could hardly avoid seeing it. It is a remarkable work of—ah—*art*."

"It is claimed that a way exists to endow it with life, and when this way is found it will then set forth to lay waste the enemies of this city and execute justice upon them. By every means we have sought to bestow life upon it; we have given it blood, which as you doubtless know is life, from every class and condition of person. Even my consort, who but a few hours ago sat beside me on this throne"—the duke wiped an imaginary tear—"now hangs, throat gashed, on yonder gibbet. Still, though, the idol declines to come alive. We need its aid, for our enemies are abroad in every corner of the world; from Ryovora to the ends of the earth they plot our downfall and destruction."

The traveller nodded. "Some of what you say is true."

"Some? Only some? What, then, is false? Tell me! And you had better be correct, or else you shall go to join that stupid chief priest who finally tired my patience! You can see what became of him!"

The traveller glanced up and spread his hands. Indeed it

was obvious, what with the second, redly oozing, mouth the priest had lately acquired below his chin.

"Well, first of all," he said, all trace of laughter fading from his tone, "there does exist a way to bring the idol to life. And, second, yes, it will then destroy the enemies of Acromel. But, third, they do not hide in distant corners of the land. They are present in the city."

"Say you so?" Duke Vaul frowned. "You may be right, for, knowing what a powerful weapon we wield against them—or shall wield, when we unknot this riddle—they may well be trying to interfere with my experiments. Good! Go on!"

"How so, short of demonstrating what I mean?"

"You?" The duke jerked forward, clutching his throne's arms so tightly his knuckles glistened white as mutton-fat. "*You* can make the idol come alive?"

The traveller gave a weary and reluctant nod.

"Then do it!" roared Duke Vaul. "But don't forget! If you fail, a worse fate awaits you than my chief priest suffered!"

"As you wish, so be it," sighed the traveller. With his staff he made a curved pass in the air. The idol moved.

Agshad in the posture of devotion did not open his clasped hands. But Lacrovas swung his sword, and Duke Vaul's bearded head sprang from his shoulders. Pellidin let fall the three crushed persons from his hand and seized the body. That he squeezed instead, and the cupped hands of Agshad in the attitude of accepting sacrifice overflowed with ducal blood, expressed like juice from a ripe fruit.

After that the idol stepped down from the altar and began to stamp on the priests.

Thoughtfully, having made his escape unnoticed in the confusion, the traveller took to the road again.

Perhaps there would be nothing worse to witness during this journey than what he had beheld in Acromel. Perhaps there would be something a million times as bad. It was to establish such information that he undertook his journeyings.

In Kanish-Kulya they were fighting a war, and each side was breathing threatenings and slaughter against the other.

"Oh that fire would fall from heaven and burn up our enemies!" cried the Kanishmen.

"Oh that the earth would open and swallow up our enemies!"
cried the Kulyamen.

"As you wish," said the traveller, "so be it."

He tapped the ground with his staff, and Fegrim who was
pent in a volcano answered that tapping and heaved mightily.
Afterwards, when the country was beginning to sprout again —
for lava makes fertile soil — men dug up bones and skulls as
they prepared the land for planting.

On the shores of Lake Taxhling, men sat around their canoes
swapping lies while they waited for a particular favorable star
to ascend above the horizon. One lied better than all the rest.

But he lied not as his companions lied — to pass the time,
to amuse each other harmlessly. He lied to feed a consuming
vanity hungrier than all the bellies of all the people in the
villages along the shores of the lake, who waited day in, day
out, with inexhaustible patience for their menfolk to return
with their catch.

Said the braggart, "If only I could meet with such another
fish as I caught single-handed in Lake Moroho when I was a
stripling of fifteen! *Then* you would understand the fisherman's
art! Alas, though" — with a sigh — "there are only piddling fish
in Lake Taxhling!"

"As you wish, so be it," said the traveller, who had accepted
the offer of food by their fire. Duly, the next dawn, the boaster
came home shouting with excitement about a huge fish he had
caught, the same size as the one from Lake Moroho. His companions crowded round to see it — and the mountains rang with
their laughter, because it was smaller than most of what they
themselves had taken during the night.

Thus shamed, the braggart fled, and was no more heard of
in those parts.

"I do not wish a man to love me for my looks or my fortune,"
declared the haughty daughter of a landed lord in the city
Barbizond, where there was always a rainbow in the sky owing
to the presence of the bright being Sardhin chained inside a

thundercloud with fetters of lightning. The girl was beautiful, and rich, and inordinately proud.

"No!" she continually insisted, dismissing suitor after suitor. "I wish to be loved for myself, for what I am!"

"As you wish, so be it," said the traveller, who had come in the guise of a pilgrim to one of the jousts organized that this lady might view potential husbands. Nine men had died in the lists that afternoon, and she had thrown her glove in the champion's face and gone to supper.

The next time a tourney was announced, no challenger appeared. Pulling a face, the girl demanded that more heralds be sent forth. Her father summoned a hundred of them. The news was noised abroad in every city. And in each, all the personable young men said, "Fight for a stuck-up shrew like her? Ho-ho! I've better ways to pass my time, and so've my friends!"

This news was brought to her, and made for misery.

On learning later, in the way of gossip, how many of those whom she had fancied in her heart of hearts had married other girls—some, even common wenches from a shop or farm—in preference to herself, she felt her pride evaporate. She learned to curb her mocking tongue and hoity-toity ways; she recognized that so behaving had not made her happy, but only fed her vaunting self-esteem.

One night, at last, a young man was obliged by chance to ask for lodging at her father's mansion, that on the strength of her ill repute he had intended to avoid, and found not the precocious termagant old friends had warned him of, but a pretty, pleasant, ordinary girl, and married her.

Thus the journey approached its end. The traveller felt a natural relief that nothing unduly alarming had occurred as he hastened his footsteps towards the goal and climax of his excursion—towards Ryovora, where folk were sensible and clear-sighted, and made no trouble that he had to rectify. After this final visit, he could be assured his duty was fulfilled.

Not that all was well by any means. There were enchanters still, and ogres, and certain elementals roamed at large, and of human problems there might be no end. Still, the worst of his afflictions were growing fewer. One by one, the imprints of aboriginal chaos were fading away, like the footmarks of travellers on the road above the hill where Laprivan was prisoned.

Then, as the gold and silver towers of Ryovora came to view, he saw that an aura surrounded them as of a brewing storm, and his hope and trust in the people of that city melted clean away.

III

AT THE CITY BARBIZOND, where he had been but recently, there was likewise an aura around the tallest towers. There, however, it was a fair thing and pleasant to look upon, imbued with the essence of bright—if cruel, not the less lovely—Sardhin, chained in his unmoving cloud.

Since time immemorial, though, Ryovora had been immune from such disadvantageous infestations as elementals, principalities and powers; the citizens prided themselves on being gifted with hard plain sense, sober in the making of decisions, practical and rational and causing a minimum of trouble to the world.

That something had happened to alter this state of affairs . . . ! There was an enigma to make the very cosmos shiver with foreboding!

The traveller turned aside from the regular track, making no attempt to unfurrow his forehead, and instead of pursuing a direct course into the city diverged across a verdant meadow in the midst of which hovered a mist like the mists of early morning, but more dense. When its grey wisps had closed around him entirely, to the point where they would have incapacitated the vision of any ordinary trespasser, he dissolved one of the forces which curdled the light composing his staff, and a clear bright beam penetrated the opacity. It had barely sheared the vapor when a quiet voice addressed him.

"Since you know where you are, I know who you are. Enter my dwelling, and be welcome."

The haze vanished, and the traveller advanced across the drawbridge of a castle that reared seemingly to heaven. At each corner rose a tower, haloed with cloud; two dragons chained beside the portcullis bowed their heads fawningly; four man-like persons whose bodies were of burnished steel came to escort him—one before, one behind, one at each side—through the gateway and across the courtyard; as he ascended steps towards the chief tower and the keep, twenty trumpeters sounded a blast from a gallery, and they were as metallic as their instruments.

There was a scent of magic in the air. Echoes of half-forgotten cantrips resounded, incredibly faint, from the masonry of the walls. Here and there blue light dripped from a projecting cornice; shadows moved with none to cast them.

Then a door of oak studded with brass swung open on silent hinges, giving access to a room across which slanted a thick bar of sunlight from a window standing wide. The beam illuminated the shrivelled mummy of a mandrake. In jars covered with black cloth, ranged on an oak shelf, were twenty homunculi. A brazier burned, giving off a thick, very pleasant smell like warm honey.

From behind a table on which were piled massy books that also served as a perch for a drowsy owl, a personage in dark red robes rose to greet the traveller, and spoke in a tone between delight and resignation.

"It is traditional that no one shall pierce the mist with which I guard my privacy save an invited guest or one who has a single nature. And, the universe being as it is, the latter class possesses but a single member. As you must know, I am the enchanter Manuus. Be welcome."

The visitor bent his head in acknowledgment. A chair was placed for him, not by visible hands; he sat down, disposing his cloak comfortably over its arms. From a cupboard Manuus took a large flask and two pottery mugs ornamented with complex symbols in blue enamel. From the flask—which bore similar symbols, but in green—he spilled a few drops of sparkling liquid, muttering words that made the walls hum faintly. The drops vanished before they reached the floor, and the enchanter gave a smile of satisfaction as he filled the mugs.

"What business causes you to honor my abode with your presence?" he inquired, resuming his own chair after handing one mug to his caller.

"There is an aura surrounding Ryovora," said the traveller. "Before I enter the city I wish to ascertain its cause."

Manuus nodded thoughtfully, stroking the wispy beard that clung at his chin. It was as grey as the mist he used to guard his home from casual prying.

"You will forgive me mentioning the fact," he said in an apologetic tone, "but it is asserted in one of my books—a volume, moreover, in which I have come to place some degree of confidence—that if your nature is single, then it must logically follow that you answer questions as well as asking them, and that you are obliged to do so one for one."

"That is so. And I see plainly that you trust the tome of which you speak. The faceless drinker to whom you just poured libation is not elsewhere referred to."

Silence ensued for a space while each contemplated the other. There was, though, a distinction, inasmuch as the enchanter might only study the outward guise of the traveller, whereas the latter examined the totality of his host.

"Ask away, then," the traveller invited at length. "And I may say that the more involved your question, the simpler and harder to unravel will be my answer."

"And vice versa?" suggested Manuus, his old eyes twinkling.

"Exactly."

"Very well, then. Who are you? Note, please, that I do not ask how you are called. You must have an infinity of names."

The traveller smiled. "That is a good question, frankly phrased. So I will answer frankly. I am he to whom was entrusted the task of bringing order forth from chaos. Hence the reason why I have but one nature."

"If your nature were such that you demanded honor in full measure with your worth, all the days of my life would not suffice to do you homage," said Manuus seriously. "Ask now what you would know."

"What's the trouble in Ryovora?"

Maliciously Manuus countered, "I am not bound by your laws, sir. Therefore I will answer in the human style—simply, to simple questions. There is dissatisfaction with the order of things as they are."

"Fair," the traveller conceded. "Ask away."

The enchanter hesitated. "Who," he resumed at length, "imposed on you—?"

And his tongue locked in his mouth, while the traveller looked on with an expression blending cynicism and sympathy. When at last Manuus was able to speak again, he muttered, "Your pardon. It was of the nature of a test. I had seen it stated that . . ."

"That there are certain questions one is literally and physically forbidden to pose?" The traveller chuckled. "Why, then your test has served to confirm the fact. I, even I, could not answer the question I suspect you were intending to frame. However, a question that cannot be asked is *ipso facto* no question at all. You may try again."

Manuus licked his lips. What had transpired in his head during that moment of involuntary paralysis defied comprehension. He was, though, brave and enterprising, and shortly ventured, "On the other hand, I believe I may legitimately ask: what is the purpose of your undertaking?"

"You may."

"So I do"—leaning back expectant in his chair.

"Why! When all things have but one nature, they will be subsumed into the Original All. Time will stop. This conclusion is desirable."

Manuus looked sourly at the brazier. "Desirable, perhaps—but appallingly dull. Speak again."

"In what particular respect are the citizens of Ryovora dissatisfied?"

Manuus turned the question over in his brilliant mind, seeking a way to milk from it a further opportunity to interrogate his distinguished visitor. He failed, and replied:

"They are displeased because they have no gods."

Three bolts of lightning sheared the clear blue sky beyond the window; three successive claps of thunder made the room re-echo and startled the sleepy owl into giving three little hops across the great book on which he squatted. The traveller ignored these events, taking a further sip from his mug, but on his face a frown was suddenly engraved.

"Ask a third time," he invited.

"Why, this can't be altogether necessary," said Manuus in high delight. "But so I will!" He darted his gaze from place to place within the room as though in quest of inspiration, and finally lit on the proper line of inquiry.

"What was there, before things became as they are now?"

"I will show you," said the traveller, and dipped one fingertip into his mug. He drew forth a drop of liquid in which was trapped a sparkling bubble.

"Regard this bubble," he instructed. "You will see . . ."

In those days the forces were none of them chained. They raged unchecked through every corner and quarter of the cosmos. Here, for instance, ruled Laprivan of the Yellow Eyes, capricious, whimsical; when he stared worlds melted in frightful agony. There a bright being shed radiance, but the radiance was all-consuming, and that which was solid and durable—but dull—flashed into fire. At another place, creatures numbering a million strove for possession of a grain of dust; the fury of their contest laid waste solar systems.

Once—twice—a third time something burgeoned which had about it a comforting aura of rationality, predictability, stability; about this nucleus, time was generated from eternity. Time entails memory, memory entails conscience, conscience entails thought for the future, which is itself implied by the existence of time. Twice the forces of chaos raged around this focal point and swallowed it back into oblivion; then the will of Tuprid and Caschalanva, of Quorril and Lry, and of all the other elemental beings, reigned once more. But none of them was supreme, because in chaos nothing can endure, nothing can be absolute, nothing sure or certain or reliable.

In that age stars flared up like fires of straw, bright one moment, ash the next. On planets circling uncounted suns creatures who could think struggled to reduce chaos to order, and when they had most nearly achieved it, chance ordained that all their work should go for nothing, absorbed again into the faceless dark.

"But that was before me," said the traveller, and squeezed the bubble, so it burst.

"I have seen," said Manuus with inexpressible weariness. "But I have not understood."

"Man does not comprehend chaos. That is why man is man, and not of another nature." The traveller smiled. "I wish now to propound my final question; do you grant that I have well and sufficiently answered yours?"

"You have only given me another million questions to ask," sighed Manuus, shaking his grey head. "But that also, I suppose, stems from the nature of mankind. Ask away."

"Your supposition is correct. Now my last question: enchanter, what is your opinion of a god?"

"I do not know what a god is," said Manuus. "And I doubt that anybody knows, though many think they do."

"Fair enough," said the black-clad traveller, and rose.

"Have you not even one more question to put to me?" suggested the enchanter with a wan smile.

"Not even one."

Manuus gave a shrug and rose also. He said formally, "Then I can only thank you for having graced my dwelling. Few of my colleagues can have enjoyed the honor of receiving you in person."

The traveller bestowed on him a hard, forthright look.

"I have many names, but one nature," he said, "Being human, you have one name, and many more natures than two. But the essential two are these: that you shall strive to impose order on chaos, and that you shall strive to take advantage of chaos. Such folk as you are allies of the powers who preceded me."

"I resent that, sir," said Manuus frostily. "Let it not be said that I oppose you now you have informed me of the purpose of your task."

"A third component, not of your nature alone, but that of all humanity, is this: that you shall not understand what you are doing. I wish you good day—though whether it will be so is rather up to you than up to me."

Leaving his host rapt in thought, with one elbow on a book in front of him, his chin cupped in his hand, his eyes staring vacantly at his pet owl, the traveller set forward, and among the gold and silver towers of Ryovora the populace confirmed what Manuus had said.

That same argument the enchanter had put bluntly, he heard indirectly phrased before the houses of the great merchant-enchanters who conjured this city's goods from the far corners of the world; so too in market squares and private homes; so too in theaters and taverns, shops and laboratories and even brothels. When at last he came to stand upon the summit of a high shining tower and overlook the sleeping city in the small dead hours, he was convinced.

Yes, truly the folk of Ryovora were dissatisfied, and it was as Manuus had claimed. They had struggled through centuries inquiring of the mute cosmos what its purpose and the purpose of humanity might be, and they were left still hungering, to the point of growing disillusioned.

This hunger—so they declared—would be assuaged if only they had a god to turn to, as did their neighbors at Acromel. News had been brought, of course, that the god of Acromel had caused uncounted deaths and widespread misery, but they ascribed all that to the notorious stupidity of Duke Vaul. "We are sensible people!" they insisted. "We would know how to treat a god!"

The traveller stood gazing out over the placid scene. The beams of a waxing moon glinted on the roofs of splendid buildings, on ornamental trees and lakes, mansions and fine wide roads among whose dust were scattered gems to make the way more pleasant.

nk that folk who revelled in such luxury could hanker
rbitrary god . . . !

He had asked everywhere, "What is the nature of a god?"
And they had answered confidently, "We have none! How,
then, can we tell? But if we did have one – ah, then we'd
know!"

The traveller remained immobile until pink dawn-flush
tinged the east, absorbing and reviewing the desire that in-
choately washed against his mind. At last, a breath or two
before full sunrise, a smile quirked his mouth and he raised
his staff above the city and said, "As you wish, so be it."

Then, his task for the moment being accomplished, he
departed.

IV

To PARK A CAR while one goes for a walk in the woods is not
uncommon. To return and find that the car is no longer there
is not unprecedented. But to return and find that the road itself,
on which the car was parked, has likewise vanished, is a different matter entirely.

Yet for a man who rules himself by the straightforward logic
of common sense, such as a materials scientist turned civil
engineer, there is no need instantly to assume that a problem
of this magnitude is insoluble. Bernard Brown was precisely
such a person, and it was to him that this improbable event
had just occurred.

"Well!" he said, staring at the indisputably grassy surface
of the narrow ride between high hedges where to the best of
his recollection – and his memory was normally good – there

had shortly before been a tarmac road, sound enough in general albeit a far cry from the concrete superhighways he was used to helping build. "Well!" he said again, and since there was no obvious alternative sat down on a mossy rock and smoked a cigarette in a philosophical manner.

However, no one came by who might enlighten him as to the fate either of his car or of the road it had been on, so when the cigarette had reduced to a stub he dropped it on the grass, ground it out underfoot, and began to walk along the lane between the hedges.

By the straightforward logic of common sense, a road which had been here a scant hour ago could not have removed itself to another location. Therefore it must be he who was misplaced; he had no doubt missed his way in the pleasant summery woodland, and would eventually return if not to the road he had first followed then to some other that intersected with it.

He strolled along jauntily enough, not much worried by the turn of affairs, and whistled as he walked. Occasionally the hedges on either side parted after he had gone by, and eyes thoughtfully studied his retreating back, but since he did not notice it this fact failed to disturb him.

At length the hedges ended, and with them the trees of the wood, and he emerged on a rutted track between two ploughed fields. On the near edge of one of these fields a man whose only clothing was a kerchief tied around his neck and whose legs were soiled to the knee with dirt was backing up a large obstreperous horse, harnessed to a cart whose contents were indeterminate but stank incredibly. Ignoring both reek and nudity as best he could, Bernard addressed the fellow in his politest tones.

"Excuse me! Can you tell me the way to the London road?"

The man considered for a moment. Then he spat in the earth where it was new-turned by his horse's enormous hooves, and said bluntly, "No!"

Well, that was at least an answer, if not a very helpful one. Bernard shrugged and wandered on.

Again the grassy ride passed between hedges, and began to wind so that at any given moment only twenty paces of it were in clear view before and behind. From around a bend ahead a voice could be heard raised in song and growing louder. This voice was of intersexual quality, neither altogether male nor altogether female, and shrilled occasionally on the highest notes with shiver-provoking acidity.

Shortly the singer came in sight, and Bernard found himself confronted by a young man, with silvery white hair cut short around his head, riding negligently on a gaily caparisoned horse that moved its head in time with the beat of its master's song. His attire was extraordinary, for he wore a checkered shirt of red and yellow and loose breeches of bright green, the color of a sour apple, and his steed was if anything more surprising, inasmuch as it was skewbald of purple and pale blue. This rider accompanied his vocalizing on a small plucked instrument, the strings of which chirruped like birds.

When he perceived Bernard, he abandoned his song in midphrase, let his instrument fall on a baldric to his side, and reined in his mount. Then he leaned forward, one hand on the pommel of his saddle, and fixed the pedestrian with bright hard eyes; these were violet.

"Good morrow, stranger," he said in a light tone. "And what's your business here?"

"I'm trying to find my way back to the London road," said Bernard, trying to stop his eyebrows rising in astonishment at this spectacle.

"There is no road of that name near here," said the young man, and shook his head sorrowfully. "I know that to be a fact, for all the roads in this vicinity belong to me."

"Now this is all very well," said Bernard, and forced a smile to show he was party to the joke. "But while it may amuse you to make such grandiose assertions, it does not amuse me to be denied essential guidance. I've lost my way somehow, through taking a wrong turning in the woods, and I badly need directions."

The young man drew himself upright and urged his horse forward—and it could be seen now that this was not a young man riding a horse, nor was there in fact a horse being ridden, but some sort of confusion of the two, in that the youth's legs were not separated from his mount. They ended in fleshy stalks, uniting with the belly of that part of the composite animal resembling a horse.

"This is weird!" thought Bernard to himself, but being mannerly he forbore to remark on the combination.

The man-portion of the creature stared at him harshly, hand falling to his thigh where a sword rested in a black scabbard. "Who are you?" he demanded. "And where are you from, that you don't recognize me?"

Nettled, Bernard rejoined, "Unless you had taken part in a circus, or been exhibited at the zoo, I would not presume to do so!"

Horse-head and man-head reared back together in appalled amazement, and the sword whined brightly through the air. Feeling he must have to do with a creature whose mind was as abnormal as its body, Bernard had already stepped discreetly out of range when the blade flashed by.

"I am Jorkas!" shrieked the man-horse creature. "Now dare you still say you do not know me?"

Alarmed at the behavior of this composite personage, Bernard replied in a tone as civil as could be expected, given the attack with the sword, "No, sir, I do not, and I may say that your actions give me little cause to wish we had become acquainted earlier."

The man-face contorted with unbelievable rage, and the sword swung aloft for a second blow as the horse-body danced three steps towards Bernard. He was on the point of making an inglorious—and predictably ill-fated—retreat when a sudden ringing noise indicated that the weapon had struck something very resistant indeed in its downward passage. Indeed, the creature was shaking its sword-arm as though it had been numbed clear to the shoulder.

The obstacle the blade had encountered was a glittering staff, upheld in the firm grip of a black-clad man who had somehow contrived to approach without being noticed. This person was now standing back, leaning on the staff, and regarding Jorkas with a wry expression.

Jorkas shrugged, sheathed his sword, and took up his instrument again. His horse-legs bore him cantering away, and when he was out of sight around the next bend his countertenor voice was once more heard raised in song.

"It seems, sir," Bernard said to his rescuer, wiping his face and not unduly surprised to find he was perspiring, "that I owe you a debt of gratitude. I confess I was not prepared to meet anyone—or anything—like that in this quiet lane."

The black-clad one smiled, a faraway look in his eyes. "It's true," he said matter-of-factly, "I did render some small service, but you'll have the chance to pay it back a hundredfold. Meantime, I'd add a smidgin of advice. If you expect nothing and everything, you will do well."

Settling his jacket more comfortably around his shoulders, Bernard blinked several times in succession. "Well, sir, taken whichever way, I cannot see your advice proving unsound. Particularly if this neighborhood is populated by more amazing freaks like Jorkas!"

"Yes, he bears the imprint of chaos," said the man in black. "He is left over, so to speak. He is fairly harmless now; events have passed him by, and his power grows small."

"That sword, had it attained its target, would scarcely have been harmless," Bernard pointed out. "One blow could have disposed of me. . . . Has he escaped from some—some fantastic menagerie?"

"He has rather endured from a period of confusion," was the reply, which though apparently meaningful served not at all to lessen either Bernard's puzzlement or his alarm. He decided, nonetheless, to forgo further inquiry into the matter, and to revert to his primary preoccupation.

"Can you, sir, tell me: where's the London road?"

"I can," said the other with a chuckle. "But it would be of small help if I did, since you cannot come to it from here. No, pay attention, and I will give directions that will eventually bring you where you wish to be."

Since that was the best the stranger was willing to offer, Bernard had perforce to nod acceptance.

"Go forward from here," said his mentor, "until you reach three alder trees standing alone in a meadow. You will recognize them readily enough. Stand before them and bow three times, then take the path around them. In a little while it will bring you to a city. And whatever you do, do *not* speak with a woman in clothing the color of blood. Otherwise I cannot answer for the outcome."

"What nonsense!" thought Bernard to himself. But since he had no choice he thanked the other in a civil fashion and went on circumspectly down the lane.

The alder trees poked up, white and gnarled, from the grass of the promised meadow, like the fingers of a skeleton. Bernard hesitated, looking around. He knew he would feel foolish if he acted as he had been advised. Still, so far as he could tell no one was watching, and the logic of common sense had long ago enabled him to conclude that he was not at present in a region where common sense was greatly prized.

He was troubled, though, that he could discern no sign at all of a road beyond this point, so that unless he did what he had been told, and it—ah—worked, he would have to retrace his steps, with the concomitant prospect of a second encounter with Jorkas. For that he had no stomach. Accordingly, he bowed his head three times, rather as he an unbeliever might have done in church, and was taken aback to find he was suddenly standing on a well-defined path. Which, he instantly noticed, led nowhere save around the alders.

Well, the black-clad man had said he should take the path which led around them. He turned to his left and resolutely made three circuits, hopeful of getting somewhere else eventually.

Starting his third turn, when he was feeling distinctly embarrassed by his own silliness, he glanced towards the trees again and saw a slender woman standing among them. She had a face of perfect oval shape, skin like mother-of-pearl, and hair blacker than the midnight sky. But she was gowned from shoulders to ankles in a dress as red as blood.

She spoke to him in a musical voice, sarcastically. "And where do you think your circumambulations will carry you, my foolish friend? Did no one ever warn you that if you walk in circles you'll get nowhere? Why not head onward? See!"

She raised an arm on which golden bracelets jangled, and when Bernard followed her pointing finger he saw a city of black houses clustered round a lofty tower, whose top resembled onyx and whose shaft resembled agate.

A strange sort of city! Yet at least a zone of habitation, not a further stretch of deserted countryside. He was half minded to make towards it with all haste, yet felt a vague foreboding. There was a sense of menace in the air. . . .

He spoke aloud, but to himself, not the woman in red, and said, "The man who saved me from Jorkas advised me not to speak with a woman in a dress the color of blood. I assume this advice extends to not following any suggestion she may make."

Doggedly he completed his rotatory progress, while the woman's laughter tinkled irritatingly in his ears, and was rewarded on his final circuit to see that she had gone. Somewhere. Somehow.

Moreover, another city was in sight, and this was not so disturbing. Its towers were of gold and silver, and although the sky about it was of an electrical blue shade that seemed to presage nothing less familiar than the advent of a storm.

"There, perhaps," reasoned Bernard, "I may escape this conglomeration of cryptic nonmeaningful events, and may even track down someone who can tell me how to get home."

He struck out across the meadow, and shortly came to a wide though dusty road, which led straight towards the city with the gold and silver towers. Determined to reach it in the least possible time, he thrust the road behind him with feet that now began to ache more than a little.

"So!" said the enchanter Manuus, leaning back in his chair with a chuckle. "So!" he said again, dropping the cover—made of bat's skin as fine and supple as silk—over his scrying-glass. "Well, well, well, well, *well!*"

V

AT THE HEAD of the council table—which, because the weather was oppressive, he had caused to be set out under the sycamore trees in the Moth Garden—the Margrave of Ryovora sat frowning terribly.

Before him, the table stretched almost a hundred feet, in sections that were so cleverly joined the overarching trees could admire their reflections intact in its polished top. Nothing spoiled the perfection of the table, except the purplish sheen it had acquired from the close and sluggish air.

To right and left of him, ranked in their chairs, sat the nobility of Ryovora, men and women of vast individual distinction: the merchant-enchanters, the persons of inquiring mind, the thinkers, the creators, all those to whom this city owed its fame and reputation.

The margrave spoke, not looking at his audience.

"Tell us what has transpired in your section of the city, Petrovic."

Petrovic, a dry little man with a withered face like an old apple, coughed apologetically and said, "There are omens. I have cast runes to ascertain their meaning. They have no known significance. But in my demesne milk has soured in the pan four mornings running."

"And Ruman?"

Ruman was a man bodied like an oak tree, whose thick gnarled hands were twisting restlessly in his lap. He said, "I have slaughtered an ox and an ass to divine what may be read in their entrails. I agree with Petrovic; these omens have no

29

discernible significance. But two springs under the wall of the city, which have not failed in more centuries than I can discover, are dry this morning."

"And Gostala?"

Gostala was a woman with a queenly bosom and a queenly diadem of white hair plaited around her head. She said, "I have watched the flight of birds each dawn for seven days, and also at sunset. The results are confused. But a two-headed lamb has been born in the village of Dunwray."

"And Eadwil?"

Eadwil was hardly more than a boy. His chin was innocent of a beard and when he spoke his voice was like a reed pipe; still, they must respect his precocious wisdom. He said, "I have analyzed the respective positions of the stars and planets, and am driven to the hypotheses that *either* we know nothing at all of their effects *or* some undetected celestial body is influencing events—perhaps a comet. But yesterday lightning struck three times out of a clear sky, and—and, Margrave, I'm frightened!"

The margrave made a comforting gesture in the air. It didn't help much. He said, "This, though, cannot be the whole story. I move that we—here, now, in full council—ask Him Who Must Know."

Eadwil rose to his feet. On his youthful lips trembled a sob, which he stoutly repressed.

"I request your permission to withdraw, then. It is well known how He Who Must Know deals with those—uh—in my condition."

The margrave nodded approval of the discreet reference. Eadwil owed some of his precocity to the postponement of a major upheaval in his physiology, and the elemental they were considering found virgins vulnerable to his powers.

"Agreed," he said, and Eadwil departed, sighing with relief.

Before they could proceed with the business in hand, however, there was a rustling sound from far down the table, and a voice spoke like the soughing of wind in bare winter woods.

"Margrave, I suggest otherwise."

The margrave shifted uncomfortably in his chair. That was

Tyllwin who spoke, a figure as gaunt as a scarecrow and as thin as a rake, who sat among them by courtesy because no one knew where he had come from or how old he was, but everybody knew he had many and peculiar powers which had never been put to use. Just as well, maybe. Whenever he spoke, untoward events ensued. The margrave saw with alarm that blossoms on several nearby trees were withering.

"Speak, Tyllwin," he muttered, and braced himself.

Tyllwin chuckled, a scratching noise, and the flowers on the whole of one tree turned to fruit and rotted where they hung. His nearest neighbors hastily left their seats and moved towards the margrave's end of the table.

Tyllwin's huge round head, like a turnip ghost's, turned to watch them, and a smile curved his dusty lips. He said, "Is it not certain, lords of Ryovora, that these things foreshadow an important event?"

The rotten fruits fell with a succession of squelching sounds, and ants hurried from among the roots of the trees to investigate. The company hardly dared do more than nod.

"Therefore," said Tyllwin, "I suggest we investigate the commotion which is shortly to take place at the main gate."

He fell silent. A few dead leaves blew across the table. Most of them clustered before his place, and he touched them with a bony hand, whereat they dissolved. The watchers trembled.

Still, the margrave was relieved to find that nothing more outrageous was going to follow Tyllwin's unexpected loquacity. He said, "What is the opinion of the council?"

Ruman spoke up, with a glance towards Tyllwin that lasted half a second after meeting Tyllwin's eyes. He said, "I have not scried any such commotion."

"But you have not scried since yesterday," countered Gostala with feminine practicality.

"True, true. Then I am with Tyllwin."

"Petrovic?" inquired the margrave.

"I am aware," that dried-up individual said in a doubtful tone, "that the people believe all our troubles would be at an end if we had a god, as other cities do. I hope that in this instance they are wrong; they usually are. Having heard from

our neighbors at Acromel how severely they suffer from their
deity—"

"This strays far from the point," Gostala interrupted, tapping the table with a thumb-bone which had once been the
property of a man fortunate enough—or unfortunate enough—
to be her lover. "I say we do not know. Let us therefore expect
both nothing and everything."

"Rational and well spoken!" approved the margrave. "Those
in favor . . . ?"

All present laid their right hands on the table, except Tuc,
who had left his in the mouth of a dragon beyond an interesting
sea of fire far to the north. Even Tyllwin moved with the rest,
causing yet more leaves to wither and tremble on the tree that
had suffered most since he broke from his impassivity.

"Agreed, then," said the margrave. "Let us go thither."

The company rose with a bustle and began to adjourn to
the main gate. The margrave, however, delayed a moment,
contemplating Tyllwin, who had not vacated his place.

When the others were at a distance he judged safe, he addressed the round-headed enchanter in a low voice.

"Tyllwin, what is your opinion of a god?"

Tyllwin uttered a creaking laugh. "I have been asked that
before," he said. "And I will answer as I did then: I do not know
what a god is, and I doubt that many men do, either."

A branch on the tree overhanging him split with a warning
cry, so that the margrave flung up his hand reflexively before
his face. When he looked again, Tyllwin was gone.

The commotion at the gate, foreseen by Tyllwin and by no
other of the council members, had already begun when the
stately procession entered the avenue leading thither. Each
enchanter had come after his or her own style: Petrovic walking
with his staff called Nitra, from which voices could sometimes
be heard when the moon was full; Gostala riding on a creature
she had summoned out of the deep water which was its natural
element, that cried aloud in heartrending agony at every step;
Ruman on the shoulders of a giant ape fettered with brass;
Eadwil on his own young legs although his feet flashed red-
hot at every tenth pace—this was to do with a geas about which

no one ever inquired closely. The air about them crackled with strife between protective conjurations and the tense oppressive aura that enshrouded Ryovora.

In the wide street before the gatehouse a crowd had gathered, laughing, shouting, exclaiming with wonderment. At its center, a man wearing outlandish attire, his face in a perpetual frown of puzzlement, was vainly trying to contend with a hundred questions simultaneously.

The crowd parted to let the nobles approach him, and at once closed in again, like water around a slow-moving boat.

The margrave came up behind the rest, panting somewhat, for he was growing fat, and looked the stranger over with dismay, while the people's voices rose to a roar and then sank again into a muttering buzz. At last, having cast a beseeching glance at his companions and received no offers of assistance, he was compelled to address the newcomer.

"Sir, who are you and what do you want?"

In the terribly patient tone of one dealing with lunatics, the stranger said, "My name is Bernard Brown, and all I want is to go home."

"That is easy enough to arrange," said the margrave in relief—though had he paused to reflect that Tyllwin was concerned with this man's arrival, he would not so soon have been optimistic. He rounded on Petrovic. "Will you oblige?"

Petrovic looked up in the air and down at the ground. He scratched a number of ideograms in the dust with his staff Nitra, then hastily scuffed them over with his sandal. He said flatly, "No."

"Well, if you won't you won't," sighed the margrave. He appealed next to Gostala, who merely shook her regal head and went on scrutinizing Bernard Brown.

"Eadwil!" cried the margrave.

The boy, whose face had turned perfectly pale, stammered a few incomprehensible words and burst into tears.

"See? They can't! What did I tell you?" bellowed a voice from the crowd, and the margrave shot a glance at the speaker as sharp as a spear.

"Come forth!" he commanded, and with the aid of a number of bystanders the fellow pushed and shoved until he stood before his ruler. He was an insolent-faced churl with a shock of corn-colored hair, and wore a leather apron with large pockets in which reposed the tools of his trade. He appeared to be some kind of worker in metal.

"You are . . ." said the margrave, and ran through a short formula in his mind. "You are Brim, a locksmith. What did you mean by what you just said?"

"What my words meant and neither more nor less," the locksmith retorted, seeming amused. "Why, anyone can *see* he's not to be pushed around by ordinary folk!"

"Explain further," the margrave commanded.

"Why, 'tis simple as your mind . . . *sir*." Brim thrust an errant lock of hair back into place with one blunt thumb. "I see it plain, and so do all of us. Here we've been saying these years past that what's amiss with Ryovora is, we haven't got a god like all those towns around the world every wherever. And now, today, what do the omens say? Can all your magicking unriddle them?"

He thrust a stubby finger at the margrave's chest. The latter recoiled and looked at him distastefully. But he was by temperament an honest man, so he had to admit that although the noble enchanters had speculated long and long about the recent omens they had failed to arrive at any conclusion.

"There, mates! What did I tell you?" thundered Brim, whirling to face the crowd. There was an answering yell, and in a moment the situation had turned topsy-turvy. The throng had closed in on Bernard Brown, unmindful that they trod on noble toes, and had seized him and gone chairing him down the avenue, while men, women and children ran and skipped behind him, singing a rhythmic song and laughing like hyenas.

"Well!" said the margrave in vexation. "This is a most improper and irregular state of affairs!"

VI

THE MARGRAVE HAD CAUSE to repeat those words, with still greater emphasis and an even more somber expression, the following morning. He sat once more at the head of the long table in the Moth Garden, for the air had become if anything more oppressive than yesterday; moreover, reports of omens seemed to have doubled in number.

"This is extremely aggravating!" said the margrave testily. "Virtually the entire populace is firmly convinced this stranger is a god, simply because they can't make head or tail of what he says. Accordingly they have turned me out of my own palace—I spent an uncomfortable night here in the Moth Garden!—and are at work converting it into a temple for this *character* without so much as a by-your-leave!"

Eadwil suppressed an inappropriate smile. "Moreover," he supplied, "all those persons who have voyaged extensively are being interrogated concerning the correct manner in which to pay homage to a new deity. Brim the locksmith, around whom this ferment seems to be most turbulent, has travelled to Acromel and is vociferous for human sacrifice; there is a group of women who in their youth were captives in Barbizond and wish to hold daily single combats before the altar; a man who formerly fished Lake Taxhling declares that the sole method of adopting the god is to burn down the city twice a year and rebuild it, as the fisherfolk do with their reed-hut villages. . . ."

Petrovic shook his withered head and opined, "No good will come of this."

"Has anyone knowledge of Tylwin's whereabouts?" inquired the margrave, for the gaunt one's place was empty today.

A shudder went down the table, and those in earshot shook their heads, not without exclamations of relief.

"Well, then, let us proceed to a course of action," said the margrave. He shifted in his chair; his night in the open, although the weather was warm, had left him feeling bruised all over.

"The first point to establish," said Gostala sensibly, "is whether this Bernard Brown is indeed a god. If not—well!"

"Agreed!" came a chorus in reply.

Snorting, Ruman thumped the table with a hamlike fist. "And how, pray, do we set about that?" he demanded with honey-sweet sarcasm. "For we have all previously confessed that we do not know what a god is. Was that not the reason why we never acquired one in the old days?"

"I fear very much," said the margrave heavily, "that the days of ordered rationality in Ryovora may be finished. It would appear that the populace are already treating Bernard Brown in all the ways they think it proper to honor a god; unless, then, we arrive at disproofs adequate to disabuse them, life in our city is doomed to become insufferable."

"Hah!" said Gostala without mirth.

"I have a suggestion," ventured Eadwil. "A god is presumed to have knowledge and power beyond what mere humans may command. Let us therefore interrogate Bernard Brown concerning the most recondite and esoteric of our arts. If he fails to answer well, let us challenge him before the multitude, so that it may be seen his talents are negligible compared to ours."

"The proposal is rational," conceded the margrave. "As I said, however, the days of rational thought here may be numbered. . . . However, if there is no better idea—?"

None was forthcoming. Accordingly the company betook themselves to the newly converted temple, formerly the great hall of the margrave's palace.

There they found Bernard Brown—to judge by his expression, less than delighted with his situation—seated on an ebony-and-silver throne above an enormous improvised altar. Before this throne the townsfolk were coming and going with gifts. Their most prized possessions were heaped about his feet, from their inherited table-plate to their newest garments. On the altar itself were piled luscious fruits and choice cuts of meat, together with bottles of delicious wine. Sucking at one of the fruits, Bernard was attempting to question the people as they came and went. However, they would not answer him; they merely listened respectfully, then went away and wrote down what he said, with a view to creating a canon of mystical precepts.

At the entry to the hall the nobility paused to survey the scene, and Eadwil spoke privily to the margrave.

"Has not Tyllwin been here?" he said under his breath.

"You're right!" confirmed the margrave after a deep inhalation. "I can scent his power. Now what snare has that devious personage laid in our path?"

He advanced towards the altar. Taking his stand three paces distant—because of the heaped-offerings—he raised his voice and addressed the putative god.

"Sir! We, the lords of Ryovora, are here to determine whether or no you are a god, as the populace maintain!"

Bernard Brown gave a cautious nod. "I was advised about your intention," he confided. "And I have been warned not to deny the possibility. Since meeting with Jorkas on my way here, I have acquired a healthy respect for the advice I am given hereabouts, no matter how irrelevant it may seem. Contrariwise, however, in all honesty I must state that prior to my arrival in your city the notion that I *might* be a god had never crossed my mind."

Was it possible for a god not to be aware that he was one? That paradox was not addressed in any of the books the margrave had studied. He exchanged frustrated glances first with Eadwil and then with Ruman, who snorted characteristically and called to Bernard Brown.

"Are we, then, to take it that you believe it possible you may be a god?"

"I don't know what to believe," said Bernard unhappily. "Until yesterday I had always pictured myself as a perfectly ordinary person. But certainly I am not ordinary in your world, wherever and whatever it may be."

"Come now!" said Ruman, bridling. "This is a reputable and well-regarded city! Or was, until you chose to intrude on its traditionally sober existence."

"If you will forgive my contradicting you," Bernard sighed, "I chose nothing of the sort. All I want is to be allowed to go home. Have I not already said as much?"

"This does not sound like the utterance of a god," the margrave muttered to Eadwil, who nodded.

"Sir," he said to Bernard, "we wish to establish the extent of your powers. To what knowledge lay you claim?"

"I am competent," said Bernard cautiously, "in matters touching roads, drains and bridges and similar practical undertakings. Is that the sort of thing you want to hear about?"

"Indeed it's not! But are you acquainted with the Book of Universal Shame, and can you conjure from it?"

By now the townspeople had ceased their going and coming before the altar, and were gathering in silence to listen to this discussion. It was plain that a few of them were unconvinced, propitiating Bernard only by way of insurance, as it were.

"I never heard of it," said Bernard, swallowing.

"Then of the Book of Three Red Elephants? Perhaps of the Casket of Disbelief?"

To each name Bernard shook his head.

Eadwil turned smiling to the margrave. "It is most unlikely that this fellow is a god!"

Then in their turn Petrovic, Gostala, and Ruman questioned Bernard about the most esoteric wisdom known to them— which implied the most esoteric known to anyone. Some few individuals surpassed the enchanters of Ryovora, such as Manuus, but those persons were far beyond the commerce of everyday life and chose to exist alone with their powers, seldom intruding on mundane affairs.

To each inquiry Bernard was constrained to reply in the negative, and in the watching crowd some began to stare significantly at Brim. The locksmith grew more and more flustered and annoyed, until at last, when Ruman had completed his interrogation, he strode forward and faced the altar challengingly, hands on hips.

"Let's have it straight!" he bellowed. "Are you a god, or have you come here under false pretenses?"

"I—I was advised not to deny it," said Bernard helplessly, and the margrave clapped his hand to his forehead.

"Fool that I am, after Eadwil gave me the clue!" he cried, and thrust Brim to one side, ignoring his complaint. "It was Tyllwin who advised you thus, was it not?"

"I don't suppose it can do any harm to say who it was," Bernard decided reflectively. "Uh . . . whether it was Tyllwin or not, I'm unsure, for he gave no name. But I can describe him: a very charming elderly gentleman, with a wisp of grey beard clinging at his chin."

"Manuus!" exclaimed several of the lords together, and the margrave whirled to face his colleagues.

"How many of you had seen Tyllwin before yesterday?" he demanded.

"Why—" began three or four, and as one fell silent with expressions of amazement.

"You have it!" snapped the margrave. "He was there, and by some enchantment persuaded us he was seated by right and custom. But I for one now realize that I have no other knowledge of Tyllwin. Well, then! So Manuus is behind the matter! We must go to him and tell him we will not tolerate his meddling in Ryovora's affairs. If he chose to live among us as a responsible citizen, that would be a different cauldron of spells. But as things are, we can only respect his privacy so long as he respects ours."

There was much shuffling of feet. With juvenile dignity Eadwil spoke up. "Margrave, I regret that I dare not face Manuus in this connection. My powers are inadequate as yet. I hate to shelter behind my youth—*but*!"

And he took his leave.

One by one, shamefaced, the others of the council copied his example, until the margrave was left by himself, whereupon the townsfolk, having garnered from these events only that the nobles had failed to disprove Bernard's divinity, made haste to resume their self-imposed tasks.

"A fine lot we breed in Ryovora!" exclaimed the margrave

scornfully. The scorn, though, was a mask for his own forebodings; he was less of an adept than many who served under him, having attained his eminence by administrative skills. Nonetheless he was a resolute man, and accordingly he summoned his train and set forth to beard Manuus in his castle.

The mists parted in such fashion as to imply that this call was not unexpected, and having left his attendants huddled together in the great yard he ascended to Manuus's sanctum with determined steps. There the enchanter greeted him with warm professions of respect.

But the margrave was ill at ease in this place of discomfortable forces, and came to the point as swiftly as manners would permit. He said firmly, when he had the chance, "Sir, since you are Tyllwin's master you know the purpose of my errand."

"Correction," the enchanter parried blandly. "I *am* Tyllwin. I have certain other natures besides my own—a trait I share with all persons save one alone."

The margrave made an appropriate sign at the mention of him who has many names but one nature, and pressed on with what he had to say.

"We will not tolerate interference, sir," he declared. "Since time immemorial we in Ryovora have striven to create a tradition of calm rationality, and to rely upon hard sense. This petty trick of intruding a so-called god like a gaming piece into our affairs is hardly worthy of a personage of your distinction."

"I agree," said Manuus. "You may therefrom deduce that the act is not of my choosing."

"What?" the margrave blurted.

"In this matter," the enchanter continued, ignoring the exclamation, "you and I are on the same side: so to say, the *outside*. It will perhaps interest you to learn that he of whom we were speaking a moment ago—whose nature is single—was sitting in that same chair only two days ago."

Wondering what he had stumbled into, the margrave shivered. He said respectfully, "Manuus, your powers are beyond imagining!"

"Oh, he did not come at my bidding!"—with a thin chuckle. "Rather the reverse!"

"However that may be, I shall take leave of you," said the margrave, rising and bowing. "For if this matter is *his* concern, I dare do nothing to intervene."

Eyes twinkling, Manuus shook his head. "I'm afraid you have no choice. Like it or not, both you and I have been concatenated in this web."

At which the margrave departed, his heart so heavy he could barely lift his boots, and when he was gone Manuus fell to ceremonies of a kind that had not been performed in living memory, which strange phenomena attended. There was a storm on peaceful Lake Taxhling; in Barbizond three madmen ran screaming through the streets; on a hill near Acromel dust devils ceased their whirling. Last, but not least, certain persons in Ryovora itself saw visions of a disturbing nature, and hastened to the new-designated temple to place yet more offerings at the feet of Bernard Brown and to consult the already sizable record of his sayings.

Studying them, they found no comfort.

VII

AND THUS the matter was to remain for another day. The margrave, making as was his custom the best of a bad job, called up an obliging spirit and had a pavilion erected in the Moth Garden to serve as a temporary surrogate for his palace; there he sat, swearing mightily, far into the night, while he pondered the information Manuus had divulged.

Those other nobles of Ryovora who were best skilled in the art of magic met to discuss in low tones over their wine the riddle of how to distinguish divinity from humanity. They

remained unswayed by both the clamor of the populace, led
by Brim, and the scant evidence furnished by their interrogation of Bernard Brown. It seemed implausible, they allowed,
that a person who claimed to know merely about matters as
base as roads and bridges should be a god; nonetheless, one
must respect the powers of Manuus, and perhaps in a mood to
make a jest of Ryovora he *could* have conjured up an authentic
deity and disguised him. . . . Did he not have the power to
disguise himself, even from them?

The common folk, likewise, found themselves impaled by
a dilemma. However, they had been longing for a god of whatever sort for a considerable while; indisputably someone strange
had come among them, preceded by complex indecipherable
omens, and it was generally deemed advisable to act as though
Bernard were a genuine god until some incontestable argument
to the contrary should be advanced.

So the night passed; and of those who spent it restlessly,
not the least fervent seeker of repose was Bernard Brown, for
all that his couch was a vast stack of gorgeous offerings in
velvet and satin.

Then came the dawn.

It had been centuries since another city marched against
Ryovora. The citizens had long ago deduced that their best
protection was their reputation; who after all would dare attack
that city where pre-eminently the populace enjoyed the gift
to plan and reason? No general, for sure, who depended on
ordinary and obedient soldiers, deprived by systematic training
of imagination and initiative!

Perennially cautious, though, in a world where even yet an
army might be raised of elemental spirits, they financed the
wages of a team of watchmen . . . and next day, as the sun
was rising, the current incumbent of the watchman's post en
route to his customary breakfast cast a casual glance across the
country separating Acromel from Ryovora.

And saw with astonishment – not to mention disbelief – that
a red idol a hundred feet high was striding with enormous yells
towards him.

Such an idol, the watchman realized, could be none other than the Quadruple God of Acromel.

Around the monstrous crimson feet were fetters of riveted steel; before and behind, men went with blazing torches on long poles, prodding and driving it in a desired direction. Sometimes the thing's yelling howled into a ridiculous falsetto when a torch made contact with its blood-colored limbs, and the drovers had to scatter and flee from the blows of eight gigantic fists. But they returned, and it became plain that they now well understood the reactions of the idol, and could drive it like a maddened bull because its rage made it unthinking.

The watchman sounded an alarm, and panic spread through the streets of Ryovora like floodwaters through a burst levee. Men, women, even children, roused from sleep to dash hither and thither in confusion.

One by one the nobles were summoned, and assembled on the ramparts with their retinues: an impressive band. Calmed by an enchantment that they spoke in unison, thousand by thousand the common folk acquired makeshift weapons—knives, axes, scythes—and numbered off into centuries to prepare for battle.

So arrayed they waited tensely while the sun cleared the horizon and the Quadruple God with his attendants came to take station before the city walls.

At a sign from one who seemed to be the leader, the torch-wielders compelled the god to halt, and he stood screaming empty threats at the unresponsive sky. Then this same man advanced to stand on a low knoll and gaze insolently at the Ryovoran nobles.

"Greetings!" he called merrily. "News has come to us in Acromel that in the past few days you've been fortunate enough to acquire a god! Well, as it happens we in Acromel have been fortunate in more ways than one—we've lost Duke Vaul, who had for many years oppressed us, and we've figured out how to make the Quadruple God do as he's told!" He gestured over his shoulder at the misshapen idol.

"It appears to us," he went on, "that our god is very foolish, although extremely strong. It is said that your god is weak, but extremely wise. We have not made head or tail of these cryptic utterances that have been relayed to us! Regardless of that, we wish to try conclusions and determine whether brute strength in a god is superior to sagacity! Sirs and ladies, we await your verdict! Failing a satisfactory response—by, let's say, the stroke of noon—we shall of course goad the Quadruple God into Ryovora, and since he overtops all but your highest towers I suspect that would be a major misfortune for the city. Naturally, however, we would retrieve whatever we could from the resulting ruins and remove it to Acromel for safe keeping! Until noon, therefore! And not a moment later!"

He bowed with a flourish of his right hand, and quit the knoll.

Scowling so deeply it seemed a ploughshare must have crossed his forehead, the margrave called the nobles into conference on the ramparts, and spoke worriedly concerning this challenge. Some were of opinion that if the personage with many names and but one nature had taken a hand, there was nothing any of them could do; others poured scorn on this fainthearted attitude, among them Ruman, whose bull laugh echoed around the walls.

"Never say die!" he boomed. "Some magic is of an order to bind even gods, and I have important knowledge of this magic. Fetch me a black goat and a white pigeon, and a mirror cracked from edge to edge, and I will discomfit the Quadruple Idiot!"

So it was ordained, and Ruman withdrew into a large black cloud with his goat, his pigeon and his mirror, and what he did to them caused thunderclaps.

But eventually the cloud blew away, and there was no trace of Ruman.

"This is ridiculous!" said Gostala with feminine directness, and Petrovic nodded his old dried-up head.

"I agree," he rasped. "Goats, forsooth! Pigeons! Mirrors! Claptrap, all of it! Now I came prepared, Margrave. I have here a phial containing the blood of an unborn child. That and my knowledge are all I require."

Thereupon Petrovic set about his task, and did what he had to do in the sight of all, which was most disturbing. The margrave, trying not to watch, wished Petrovic had had the decency to hide himself as Ruman had done.

Yet the business failed, and Petrovic returned to them at last speaking in a tongue no one could understand, and burst into tears when he realized what had transpired. Meantime the great red idol still fumed and howled and clanked his chains.

"Igoroth!" said Gostala in exasperation. "Dumedinnis! And likewise Algorethon!"

Three odd-looking gentlemen—one in blue, one in white, one in green—walked through a nearby wall and stood before her. None of them was entirely normal in appearance, though it was hard to say in what particular respect.

"Get rid of that—object!" directed Gostala forcefully.

The three peculiar personages looked at her, then at each other, then at her again. Premeditatedly they shook their heads, and departed, taking her with them.

Hastily the margrave hurled a protective charm around the city, to guard against a reappearance of the trio—for they were notoriously tough to tackle singly, let alone in concert—and bit his lip in frustration. This was a bad business altogether, and the worst fears he had carried away from his interview with Manuus were being overfulfilled.

"These are indeed magics to bind a god," said Eadwil, his boyish face white and strained because his feet were blazing hot, he having walked from his dwelling when news of the attack was brought. "But are they magics to bind one such as Manuus? Margrave, I think Tyllwin may be found in this vicinity."

"That is good plain reasoning!" the margrave said with enthusiasm. "You are a true citizen of Ryovora!"

He strode forward to the battlements and cupped his hands around his mouth. "Tyllwin!" he bellowed towards the Acromel party. "Tyllwin, ha!"

An acre of grass turned brown and died, while songbirds that had been chanting in the trees nearby fell stiffly from their perches. From the besieging company the gaunt figure of Tyllwin was borne into view on the back of a brawny slave.

"You desire converse with me, Margrave?" said that scarecrow form.

"So this *is* your doing!" exclaimed the margrave in disgust.

Tyllwin's thin chuckle carried clearly to his ears; also to those of various dogs, causing them to howl.

"Why, Margrave, did I not state that you and I are on the same side in this matter? Admit frankly that the pretended god in your palace is not to your taste! Admit that it is in our common interest to demonstrate his fallibility by matching him against this perfectly genuine god from Acromel!"

"It's for this reason you have destroyed three of the leading enchanters of our city?" countered the margrave. "Why could you not have left us to sort the matter out ourselves?"

Tyllwin's voice was suddenly as dull as doom. "Because he whose nature is single has a hand in the affair."

He fell silent. A horse neighed into the quietness, and the neigh became a scream of agony.

The margrave turned beseechingly to Eadwil, who shook his head. "Against Manuus, which of us can stand?" he said. "Moreover, the situation is escaping our control. Look down into the street. The townsfolk have gone to fetch their god, supplicating him for protection."

Indeed, down the broad avenue leading to the main gate they saw a pressing throng of citizens, and among them a figure in outlandish costume who was crying out for aid and receiving none. Brim the locksmith could be discerned grasping him by the elbow, hurrying him along willy-nilly, and occasional voices rang out distinct above the general uproar.

"Save us! Defeat the enemy god! We have no hope except in you!"

"Hah!" sighed the margrave in mingled pity and annoyance. "So nothing will convince them the poor wretch is not a god but that he be laid low by the Quadruple One. Well, now at least we know which way the lot is cast."

Eadwil summoned the ghost of a smile. "I wonder!" he said, "I wonder . . . !"

Shortly, the ringleaders among the crowd opened the gates, and the folk poured forth onto an open level space where they could confront the menacing array of troops from Acromel. On seeing those armored ranks—for the enemy had made careful preparations, whereas the folk of Ryovora had been taken by surprise—many felt qualms and tried to draw back, but the press was too great, and at length the mass of them, in number three or four thousand, simmered and seethed but stood still.

Urging his god forward, glistening with sweat, Brim the locksmith forced a path to the front of the crowd. "There!" he shouted, throwing up his arm to indicate the hideous red idol. "That's the best they can muster against you! Hark at his howling! Why, already he fears your mere presence!"

"I must go down," said the margrave in low tones. "I have no stomach to stand up here and watch the poor fools massacred."

"I'll come with you," Eadwil said.

Accordingly they descended together to the gate. Among muttered threats from the commoners, saying that if these nobles were going to interfere out of spite they would earn short shrift, they elbowed closer and closer to Bernard. The heat of Eadwil's feet helped clear a path.

At last the margrave stood face to face with Bernard Brown, and cast on him a look eloquent of sympathy.

"This is none of our doing," he said in apologetic tones. "It seems the people of Ryovora, so long accounted sensible, have finally taken leave of their good sense."

Bernard blinked at him unhappily. "I fear you are right, sir," he agreed. "Especially since this galumphing monstrosity is plainly nothing more than an overgrown child."

"A—*what?*" said the margrave, and Eadwil was seen to be grinning almost from ear to ear.

"An overgrown child," repeated Bernard patiently. "Why, he howls and strikes out and breaks things at random! This is not the behavior of an intelligent, adult personality! Moreover, one must assume that the folk of Acromel have attempted to establish communication with their idol, must one not?"

"Why—ah . . ." The margrave was bewildered. "One would imagine so, yes!"

"Yet their preferred mode of converse proves to be torches on long sticks." Bernard spread his hands. "One may deduce that we have here a case of arrested development, not entirely on the idol's part, so what I would propose . . ."

VIII

WAVE UPON WAVE of laughter rang out around the walls of
Ryovora, and at once the citizens, aided and abetted by the
margrave, set about implementing Bernard's plan. Eadwil stood
a little apart, his lips set in a smile that bid fair to become
permanent.

Meanwhile the sky attained full brightness and the sun
hoisted itself towards the meridian. Among the ranks of those
from Acromel a certain impatience grew manifest. The torches
which served to goad the idol were withdrawn one by one,
soaked in fresh pitch, and relit; the chains which tethered his
sixteen limbs were firmly anchored to posts hammered deep
in the ground, so that the teams of men afoot and ahorse who
weighed him down when he was on the move might relax for
a while; but in the comings and goings of the mass there was
more restlessness than purpose.

Ultimately, close upon midday, the spokesman who had
previously addressed the nobility of Ryovora again ascended
his knoll and called for the margrave. Sweating from hard
work, hands filthy, his richly embroidered sleeves turned back
above his elbows, that official leaned over the ramparts and
responded with a wave.

"Ah, there you are, your honor! It's time to remind you that
our god is restive! Time wastes—it's almost noon—and we hunger to learn the outcome of this matter!"

The margrave glanced down into the avenue paralleling the
wall, where work had proceeded apace under Bernard Brown's

direction. Far below, Eadwil raised both arms to signal that all was ready.

"Good!" said the margrave privately, and shouted to the spokesman for Acromel.

"Our city's god is prepared to meet yours!"

At once the man from Acromel yelled to those charged with loosing the Quadruple God from his chains. A moment passed; then, from amid the crowd before the gate of Ryovora, diffidently yet with unfaltering strides, Bernard Brown marched forth to face the enemy.

A gust of merriment ascended, and the welkin rang with scornful gibes. But Bernard kept on plodding towards the Quadruple God.

And the huge red idol paid him no attention.

Because behind the approaching man, behind the ramparts of the city, another figure was appearing amid a cloud of smoke—a figure so gigantic, so bloated, so colossal, that the Quadruple God seemed a dwarf or midget by comparison. This apparition bore a head with glaring yellow eyes and twenty-foot-long fangs in its gash of a mouth; it had arms like a hundred barrels; it had legs planted either side of a tall building.

And this figure was growing. It was rising as though from the depths of the earth, and all four heads of the Quadruple God were striving to fix their eyes on it at once.

Gracefully, considering its bulk—this was thanks to an afterthought of Eadwil's—the bloated colossus raised its arms into a posture of menace. From the camp of the men of Acromel the naked eye could not detect the fine silk cords governing its motions.

And then this construct of inflated wineskins, of paint and osier and waxed fabric supported by hot air—a smidgin supplemented by that quick charm of Eadwil's—spoke with the massed voices of all the citizens of Ryovora, a sound like the crashing of a landslide.

"Go away!" said the monster with terrible emphasis. "*Go away!*"

Whereat the Quadruple God burst his chains, stamped on the torchbearers, and took to his multiple heels.

Only once was his panicky progress interrupted before he regained the familiar sanctuary of his temple at Acromel.

That was when a gaunt and scarecrowlike person rushed into his path, crying in a voice which though thin and reedy caused cracks to open in the surface of the land and strange colors to muddy the clear blue of the heavens.

The Quadruple God trampled this nuisance with three of his eight massive feet, leaving nothing but a smear like a crushed beetle to mark the spot.

Triumphantly the inhabitants of Ryovora went forward in the wake of those who had come from Acromel, and with their ad hoc weapons they wrought considerable havoc among the laggards. Not the most tongue-tied among them was Brim the locksmith, who expended more breath on shouting praise of his own perceptiveness than on catching up with the rearguard of the enemy.

But certain of his fellows who had been lukewarm in their acceptance of Bernard Brown as a ready-made god turned aside to surround Brim in a hostile fashion. "Nonsense!" they said emphatically. "If we had not been lured by fools like you away from our customary trust in common sense, we would have seen what he saw and done what he advised anyway!"

Then they set about Brim with meticulous thoroughness, impressing the extent of his stupidity upon him in such fashion as to ensure he could never again overlook their various mementos. The tools of his trade that he carried in his leather apron proved ideally adapted to the task.

That chore attended to, and the Acromel party in utter disarray, they returned with satisfaction to their homes. By nightfall the aura of blue depression which had pervaded the atmosphere these many weeks past had dissipated; the cause for rejoicing which this gave them made them forget altogether about Bernard Brown.

The margrave and his nobles assembled again in the Moth Garden. The people had begun to reclaim the offerings they had set before Bernard's altar, to feast on them and deck themselves in gaudy ceremonial attire. To preoccupy the nobles, though, there were still problems, and Eadwil spoke of the most pressing when they met.

He said, "I think, sirs and ladies, that the era of enchantment is passing."

The margrave nodded. So did many others. All of them glanced at the place which had been—briefly—Tyllwin's.

"Regard it this way," said Eadwil musingly. "Of its nature enchantment, magic, whatever term you give the art, is a survival of the chaos which we know reigned before time. But the imprint of that chaos is fading from the world. The confusion which causes stone idols to walk, elementals to be personified in storm-clouds, humans to blend with animals, and spirits to speak from fire and water, is gradually succumbing to that same hard plain sense on which we of Ryovora traditionally rely."

"Well spoken!" applauded the margrave. Eadwil cast him a sidelong glance and concluded thus.

"Whether as Tyllwin or himself, Manuus is—was?—a master of chaos. So are we all in lesser degree. But the greatest master of us all has proved to be a simple stranger lacking all acquaintance with the esoteric arts. Colleagues and friends, magic is of the past. Rationality and logic will rule the future." He bent his gaze below the table. "My feet, I may add, have not pained me since I arrived at this conclusion. So I think I shall forthwith take steps to set right the other disadvantage consequent upon my command of magic. Excuse me."

And with a hop and a skip he departed in the wake of a saucy-eyed girl who was bearing fruit from the garden to the feast the people were preparing.

Another who stood unobserved among the vines and trellises was a black-clad traveller, whose face twitched into a smile when he heard Eadwil's words. He did not need to wait longer or listen more.

IX

ON THAT SAME KNOLL from which the spokesman of Acromel's forces had addressed the margrave, Bernard Brown sat with his chin in his hands, staring gloomily at nothing. His dismal contemplation was interrupted at length by one who was not a stranger, who stood before him leaning on a remarkable staff.

"I've seen you before," said Bernard slowly. "Well, who are you?"

The black-clad one chuckled. "He to whom the task was given of bringing order forth from chaos in this corner of the universe. And who are you?"

"I'm not sure I know any longer," Bernard admitted after a pause. "Until recently I thought I was Bernard Brown, an ordinary sort of person with an ordinary kind of job. But these past few days people have been telling me so repeatedly I'm a god that I've almost been convinced of the idea."

The black-clad man clucked his tongue. "I'm afraid that isn't true at all," he said. "So—since I was responsible for involving you with all this—I'd better explain."

He sat down companionably alongside Bernard, and made a gesture in the air with his staff. A short distance away, in a pleasant meadow, some clinging ground mist cleared to reveal the ruins of a castle, smoking quietly.

"An enchanter called Manuus dwelt there," he said. "A person with—so to speak—a vested interest in the chaos which formerly pervaded the All. *This* sort of thing."

He gestured again, and out of a hill a mile or two this side of Acromel a—a—a . . . Well, a pair of yellow eyes peered for

52

an instant. What could be seen in those eyes defied description. It made Bernard shudder with amazement and repugnance.

"So where am I?" he demanded. "Or is it a question of *when* am I?"

"Neither. We are speaking of a borderland between chaos, existing in eternity, and reason, existing in time. At this moment the balance is uncertain, but it is tilting, bit by bit. You have been quite invaluable in tipping it beyond a crucial point."

"I don't understand," complained Bernard.

"No matter. If you did understand the nature of chaos, men being what they are, you would certainly be conceited enough to wish to exploit it. This in fact is what those vain enchanters do: turn the forces of chaos to their own advantage. But, logically, to control chaos with reason is to impose lasting order on it. This implies in turn that sooner or later chaos will reign no longer."

Bernard's face exhibited sudden comprehension. "I see!" he exclaimed. "In other words, these magicians or whatever necessarily destroy what they most desire to preserve."

"You grasp the point exactly," said the one in black.

"And it's up to you to ensure things come out right?"

"That is the case."

"Hmm!" Bernard rubbed his chin. "That sounds like a tough chore. Who landed you with it, if I may ask?"

"You may not. I'm very sorry." The tone was final; still, the words were succeeded by a chuckle. This black-garbed fellow was really very pleasant, Bernard reflected. Casting around for the other question he had meant to put, he recalled it.

"Well, then! May I at least ask what it was I *did?*"

"That, yes! You see, there was dissatisfaction in Ryovora so long as the people felt they had to have a god. So I gave them one . . . of a kind. And in the end they realized their god— you!—had done nothing for them which they themselves could not have achieved by using their heads. My compliments, by the way, on the elegant manner in which you demonstrated that."

"I was scared silly," confessed Bernard.

"But you kept your wits about you, and refused to be overawed by mere size. The universe is a big place, and there are many corners of it where chaos on the grand scale still obtains. This, then, is a valuable attitude."

Bernard pondered for a while. At last he shook his head and sighed. "It's no good. I can't deal in these terms. Magic—monsters staring out of hillsides—creatures half man, half beast—stone idols that can walk . . . It's the stuff of nightmare! Even though I seem to remember seeing it, I don't believe it's real."

"Thank you," said his companion dryly. "That you speak thus is an earnest of my eventual success. Sometimes it seems a very long way off."

"What will—if this is the right way to put it—what will happen then?"

"*I* don't know," said the traveller. "Why should I care? I'll have finished my appointed task. And since you have now concluded yours . . ."

When he was alone, the traveller in black stood awhile leaning on his staff of curdled light, contemplating the wreck of Manuus's castle.

Chaos.

He decreed it out of existence. Since Manuus no longer held it tenaciously in being, it disappeared. Across the site the grass grew green and orderly.

The traveller wished that Bernard had not asked his last question. It was discomforting. Now and then he regretted that he must inevitably find out its answer.

Yet it was not in his nature—and his nature was single—to undo anything he had done. Therefore, inexorably, he was approaching that ultimate moment.

He shrugged, and then there was nothing but the knoll and the afternoon sunlight, while people made merry in Ryovora.

TWO

Break the Door of Hell

I will break the door of hell and smash the bolts; I will summon the dead to eat food with the living, and the living shall be outnumbered by the host of them.

—The Epic of Gilgamesh

I

TIME HAD COME to Ryovora.

The traveller in black contemplated the fact from the brow of the hill where he had imprisoned Laprivan, more aeons ago than it was possible to count. Leaning on his staff of light, he repressed a shiver. Single though his nature might be, unique though that attribute certainly was, he was not immune from apprehension; his endowments did not include omniscience.

Time had come to that great city; time, in which could exist order and logic and rational thought. And so it was removed from his domain forever, vanished from the borderland of chaos situated timeless in eternity.

Given the task for which his single nature fitted him, one might have expected that he should feel the satisfaction of achievement, or even pleasurable if mild conceit. He did not, and for this there were two most cogent reasons and a third which he preferred not to consider.

The first, and most piquing, was that his duty lay upon him; this season followed the conjunction of four significant planets hereabout, and he was setting forth, as he was constrained, to oversee that portion of the All which lay in his charge. And he had grown accustomed to terminating his round of inspection at Ryovora. Lapses and backsliding from common sense had occasionally minded him to alter this habit; still, he had never done so, and to discover that Ryovora was elsewhere displeased him somewhat.

The second reason was worse than displeasing. It was alarming, and dismaying, and unprecedented, and many other distressing epithets.

"In sum," the traveller in black announced to the air, "it's unheard-of!"

Another city had arisen in the borderland of chaos, and it was stamped all over with the betraying mark of time.

How was it possible? Carried in some eddy whose flow ran counter to the universal trend, so that from reason and logic it receded to the random reign of chance? Presumably. Yet the means whereby such an eddy might be created seemed inconceivable. Some great enchantment would be required, and in the grip of time such magic was impossible.

"A contradiction in terms!" exclaimed the traveller, speaking aloud again to distract his mind from the third and least palatable reason for regretting the loss of Ryovora and its substitution by another, unfamiliar, city. It was known to him that when he had accomplished his purpose all things would have but one nature; then they would be subsumed into the Original All and time would have a stop.

But if an entire city could be shifted in the wrong direction, from time into eternity, from rationality to chaos, it followed that someone, or something, or some impersonal force must be arrayed against him that he had never previously guessed at!

This conclusion was disturbing. Yet inevitable.

He glanced around the hillside. As ever, among the sparse and grey-leaved bushes, dust devils were sifting their substance, fine as ashes, over the footprints he had left on the path. Raising his staff, he tapped it on a rock: once, twice, and again.

At the third tap the elemental Laprivan of the Yellow Eyes heaved in his underground prison and cracks appeared in the road. From these his voice boomed, monstrous, making the welkin echo.

"Leave me be!"

"What do you know of the city that stands yonder?" said the traveller in black.

"Nothing," responded Laprivan with sullenness.

"Nothing? You say so to spare yourself the pain of memory!

Shall I send you where Ryovora has gone, into the domain of time? There memories cannot be expunged by whirling dust!"

The whole hill shuddered, and an avalanche of pale rock rattled on its further side. The sourceless voice moaned, "What should I know of yonder city? No one has come from it and passed this way."

"Bad," said the traveller thoughtfully. "Very bad."

After that he was silent a long while, until at last the elemental pleaded, "Leave me be! Leave me to wipe clean the slate of yesterday!"

"As you wish, so be it," said the traveller absently, and tapped with his staff again. The cracks in the ground closed; the dust devils resumed their gyrations.

Ignoring all this, the traveller gazed over the green and gracious meadows of the valley. There the strange city lay in noontide sunlight like a worn-out toy cast aside by a giant-child. The heedless ruin of time was everywhere about it, toothmarks of the greatest leveller on brick and stone and metal. It had been fair and rich, that was plain; its gates were of oak and bronze—but the bronze was corroded green; its towers were of silver and orichalcum—but their bright sheen was overlaid with a dull mist like the foul breath of a swamp; its streets were broad and paved with marble—but the flags lifted to the roots of wild plants, and here and there one found holes filled by rain and noxious with algae and the larvae of biting insects.

Out of time and into chaos. Almost beyond belief.

At length he bestirred himself. There was nothing else for it—so he reasoned—but to set off on his journey of obligation, and come at last not to familiar, welcome Ryovora but to this enigma wished on him by fate and boding no good whatsoever.

Anxiety carried him far and fast, and little by little it was mitigated by relief. To learn that Acromel still stood where it had, albeit altered; to find that they yet fished Lake Taxhling when the proper stars came out, and that the river Metamorphia fed it with strange unspawned creatures, greedy and unwholesome—this was reassuring, an earnest of balance continued in the cosmos.

And at these places, and many many more, he did what on this as on all his journeys was required of him.

A lonely hut stood on the shelf edge of a mountain pasture in the land called Eyneran; here, when he paused to ask a crust of bread and a sup of ewe's milk from the flock high and distant as clouds on the steep meadow, a woman with a frightened face opened the ill-carpentered door to him, and met his request with a silent shake of the head.

She was wrinkled and worn out beyond her years; yet the hut was sound, a savory smell filled the air, and the clean floor and many copper pots the traveller could see assorted badly with her ragged gown and bare feet. He waited. Shortly a cry rang out, man-deep, yet edged with a spoilt child's petulance.

"Mother, come here! The pot's boiling over! What's keeping you, you lazy slut?"

"Mintra!" whispered the woman, and a patter of feet announced the passage of a girl, some twelve years old, across the single room to tend the pot.

Another cry, still louder: "Mother, I told you to come here! Mintra can't lift the pot when it's full, you stupid old bag of bones!"

"We can't give you food," the woman said to the traveller. "All of it is for my son."

The traveller nodded, but waited still. Then at last with great heaving and panting the son came into view: bulging-bellied in his apparel of velvet worked with gilt wire and stained with slobberings of food, so tall he nearly scraped the roof with his pate, yet so fat he breathed hard for the simple effort of standing upright. His fist, big as a ham, cracked his mother behind the ear.

"Why don't you die, you lazy old cow, and get it over with?" he bellowed.

"It'd be a merciful relief," the woman whimpered. "And die I would of my own free will, but that I stand alone between you and Mintra! With me gone you'd take her like a harlot, sister or no!"

"And wouldn't she be a tasty bit for my bed?" chortled the

son with an evil grin, his tongue emerging thick as an ox's to stroke his lips lasciviously.

"As you wish," said the traveller, "so be it." And he knocked his staff on the threshold and took his leave.

That night plague stole silent from the mountain mist, and took the mother as the son had wished; then the girl Mintra fled on light feet down the hill trails and the fever-giddy glutton went calling her among the heedless sheep until his gross weight dislodged a rock and sent him over a precipice to feed the crows.

In the rich city Gryte a thief spoke to curse the briefness of the summer night, which had cut short his plan to break the wall of a merchant's countinghouse.

"Oh that dawn never overtook me!" he cried. "Oh that I had lasting darkness whereby to ply my trade!"

"As you wish," said the traveller, "so be it." And darkness came: two thick grey cataracts that shut the light away.

Likewise in Medham was another rogue, striving to seduce a lady who feared her charms were passing with the years so that he might win to a coffer of gold secreted in her chamber. "I love you!" declared this smooth-tongued deceiver. "I'd wed you had you no more than rags and a shack!"

"As you wish, so be it," said the traveller, and bailiffs came to advise the lady that her house and treasure were forfeit on another's debt. Upon which the liar turned and ran, not staying to hear a city officer hard on the bailiffs' heels, come to report the honoring of the debt a day past due.

So too in Wocrahin a swaggering bully came down the street on market day, cuffing aside children with the back of his hand and housewives with the flat of his sword. "Oh that my way were not cluttered with such riffraff!" he exclaimed, his shoulder butting the traveller in the chest.

"As you wish, so be it," said the latter, and when the bully turned the corner the street he walked was empty under a leaden sky—and the buildings on either side, and the taverns, and the shops. Nor did he again in all eternity have to push aside the riffraff he had cursed; he was alone.

* * *

This, however, was not the sum total of the traveller's doings as he passed from place to place within his realm. In Kanish-Kulya they had built a wall to keep Kanishmen and Kulyamen apart, and from either side, set into the masonry, grinned down the skulls of those dead in a war for which the reason had long been forgotten. In this strange and dreadful place Fegrim was pent under a volcano; shadowed by its cone the traveller halted and spoke long and seriously with that elemental, and when he was done the country for a mile on every side was dusted with cinders, little and bright as fireflies.

At Gander's Well, branched Yorbeth brooded in the guise of a tall tree whose main root tapped a wonderful subterranean spring and whose boughs, fed with miraculous sap, sprouted leaves and fruit the like of which had not been seen under any sun before. The traveller spent an hour in the shade of that tree, and for the questions he asked was constrained to carry away a red twig and later catch a cat and perform a ceremony with these two items—a price he paid with heavy heart, for he had been told nothing of any great use in his inquiries.

Also he consulted with Farchgrind, and in Leppersley he cast the bones of a girl's foot to read the runes they formed, and after great labor he incarcerated Wolpec in a candle over whose flame he smoked a piece of glass which thereupon showed three truths: one ineluctable, one debatable, and one incomprehensible. That was in Teq, when the end of his journey was near.

So presently he came to Barbizond, where there was always a rainbow in the sky because of the bright being Sardhin, chained inside a thundercloud with fetters of lightning. Three courses remained to him: he might free Sardhin and let him speak, and from here to the horizon nothing would be left save himself, the elemental, and that which was of its nature bright, as jewels, or fire, or the edge of a keen-bladed knife; or he might do as once he had done under similar circumstances—address himself to an enchanter and make use of powers that trespassed too far towards naked chaos to be within his own scope—or, finally, he might go forward in ignorance to the strange city and confront the challenge of fate without the armor of foreknowledge.

Some little while remained before he needed to take his irreversible decision. Coming to Barbizond, therefore, he made his way down a fine broad avenue where plane and lime trees alternated in the direction of a steel-blue temple. There stood the altar of Hnua-Threl, who was also Sardhin when he chose to be; the people invoked him with daily single combats on the temple floor. They were not a gentle folk, these inhabitants of Barbizond, but they were stately, and died—in tournaments, or by the assassin's knife, or by their own hand—with dignity.

A death had lately occurred, that was plain, for approaching the city gate came a funeral procession: on a high-wheeled cart drawn by apes in brazen harness, the corpse wrapped in sheets of lead and gold and interwoven leaves; a band of gongmen beating a slow measure to accompany musicians whistling on bird-toned pipes no longer than a finger; eight female slaves naked to the ceaseless warm rain; and at last a straggle of mourners, conducting themselves for the most part with appropriate solemnity.

He who passed penultimately of the mourners, however, was a fat and jolly person on each of whose shoulders perched a boy-child, and the two were playing peekaboo around the brim of his enormous leather hat. The traveller stared long at him before stepping out from the shelter of the nearest tree and addressing him courteously.

"Your pardon, sir, but are you not named Eadwil?"

"I am," the fat one said, not loath to let the funeral wend its way to the graveyard without his assistance. "Should I know you as you apparently know me?"

"Perhaps not," said the traveller in black. "I'd not expected to see you here; you were formerly one of the chief merchant-enchanters of Ryovora."

"A long time ago," Eadwil answered with a deprecating smile. The children on his shoulders giggled; one of them tried to catch hold of the traveller's staff, almost lost his balance, and righted himself with the aid of a pat from Eadwil's broad soft hand.

"May I ask what brought about your change of residence?" the traveller murmured.

"My change of employment." Eadwil shrugged, again nearly dislodging the more venturesome boy. "You spoke of me as a merchant-enchanter; so I was! But when the decision was taken, back in the days of my youth, to let rational thought rule Ryovora and put an end to conjurations there, certain consequences followed. For myself I have no regrets; there was a geas on me which made my feet glow red-hot when I walked, and now nothing worse attends a long tramp like today's than an occasional blister. And these my grandsons too—hey, you little nuisances?—they'd not be here today if I'd continued to submit to the other main restriction that purchased my powers." He rubbed the boys' backs affectionately, and they responded by pulling his ears.

This was quite true, as the traveller was aware. Eadwil had postponed the growing of his beard until unusually late in life by making the trade on which his command of magic had been founded.

"So there came an end to my conjuring of spices and fine silks, of rare wines and exotic perfumes!" Eadwil pursed his lips. "And there were, one must confess, certain persons in Ryovora who felt the lack of these luxuries and accused us retired enchanters of—ha-hm!—betraying them. Therefore I removed to Barbizond. It's a fair city in its way, and even though the local customs are not wholly to my taste, here they do at least have scores of enchanters of their own, so that no one plagues me to be about magical doings. . . . You have late news of Ryovora, sir? For it comes to my mind that I've heard nothing from my old home in quite a while."

The traveller gave a wry smile. "It's a fair span since I set foot there, too. Indeed, I was hoping you might be able to give me certain crucial information which I lack, rather than vice versa."

Eadwil looked politely downcast at being of no help; then one of the boys grew impatient and started to fidget.

"Home?" said his grandfather, and laughed indulgently. "Very well—old Harpentile is in no state to notice that we failed to attend his burying. Good day to you, sir," he added to the traveller. "It's been pleasant to renew our acquaintance, and

I greatly hope you'll soon find someone who can aid in your inquiries."

"As you wish, so be it," said the traveller under his breath, and a vast weight seemed to recede from his heart.

II

THAT ACCOMPLISHED, there was no more to do than sit and wait until the course of fate worked itself out. The traveller took a chair at a curbside tavern; with his elbows on a green tabletop, protected from the rain by a round blue umbrella fringed with pink, he watched the passers-by and wondered in what guise his helper would appear.

As the day wasted the avenue grew ever more crowded. Horsemen in bright jerkins came by with armor clanking at their saddlebows, challengers in some tourney for the hand of an heiress; also there were pedlars, and wonder-workers possessed of a few small tricks—for which they had paid excessively, to judge by their reddened eyes, pocked cheeks, limping gait, or boy-shrill voices. . . . No wonder, the traveller reflected, Eadwil felt his grandsons were the better bargain.

Women too passed: high-wimpled dames attended by maids and dandling curious unnamable pets; harlots in diaphanous cloaks through which it was not quite possible to tell if they were diseased; goodwives with panniers of stinking salted fish, loaves of fresh bread, and sealed jars of pollywogs for use in the commonplace home enchantments of this city.

And children likewise: many naked, not necessarily from poverty but because skin was the best raincoat under Barbizond's light continual shower, others in fantastical costumes to match their parents' whims—helmets of huge eggshells, bodices of leaves glued like scales, breeches made to resemble plant stems in springtime. With spinning windmills, toy lances, tops and hoops and skipping-ropes, they darted among the adults and left a trail of joyful disorder.

There was no joy in the heart of the traveller in black—only a dulled apprehension.

The places at the tables before the tavern filled with customers, until only one was left—the second chair at the table where the traveller waited. Then, to the instant, appeared a curious bewildered figure from the direction of the southern gate: a pale-faced, wild-haired man in a russet cape, clutching a pitiful bag of belongings like a baulk of timber in an ocean of insanity. Time had etched his brow with suffering, and the traveller knew, the moment he clapped eyes on him, that this was the person he expected.

Abreast of the tavern the stranger stopped. Enviously he scanned the delicacies placed before the customers: fragrant stoups of wine, dumplings in aromatic herbal sauce, mounds of mashed fruit stuck with crisp slivers of the moonbark that only this city's enchanters knew how to conjure safe across the freezing gulf of space. . . . Huddling his bag under his arm, he felt in his scrip for money, and produced one solitary copper coin.

Hesitant, he approached the traveller in black. "Sir, by your leave," he muttered, "will this purchase anything at your tavern here?" And proffered the coin on a trembling palm.

Taking it, the traveller turned it over, and was at pains to conceal the shock he felt on seeing the name inscribed on its reverse.

Ys!

A city in the realm of time so great and famous that rumors of it had crossed the tenuous border of chaos, running ahead of those who bore its news until the stories were magnified beyond believing, until true prophecies arose caused by the recirculation of those rumors through one corner of eternity and back to time ahead of reality.

Hmm . . . !

"No?" said the stranger sadly, seeing how long the black-clad one spent staring at his only money.

"Why—!" the latter exclaimed, and rubbed the coin with his fingertips, very lightly. "I should say so, friend! Is it not good gold, that passes anywhere?"

"Gold?" The stranger snatched it back, almost dropping his shabby bag in his agitation, and scrutinized it incredulously. Through the coppery tarnish gleamed the dull warm yellow of precious metal.

Without more ado he slumped into the vacant chair beside the traveller. A waggle-hipped servant-girl came promptly to his signal. "Food and drink!" he snapped, letting the miraculous coin ring on the table. "I starve and I'm clemmed with thirst—therefore be quick!"

Eyes twinkling, the traveller regarded his new acquaintance. "And how are you called, sir?" he demanded.

"Jacques of Ys is my name," the other sighed. "Though truth to tell I'm not overmuch inclined to add my origin to my name any longer."

"Why so?"

"Would you wish to be shamed by connection with a cityful of fools?"

"Considering the matter with due reflection," said the traveller, "I think—no."

"Well, then!" Jacques ran his long bony fingers through his already tousled hair; the rain had been trying to slick it down, but half an ocean would have been unequal to the task. He was a gaunt man, neither old nor young, with burning grey eyes and a bush of tawny beard.

"So in what way are the folk of Ys so foolish?" probed the traveller.

"Oh, once they were a great people," grunted Jacques. "And that's where the trouble started, I suppose. Once we had a fleet—and not on any landlocked lake, either, but on Oceanus itself, mother of storms and gulls. Also we had an army to guard our trade routes, skillful money-changers, wise counsellors. . . . Ah, Ys was among the noblest cities of the world!"

"I believe I've heard so," the traveller agreed.

"Then, sir, your news is stale!" Jacques thumped the table.

"Listen! There came changes—in the times, in the weather, in the currents of the sea. To be expected, *I* said, for did not Heraclitus teach us 'all things flow'? But soft living and much ease had stolen the brains out of the people's heads! Faced with the silting up of our great estuary, did they turn to it and build dredgers? They did not! Faced with a landslide that closed our chief silk-road, did they send scouts to spy out other routes? They did not! Faced with long winters that killed our autumn wheat in the ground, did they sow barley or the hardy northern oat? They did not!"

"Then what did they do?" the traveller inquired. "If anything."

"Fell first to moaning and wringing their hands, and lamenting their sad fate by night and day; then, when this proved unfruitful and incapable of filling the granaries, turned to a crowning imbecility and invoked the aid of magic. I see you scowl, sir, and well you may, for all the world knows that magic is a vain and ridiculous snare laid by evil demons in the path of humankind."

This was a stubborn unobservant fellow, clearly; with his hand closed around a coin that veritable magic—and no petty domestic hearth-spell, either—had turned from copper to gold, he could still make such a blunt assertion. He would not care for this domain in which he now found himself. . . . Still, there was no help for that.

"And to what purpose tended their research in—ah—*magic?*" the traveller asked.

"To bring back the great days of the past, if you please," said Jacques with majestic scorn, and on the last word crammed his mouth full from a dish the serving-girl placed before him.

While he assuaged his hunger, his companion contemplated these new data. Yes, such an event as Jacques had outlined would account for the paradox of Ys reversing the cosmic trend and exchanging time for eternity and its attendant confusions. But there must have been a great and terrible lust in the minds of very many people for the change to come about; there must have been public foolishness on a scale unparalleled throughout the All. Thinking on this, the traveller felt his face grow grim.

Reaching for his staff, he made to depart, and Jacques glanced up with his cheeks bulging. Having swallowed frantically, he spoke. "Sir, did I intrude on your meditations? Your pardon if—"

"No, no! You merely recalled me to some unfinished business. You are correct in your description of the folk of Ys. They are fools indeed. So do not—if you will take my advice—return there."

"Where else am I to go, then?" countered Jacques, and for a second despair looked out from behind his eyes. "I set off thinking no place could be worse than my hometown had now become—yet on this brief journey I've seen horrors and marvels that make me question my good sense. I met a creature on the road that was neither man nor beast, but a blending; I saw a shining sprite washing feet like alabaster in a cloud rimmed with rainbows; and once when I bent to drink from a stream I saw pictures in the water which . . . No, I dare not say what I thought I saw."

"That would be the brook called Geirion," said the traveller, and appended a crooked smile. "Don't worry—things seen therein can never become real. The folk round about visit it to rid themselves of baseless fears."

Jacques glanced over his shoulder at the motley crowd of passersby and shivered with dismay. "Nonetheless, sir, I'm not minded to remain in this peculiar city!"

"It would be more comfortable for you to adapt to the local customs than go home," the traveller warned. "A certain rather spectacular doom is apt to overtake Ys, if things are as you say."

"Doom!" cried Jacques, and an unholy joy lit his face. "I told them so—over and again I told them! Would I could witness it, for the satisfaction of seeing how right I was!"

The traveller sighed, but there was no help for it now; his single nature bound him to single courses of action. He said sourly, "As you wish, so be it. Go hence towards the city men call Acromel, the place where honey is bitter, but do not enter it. Go rather around it towards the setting sun, and you will reach a grey hill fledged with grey bushes where there are always dust devils, which will wipe out your tracks the moment you have passed. From the top of that hill you may behold Ys at the moment of disaster."

"Now just a moment!" Jacques exclaimed, rising. "From my

boyhood up I've wandered around Ys, and I know of no such hill as you describe!"

The traveller shrugged and turned away. Jacques caught his cloak.

"Wait! What's your name, that you say such strange things and send me on such an improbable errand?"

"You may call me anything you choose," the traveller said, shaking off the other's grip with a moue of distaste.

"Hah! That's rich!" Jacques set his hands on his hips and laughed. "But still . . . Well, sir, for the sake of wanting to see how Ys goes to its doom, I'll follow your instructions. And my thanks!"

He parodied a bow, flourishing a hat that was not on his head.

"You may not thank me more than this once," said the traveller sadly, and went his way.

III

LORD VENGIS SAT in the Hall of State at Ys and surveyed the nobility assembled in his presence. He tried to ignore the sad condition of his surroundings. Once this had been a building to marvel at: mirrors higher than a man lined its walls, set between pilasters of marble, gilt, and onyx, while the arching roof had been painted by a great master with scenes in eleven bright colors, depicting the birth of Saint Clotilda, the martyrdom of Saint Gaufroy—that one was mostly in red—and the ascension of Saint Eulogos to heaven on the back of a leaping dolphin. Moreover the floor had been carpeted with ermine and bear pelts.

The pelts had gone. Or, to be more exact, some of them had gone away and returned—but in unusual fashion: they had been cut into coats for the nobles, and now enveloped impressive paunches and bosoms with the assistance of gilt girdles. Moreover, half the mirrors were fly-specked and not a few were cracked, while worst of all some of the slabs of marble forming the floor had been prized up to expose crude foundations of rubble—a rumor having run around as to the efficacy of marble for sacrificial altars—and on an irregularity due to this cause, in an ill-lit corner, Lord Vengis had twisted his ankle en route to his throne.

This hall was a condensation of the trouble afflicting the whole of Ys. The harbors that once had swallowed the twice-daily ocean tides were blocked with stinking silt; grass grew on the stone moles, as in the wheel-ruts on the fine old roads leading away from the city—at least, according to report; none of the personages present could vouch for the assertion, all having declined to venture out of Ys since things took this turn for the worse. So also in the gardens of the great houses a plant like, but not identical with, mistletoe had spread over the handsome trees, letting fall a horrid sticky fruit on those who walked beneath; in the deep sweet-water wells servants claimed that they heard ominous voices, so that now they refused to let down buckets for fear of drawing up those who spoke; last week's market had reduced to two old men squabbling over a cracked earthen pot and a comb of dirty wild honey. . . .

Lord Vengis glowered at the company, and they fell silent by degrees. Their attendants moved, silent as shadows—which some of them were—to the double doors of entrance, closed them, barred them against all intrusion with the necessary charms, for this was no discussion that the common people might be permitted to overhear.

With the clanging down of the final bar, one leapt to his feet at the end of the front rank of gilded chairs, uttering a groan and cramming his fingers in his mouth. All eyes turned.

"Fool, Bardolus!" Lord Vengis rapped. "What ails you?"

"In that mirror!" Bardolus gibbered, trying to point and finding his shaky arm disobedient to his will. "I saw in the mirror—"

"What? What?" chorused a dozen fearful voices.

Bardolus was a small man whose manner was never better than diffident; he was accounted clever, but in a sly fashion that had won him few friends and none that would trust him. He said now, mopping sweat, "I don't know. I saw something in the mirror that was not also in this hall."

Time hesitated in its course, until Lord Vengis gave a harsh laugh and slapped the arm of his throne.

"You'll have to grow accustomed to manifestations like that!" he gibed. "So long as the *things* stay behind the mirror, what's to worry you? It's when they emerge into the everyday world that you must look out. Why, only the other day, when I was in my thaumaturgical cabinet testing a certain formula— But enough of that." He coughed, and behind his polite covering hand glanced to see whether his words had had the desired effect. They had, even though the episode to which he referred was an invention. True, he had spent much time in his cabinet; true, he had rehearsed many formulae; alas, nothing so far had come of his efforts, not even a harmless specter in a mirror.

Still, that would change. One could tell by the very feel of the air. There were forces in it that no man could put a name to, and sometimes scalps prickled as before a thunderstorm.

"We are here for a reason you know," he said after an impressive pause. "We are agreed on the sole course open to us. We admit that modern Ys stands on the shoulders of great men and women. Yet to what has their ambition led us? Unkind fate has burdened us with such difficulties as they never encountered. We eat stale bread and rancid meat where they gorged pies running with gravy and soft delicious fruits from the ends of the earth. We drink brackish water, none too clean, where they enjoyed wine and mead, and beer like brown crystal!

"We have concluded that for all their—admitted—greatness, *they* are responsible, not us! We did not ask to be born at a time when our trees rot, our crops wither, our harbor is blocked. In every way they are responsible: for siting Ys where it stands, for breeding children to inherit such a miserable legacy!"

"Aye!" came a rumble of assent from around the hall.

"Some fainthearts, some ignorant fools, have argued against us," Vengis went on, warming to a speech he had not intended to deliver. "These, of course, were baseborn, lacking the insight which is the birthright of nobility. Jacques the scrivener, for example, would have had us turn to with hoes and shovels and clear the harbor—and if hoes and shovels lacked, with our *bare hands!*"

This time the response lay between a shudder and a chuckle.

"What's become of Jacques, by the way?" someone asked audibly.

"Does it matter?" Vengis countered, drawing his beetling brows together. "We know we are adopting the right course. We have decided that we must employ more potent tools than crude—ah—agricultural implements to cope with so massive a disaster. We must, in short, restore all our fortunes, and the splendor of our city, *and* root out once for all the disaffection among the rabble spread by such as Jacques, by exploiting the mightiest means available to us. Magically, by decree of the will, by harnessing supernatural forces, we shall again make Ys the envy of the world!"

A roar of approval followed, and a barrage of clapping. Unnoticed in the shadows, one listener alone did not applaud; instead, he stood leaning on his staff, shaking his head from time to time.

"Let us have news, then—encouraging news of our progress!" Vengis cried. "I call first upon Dame Seulte, around whose home last time I rode by I could not help noticing an aura pregnant with remarkable phenomena."

Silence. At length a portly woman near the back of the hall rose—with some difficulty, for her weight—and spoke.

"Dame Seulte, as you know, is my close neighbor, and as she is not here I think perhaps I ought to mention that yesterday I found her in high spirits and confident of success in her experiments. She had obtained a freewill gift of a child to offer to—well, to a creature best not named directly. When I met her she was leading the pretty thing home on a leash of green leather. Such a charming sight!"

"Dame Rosa!" said a young man from nearer the front, turning on his chair. "A freewill gift? Are you entirely sure?"

And his companion, a pale girl of no more than eighteen

in a brown velvet dress, said doubtfully, "My maid referred to a fire at Dame Seulte's house this morning . . ."

Vengis slapped the arm of his throne again, making a sound as sharp as a gavel's rap. He said sternly, "No more defeatist talk *if* you please, Lady Vivette!"

"But are you sure it was a freewill gift?" persisted the young man at Vivette's side.

Dame Rosa said stiffly, "Dame Seulte had promised to treat the child as she would her own, and the parents were poor and hungry; they parted with it willingly. She said so."

"Then there was undoubtedly a fire at her home this morning," said the young man, and shrugged. "I warned her—I did warn her, more than once! Our copy of the book she conjured from includes a leaf that Dame Seulte's lacks, and on it the authorities are cited by the dozen. Ingredients obtained by deception, it states plainly, are of no avail when one strives to bind a pyrophoric elemental."

There was a stunned pause. Dame Seulte, after all, had only been trying to achieve a comparatively low-grade manifestation.

"I have more cheerful news," said a sweet enticing voice from the opposite side of the assembly. They turned gratefully; this was Lady Meleagra, whose eyes like sapphires, lips like rose-petals, and skin like fresh snow overlying frozen blood had broken hearts for ten of her twenty-one years. As Eadwil had once done in Ryovora—though she was unaware of that precedent—she had purchased her ability on terms. Herself, she had not yet suffered unduly in consequence; she was, though, constrained to impose a most regrettable proviso on anyone who craved to share the pleasures of her bedchamber. It was an efficacious precaution against undesired supernatural intervention, but it had signally reduced the number of her suitors.

"I sense a change in Ys," she mused aloud. "A great wonder has overtaken our city. So far I do not know its precise nature, but the fact is indisputable. See!"

She extended one graceful arm, swathed in white lace so fine her skin tinted it pink, and in the central aisle dividing the company a *thing* appeared. It was dark, and it writhed;

apart from that it had no describable attributes save two glowing eyes alive with hatred. It lasted half a minute before it faded, and at its going the air was permeated by a dank steamy odor against which those foresighted enough to have brought them buried their noses in bouquets of flowers.

By degrees a clamor arose, and on all sides the nobles strove to show they had been equally successful. "Look!" cried Messer Hautnoix, and between his hands he strung a chain of gleaming bubbles from nowhere, and again, and yet a third time before the glamor faded. And: "See!" cried Dame Faussein, beating a drum made of a gourd capped either end with tattooed skin from a drowned sailor; this made the hall pitch-black for as long as it sounded, and all present had the eerie sensation of being adrift in an infinite void. And: "Watch!" bellowed rough old Messer d'Icque, spreading a scarlet cloth at the full stretch of both arms; on the cloth, a mouth opened and uttered five sonorous words that no one present understood.

Smiles greeted these achievements, and loud approbation gave place to a babble of inquiry as to means. "Five nights drunk under a gallows!" boasted Messer Hautnoix—"A day and a night and a day kissing the mouth of the man who bequeathed his skin!" bragged Dame Faussein—"Doing things to a goat that I can't discuss with ladies present," muttered Messer d'Icque behind his hand.

"But Ub-Shebbab came to me when I did no more than whisper his name," said Meleagra, and at this disturbing news those closest to her chair drew aside as far as they could without appearing rude.

Vengis on his high throne joined neither in the praise nor in the questioning; his heavy-jowled face remained as set as stone. Had he not submitted himself to worse indignities? Had he not made pledges that in retrospect caused him to quail? And what had derived from his struggles? Nothing! Not even a pretty tricksiness like Messer Hautnoix's bubbles!

He thumped on his chair-side again, and cut through the chatter with a furious roar.

"Enough! Enough! Are you children early out of school, that you disgrace our meeting with mere gossip? How far do these cantrips advance us to our goal? That's the question!"

Visibly embarrassed, the company subsided into a phase of asking one another with their eyes whether any would be bold enough to claim progress in their central problem. At first they avoided looking at Meleagra; then, no other offer being forthcoming, they took that plunge and were rewarded with a sigh and a shake of the head.

"As I thought!" Vengis crowed in scorn. "You're overwhelmed with superficial spectacle, and have forgotten the urgent purpose confronting us. Next time you go to conjure, first ask this: if I succeed, what comes by way of benefit? Can I eat the outcome? Can I put it on my back, or mend my roof with it? Best of all, will it mend my and others' roofs without additional instruction? In fine, how will it serve not only me, but the nobility and commonalty of Ys?"

He glared at the now fidgety assembly. "It's not going to be easy, I know that well. I've had no success to speak of, myself. But at least I haven't been diverted down superfluous byways!"

At the back of the hall the one standing in shadow shook his head anew. Here truly was a company of fools, and chief of them was their chief Vengis: a man of consuming arrogance and vanity, blind to his faults and proud beyond description. This being so . . .

He touched one of the mirrors with his staff. It split with a whimper like a dying bird and heads whisked to seek the source of the sound. Vengis, astonished, half rose from his seat.

"What are you doing here?" he thundered. "Who let you in without my leave?"

The traveller in black advanced along the aisle dividing the company until he was face to face with Vengis, and there was that in his eyes which stifled further speech prior to the answering of that double question.

He said at last, "As for what I'm doing here—why, listening to and pondering on what you've said. As for leave being granted me to join you, I go where my presence is required, whether or not those whom I attend upon desire it."

The ranked nobles held their breath. This was the utterance of one holding an authority they dared not challenge.

"What – what do you want of us?" whispered Vengis when he had regained some of his composure.

"Say rather what you want of me," the traveller riposted with a sardonic cock of his head. "From the confusion of your dispute I've been unable to make it out. Put it in plain words. That is, if you have any clear idea of your ambitions . . . ?"

There was a gently insulting turn to that last phrase. Vengis bridled.

"Of course we do!" he blustered. "Have you not seen the pitiable pass to which our fair city is reduced?"

"I have," acknowledged the black-garbed intruder. "And as nearly as I can discern, you hold your ancestors to blame."

"We do so!" Vengis snapped. "And we crave to make them rectify their crime. We strive to call them back, that they may behold the ruin they've bequeathed us, and compel them to set matters right."

"Say nothing to me of compulsion," warned the traveller. "I am acquainted better with free choice. . . . Collectively and voluntarily, you have agreed this plan?"

There was a general cry of confirmation.

"What then restrains you from action?"

"What do you think?" That from Bardolus, half frantic with the tension of the moment. "For years we've quested after the power to bring about this end, and so far all we've managed to achieve is a few minor manifestations and several personal calamities!"

"Such as the one that overtook Dame Seulte?"

"Ah . . . Well, yes, I suppose!"

"Despite which ominous event, Vengis has expressed the common desire of you all?" said the traveller with very great sadness, casting his gaze to the furthest corners of the company.

"Aye!" came a chorus of replies.

"As you wish," said the traveller, "so be it." And departed.

IV

WHERE HE WENT, none of them saw. He passed among them swift as thought and silent as a shadow, and they had no more stomach for their consultations.

Yet they felt a lightness, a sense of promise, as they called the servants to unbar the doors and made their several ways towards their homes. The streets by which they passed seemed more crowded than of late, and not a few of them had the impression that they recognized among the throng a familiar face, a known gait, or the cut of a distinctive garment. However, such fancies were of a piece with the general mood, and served mainly to heighten the taut anticipation they had brought away from the Hall of State.

"What think you of Dame Seulte's fate?" said the Lady Vivette to her companion—who was also her brother, but they had judged that an advantage in making their earlier experiments. She spoke as their carriage creaked and jolted into the courtyard of their ancestral home; behind, as strong retainers forced them to, gate-hinges screamed for rust and lack of oil.

"I think she was unwise," her brother said. His name was Ormond to the world, but recently he had adopted another during a midnight ritual, and Vivette knew what it was and held some power over him in consequence.

"Do you believe we have been gifted by this—this personage?" Vivette inquired. "I have a feeling, myself, that perhaps we have."

78

Ormond shrugged. "We can but put the matter to the test. Shall we do so now, or wait until after dinner?"

"Now!" Vivette said positively.

So, duly, they made their preparations: donning fantastical garments that contained unexpected lacunae, and over them various organic items relinquished by their original owners, such as a necklace of children's eyes embedded in glass for Vivette and a mask made from a horse's head for Ormond. So arrayed, they repaired to a room in the highest tower of their mansion, where by custom deceased heads of their family had, since generations ago, been laid in state for a day and a night and a day before interment.

There, within a pentacle bounded by four braziers and a pot of wax boiling over a lamp, they indulged in some not unpleasurable pastimes, taking care to recite continually turn and turn about a series of impressive cantrips. The room darkened as the work went on, and great excitement almost interrupted their concentration, but they clung to it, and . . .

"Look!" whispered Vivette, and pointed to the catafalque removed to one corner of the room. Under black velvet draperies a form was lying—that of a man armed and armored.

"Why!" cried Ormond. "Just so, in the picture downstairs, did Honorius our great-grandfather lie when he was awaiting burial!" Leaping to his feet, he tugged the velvet aside.

Impassive, a steel visor confronted them. Vivette eased it open, and in the dark interior of the helmet eyes gleamed and a rush of fetid breath escaped. Stiffly, with vast effort, the occupant of the armor arose from the catafalque.

"Come, my descendants, let me kiss you both," said a rusty voice, and iron arms encircled them resistlessly. "What, have you no affection to your kinsman?"

There was a hollow hideous chuckle as the embrace grew tighter; the necklace of eyes cracked like a handful of cobnuts, the horse mask fell thudding to the floor, and spittle-wet lips clamped on one mouth, then the other.

Vivette and Ormond fainted.

When they recovered, the figure in armor was gone, but where it had taken shape on the catafalque lay a manuscript book in bindings of leather and brass, open to the page recording the death of Honorius from a contagious fever against which no medicine might serve, in the three-and-thirtieth year of his age.

Dame Rosa, in her palanquin borne between two white female donkeys, passed the corner on which stood the house formerly owned by Dame Seulte, and drew aside the curtains to peer curiously upward. Sure enough, as her maid had declared, from the window of the room in which Seulte had been accustomed to conduct her experiments, a licking tongue of greasy black smoke had smeared the wall.

She heaved a sigh. Poor Seulte! Had she but waited one more day she might have enjoyed the fruit of her efforts. That at least was Dame Rosa's belief; she trusted the promise that the one in black had made, and looked forward with impatience to the earliest opportunity of closeting herself with her books and apparatus and rehearsing with improvements the most relevant of her formulae.

Her family had in the past been counted among the most lascivious of Ys, and excessive indulgence by its womenfolk in the pleasures of the bedroom had often threatened to overpopulate the resources of their not inconsiderable estates. Accordingly there was a cellar where surplus children had for generations discreetly been disposed of, not by cruel and brutal means but by consigning the problem of their nourishment to the fates. She entered this cellar by a bronze door, which she locked behind her with a heavy key, and passed between rows of wooden stalls in each of which a set of rat-gnawed bones reposed on filthy straw, corroded gyves about each ankle.

She had chosen this place after much pondering. Surely she reasoned, the point of departure to eternity of so many spirits must be imbued with a peculiar potency!

Her method of working involved feathers, four liquids of which the least noxious was blood, and long silent concentration while seated on a stool of unique design, with no other covering for her ample frame than her age-sparse hair afforded. Briskly she carried out the introductory rites; then she sat down and closed her eyes, shivering more from excitement than from cold.

She had, stated the book she most believed in, to keep her eyes shut until she had completed the recital of an extended cantrip that occupied eight whole pages in minuscule script. There were still two pages to go when she heard the first rustlings and clicketings behind her. There was one page to go when the first touch brushed her fleshy thigh. Desperate to know what marvels her work had brought about, she raced through that final page, and hard on the concluding word came the first *bite*.

Thirty starving children mad with hunger, their teeth as sharp as any rat's, left gnaw-marks on her bones too.

Bardolus trembled as he piled high many curious ingredients on the brazier before his gilt-framed pier-glass. He had selected the mirror spell among the many known to him because he had, after all, come closest to success with it before—even if he had been taken aback to see a manifestation of it in the unconstrained mirrors of the Hall of State. Perhaps, though, that had been due to the intervention of the unwelcome black-clad stranger. . . .

He wished he could summon enough resolution to abandon the entire project, but fear and conceit combined to drive him on. He was beside himself with jealousy to think that a slip of a girl like Meleagra—not to mention that coarse peasant type d'Icque, or stupid complacent Dame Faussein!—had mastered magical powers in such a matter-of-fact fashion, while he still cried out in terror at the consequences of his own thaumaturgy.

He struck a flint-and-tinder spark, and blew. The pile ignited. Saturated with the fat of a sow that had devoured her own farrow, it gave off a choking smoke that veiled the mirror.

When all the fuel was consumed, the air cleared, and in the glass he recognized a face he knew: that of his mother, who was dead.

"My darling Bardolus," she said with fawning sweetness. "Look behind you! There stands an oaken cupboard you have known since you were a child. Press the left knob of the carved design, and a secret drawer will open. Within it lies what gave me power over your father. Accept it as my gift."

The image faded. A little puzzled, Bardolus hesitated before doing as directed. He remembered his father only dimly; he had been a strange man, alternating between hysterical gaiety and depression so deep he would sit by the hour contemplating a knife or a dish of poison, plucking up the courage to take his own life, the which at last he did.

Yet . . . *power.*

He pressed the knob and the drawer slid open, revealing a packet folded of strange yellow paper and sealed with green wax. Convulsively he broke the seal, and a fine powder spurted at his face, seeming to seek his nostrils of its own accord. He tried to dodge, but that was useless; he inhaled it all, and the packet lay empty on his palm.

Another few seconds, and vast elation filled him. Why, he could do anything! He was ten feet tall, stronger than an ox, more potent than the heroes of legend, and so handsome that no wench he courted could withstand him!

He let fall the paper and raced into the street.

From the mirror drifted mists, that coalesced into the shape of his mother, and ultimately grew strong enough to lift the yellow paper in old gnarled fingers and regard it out of bleary eyes.

"You," she whispered, "deserve no better fate than the one who got you on my body 'gainst my will! One hour, Bardolus —one hour of delirium! And afterwards despair! For it will be no use hunting for more of this delicious drug! I never compounded more than one dose at a time, and it was by postponing the next mixing for a day that I held power over your brutal, hateful father. There is no one to mix it for you, Bardolus! No one at all!"

V

BUT THESE WERE NOT ALL the calamities which overtook Ys, that once-fair city. For those whom the black-clad traveller had challenged truly did not know what would rescue them from their predicament, and out of greed and laziness had demanded the utmost they could envisage. Lost in this plethora of manifestations—somewhere—was precisely and exactly what was needful; that much the traveller was bound to grant. But, as he had warned them, he could not compel anyone to do the right thing. Choice was what he dealt in.

And those who chose wrong did so because of what they were.

His friends had generally liked Messer Hautnoix, who was engagingly childlike, what with his delight in such toys as the pretty colored bubbles he had displayed in the Hall of State. It was characteristic of him that, compelled to spend five nights under a gallows for the privilege, he passed the entire time drunk to avoid excessive contemplation of his predicament.

Yet when he repaired beyond the walls to his chosen ground of the execution dock, chuckling while he mumbled charms and strangled a white cock and a black hen, the one who came in answer to his call proved to be the first bearer of his line's name, professionally the municipal hangman, who had so loved his work that more than once he bought the silence of a witness who could have saved a victim from the rope; this being discovered, they had set him swinging on his own gallows at the last.

Much time having elapsed since he last performed his office, he seized his chance, and sunset found Messer Hautnoix dangling from a noose while his forebear clumped towards the city gate, rubbing his bloated hands at the thought of what he could look forward to.

Dame Faussein, who had paid a drowned sailor so generously for the loan of his skin, made further use of her drum when she came home. It was regrettable—and she certainly did regret it, though not for long—that this time the darkness to which its thumping carried her was the musty interior of her family's ancestral vault, where the warmth of her living body gave strange solace to an aunt and two uncles whose relationship, now as in their lifetimes, was more complex than the conventional ties of kinship. Her eyes continued to perceive darkness after the three of them had gathered sufficient strength to raise the stone lid of their mausoleum and sallied forth to ascertain how things now stood with Ys.

Messer d'Icque was indeed of peasant stock—in Ys that was no secret. His inclinations were toward country matters, and it has never been any secret anywhere that events transpire in country districts at which the sophisticates of cities would be appalled or nauseated. The whole of his urban residence had been stunk out for weeks by a dungpile he had ordered in its central courtyard, because reportedly it was in the warmth of rotting manure that homunculi enlivened.

This heap of foulness he ignored today, however, for his mind was set on the proper employment of his stock of *animelles*, a springtime by-product on farms where they breed sheep and cattle. His plan, moreover, was not to fry and serve them as a seasonal delicacy.

To him, the ritual completed, came a progenitor who had felt the frustration of an aging wife, racked with childbearing beyond the point where she was capable of assuaging his desires, and who had violated the daughter of his bailiff; it then also being spring. The bailiff happened to return early from the task of which *animelles* were the outcome, and to avenge the slight on his family's honor had made prompt use of the implement in his hand. For generations the sufferer had awaited the chance to inflict on another the operation undergone by himself, and he did so without a by-your-leave. Abandoning Messer d'Icque to leak away his life's blood, he thereafter set out to multiply his trophies from all possible male sources.

No word of this had been brought to the beauteous Meleagra when she came home. She had never cared for Messer d'Icque, thinking him rough and ill-bred, and the news that he had involuntarily qualified to share her overnight company would have interested her not at all.

In a boudoir hung with lacy draperies, containing a round golden bed and a mirror abstracted from the Hall of State, as being the largest in Ys—which she had mounted cunningly on the ceiling—she caused her maids first to draw curtains at the many high windows, then to light candles which gave off a fragrant, intoxicating aroma. She suffered them to remove her clothing, to prepare her a bath in which she dissolved a handful of polychrome salts, and to sing in harmony while they sponged her from head to toe. Sweetmeats were brought on a white platter and a silver filigree dish, and twenty-four new gowns were displayed before her on the body of a dumb girl who matched the dimensions of her figure.

All the while that this was going on, she was musing over a crucial decision: should she, or should she not, act upon the promise the black-clad one had made?

That he had the power to which he laid claim, she never doubted. Two years before anyone else in Ys saw what needed to be done, she had closed a bargain concerning her virginity which she had scrupulously kept—at first partly from fear, but lately out of simple habit.

And what she had purchased by the bargain had enabled her to recognize the single nature of their unaccountable visitor.

A single nature! Surely that must imply that its possessor could neither lie nor deceive! In which case she might now employ her talents to produce results compared to which her previous achievements were dross. Her whole life since the age of eleven had been led on the edge of a precipice—and there were creatures at the bottom of the chasm whom she had eluded only by the most exact preplanning. An uncharacteristic fit of vanity had made her call Ub-Shebbab to the Hall of State; he was the meekest and mildest of the beings she had conjured up, yet her skin prickled when she thought of what might have ensued. . . .

No, disasters happened only to fools and bunglers, and she was neither. She reached her decision and dismissed her maids. Them gone, she donned a gown which had not been displayed during her bath, worked all over in gold wire with a single sentence in a forgotten language; then she unlocked a brass chest and brought forth gifts she had exacted from various suitors before information about her inflexible rule was noised abroad.

There was a twig from Yorbeth, bearing a leaf transparent as glass and a brown, blotched fruit that tinkled like a bell; there was a vial of rainwater caught at the foot of the rainbow overarching Barbizond, that had a trifle of Sardhin's essence in it; there was a block of pumice from the volcano where Fegrim slumbered; there was a jar of grey dust from the hill below which Laprivan was pent; there were a hair from the head of Farchgrind, an inch of candle that had revealed the secret thoughts of Wolpec but had been allowed to burn one instant longer than was safe, and a drawing of two birds and a crocodile made by a possessed child.

Also there was a book.

Following with care the instructions it contained, she danced around her boudoir keening, crawled twice backwards across the floor with a knife between her teeth, and at last cut her forearm and let three drops of blood fall on the carpet. When she looked for them again the stains had vanished.

Nothing else happened in the room. She had expected that. Humming, she recalled her maids to bind her arm and change her gown for something more conventional, and went down to the dining-hall where supper was due to be served.

Already as she approached it she could hear the clatter of dishes, the clamor of conversation. That boded a great company. By whatever road, her guests had made amazing time. She hurried the last few steps and flung open the door.

Every place at her great table—and there were thirty-six—

was taken; the servants had pressed into use benches from the kitchen, too, and the sideboards and the serving-tables were alike packed with a hungry horde. For all the scullions and maids could do, the food, brought on trolleys because there was more of it than a man could lift, disappeared within instants of being set down. Still the howl went up for more. The meat had gone, the wine, the bread; now it was boiled turnips and hedge-greens, broth of bones and barley, and beer too new to serve by ordinary.

Yet that was not all. Behind, between, among those who ate went others looting. The fine brocade drapes had been torn down to clothe naked bodies, leather-backed chairs stripped to afford protection to sore feet, tapestries turned to cloaks and ponchos. One wild-eyed woman, lacking anything else, had smeared herself with gravy to break up the maggot pallidity of her skin.

Meleagra stood in the doorway for the space of five heartbeats before the chief steward caught sight of her and came running to beg her help.

"Mistress, what shall we do? They are in every room—five hundred of them at the least count! And all, all have claimed the right to what you have, for they say they are your ancestors and this is their home too!"

"My ancestors," whispered Meleagra. Her gaze, drawn as by a magnet, fixed on him who had taken her seat at the head of the table, and a silence overcame the entire company.

The one at whom she stared was a cross-eyed, ill-favored fellow in a dirty doublet, unshaven and with black around his nails. He gave her a smile that displayed gapped yellow teeth, and spoke in a soft voice with a peasant's accent.

"Ah, Meleagra, sure and you set a fine table! This meal which you account an everyday affair matches the grandest feasts we held in times gone by!"

"Who—who are you?" Meleagra choked out.

"You know me not?" The fellow cocked an eyebrow traversed by a scar. "Why, Damien, o'course, who built this house and founded the family's fortune in the earliest age of Ys. And at my side Cosimo, my firstborn here—though I had by-blows aplenty in another town! And Syriax his wife and their children Ruslan, Roland, and Igraine; their children Mark, Valetta, Corin, Ludwig, Matthaus, Letty, Seamus; theirs, Orlando, Hugo, Dianne, twins Nathaniel and Enoch—"

"Stop! Stop!" Meleagra pressed her hands to her temples; the room seemed to be spinning, and from every side gross faces leered at her, or thin drawn faces gazed with stony regard, or dull faces moped, or . . .

"There is no more food!" the steward shouted. "We have killed all the poultry, the larder's bare, the wine casks are drained, the last carp is gone from the pond, the beer-barrels are exhausted and even the *well* is dry!"

"You've done this to me?" Meleagra whispered to her remotest ancestor Damien. "But I gave you breath and life, and this new opportunity—I invited you here!"

"Is that," said Damien with contempt, "the only act of any importance you can boast of? Did we your ancestors not erect this house, construct this city, its fair avenues and fine harbors and full stores? Have you done nothing save parasitize upon our leavings? I read in your eyes that that is so! Here we are alive, who died before you saw the light—do you still call yourself the mistress of this house? Hah! You are a thing not worth the thinking of, less than dust, for dust can be seen to dance in sunbeams. You are the flame of a candle guttering out. So—*poof!*"

He blew at the candle closest to him on the great table, and with the extinction of its flame there was no such person as Meleagra—never had been—never could be.

VI

LONG HOURS VENGIS HAD PACED in the high room above the
Hall of State, pondering the day's events and screwing himself to the point where he would again resume his conjurations.
The day wasted; shadows lengthened; evening cold began to
permeate the building, and he called for fire and flambeaux.

He was afraid.

He had seen in the eyes of the traveller in black a warning
which his pride forbade him to heed; he was ashamed because
he was afraid, yet shame could not break fear's grip. He wished
to do as his colleagues were doing—what if he alone remained
untalented in sorcery when blockheads like Bardolus or half-
grown chits like Vivette boasted powers unnamable?

Nonetheless, he dithered and delayed, and had not yet cast
a rune nor recited the first line of a single formula when the
sergeant of the guard came stiffly to report a disturbance in
the town.

"Be more precise!" rapped Vengis. "What manner of disturbance?"

"Why, sir"—and the sergeant rubbed his chin dolefully—
"some hours agone there were complaints of desecration in
the graveyard by the cathedral, the curate saying that a vault
was open and the bones removed. But seeing as we've had
call for similar extraordinary materials that your lordship required, I decided best not to say anything. Now, though, the
affair has ramified. For example, the side wall of this building
here is cracked where they entombed alive a woman named

89

Igraine—you've seen the plaque—accused of commerce with a familiar spirit in the guise of a cat."

From the street below came a howl as of maddened beasts, and the sergeant flinched visibly. But he continued in his best official manner.

"Then, your lordship, at dusk reports came of strangers in the city, and we called out the patrols for fear of infiltration by some jealous invader. Myself, I've stopped twenty-one persons, and all spoke with the accent of our city and gave names concordant with our nomenclature. But it seems to me I've seen such names on gravestones before now—some, indeed, earlier today, when I answered the complaint at the cathedral. And what brings me to you now, begging your indulgence, is the curious business of the man and the two wives."

"What's that?" whispered Vengis, sweat pearling on his face.

"Well, sir, there was this man, one whom I'd challenged, walking with a girl of fifteen-odd. Comes up from nowhere a woman aged as he was—forty, maybe—and says she is his wife and what's this hussy doing with her husband? So then the little girl says they were married legally and then follows insults and hair pulling and at the last we must clap 'em in the jail to cool their heels. Which is—uh—difficult. For every cell, they promise me, is full, and that's more than I can understand. This morning the turnkey's records say there were one hundred and one places vacant for new prisoners."

Vengis's voice had failed him. He chewed his nails and stared with burning eyes at the sergeant.

"What shall I do, your lordship?" the man asked finally.

"I . . . I . . ." Vengis spun around and strode to a window overlooking the main square. He thrust wide the casement and leaned out. By the last dim light of the dying day he could see a myriad people gathering. Some were colorful and substantial, but these were few. Most were gray as the stones they trod, and trailed curious wispy streamers behind them, like cobwebs. But all alike exhibited an air of bewilderment, as though they were lost in the mazes of time and eternity, and could not find a way back to the present moment.

Vengis began to babble incoherently.

There came a thundering knock at the door, and a cavernous

groaning voice said, "Open! Open in the name of the Lord of Ys!"

Shrugging, the sergeant made to obey, but Vengis ran after him, clawing at his arm. "Don't! Don't let them in!" he wailed.

"But, your lordship," said the sergeant firmly, "it is in your name that he seeks entry, so it must be a matter of importance. Besides, with your permission, I'm expecting more reports from my patrols."

Vengis searched the room with feverish eyes. In the far corner he espied a closet large enough to hold a man; he dashed to it, and slammed the door with him inside.

The sergeant, astonished, went nonetheless to answer the knock, and fell back in dismay before the apparition that confronted him. Gaunt, tall, with a second mouth gaping redly in his throat, here was the figure of legendary Lord Gazemon who had laid the foundation stone of Ys with his own two hands.

Now those hands held a broadsword; now he advanced with slow terrible steps upon the closet in which Vengis thought to secrete himself, and battered down the planks of its door to hale that miserable successor of his into the wan torchlight.

"You know me!" croaked the city's founder.

Gulping, moaning, Vengis contrived a nod, and the huge specter shook him as a terrier shakes a rat. "Oh, to what a dwarfish stature have shrunk these weaklings of today!" he bellowed. The sergeant, cowering behind an oaken table, could not tell by which mouth Gazemon spoke—his natural one, or the second that had let out his life.

Again the door rattled to an imperious knock, and he scuttled to answer before Gazemon could so order him. With trembling hands he admitted those who stood without: Lorin, who had slain Gazemon by treachery and usurped his throne; Angus, who had reclaimed that throne into the rightful line of descent; then Caed; then Dame Degrance who passed for a man and ruled like one until the physicians at her deathbed unmasked her sex; then Walter of Meux; then Auberon; then Lams, and the first Vengis who was a stout and brave leader for the one short year he survived, and others and others to the latest who had sat the chair below prior to the advent of the incumbent lord.

With axes, maces, swords, with pens and scrolls and money-changers' scales according to the form of power by which they had made Ys great, they gathered around the hapless target of their contempt.

"We have walked abroad in the city since we were called from rest," Gazemon rumbled, his grip still fast on Vengis's shoulder. "We have seen stagnant puddles in the streets, shutters dangling by one hinge from the cracked walls of once-splendid houses; we have been followed by beggars and starving children in Ys which we devoted our lives to, making it a city that the world should envy! You have given our golden towers to tarnish, our iron doors to rust; you have abandoned our fine harbor to the mud and our fat grainfields to the weeds; you have squandered our treasury on baubles, forgetful that we paid for it with blood. How say you all, you who listen here? It is not time that we held an accounting?"

"Aye, time," they said as one, and hearing the menace in their voices Vengis rolled his eyeballs upward in their sockets and let go his hold on life.

VII

"Oh, there you are!"

Perched on a grey rock atop a grey hill, Jacques the scrivener forwent his gazing at sunset-gilded Ys in favor of a scowl directed at the traveller in black who had come to join him. There were no footprints to show by what path he had arrived; still, where Laprivan wiped away the past that was no wonder.

"I've sat here long enough, in all conscience," Jacques complained. "This wind is cold! And, for all you promised I should witness the doom of Ys, I see nothing but what I've always seen when looking on the city from afar. When will this doom befall? Tell me that!"

The traveller sighed. Now the course of events was grinding to its inexorable conclusion, he felt downcast, despite there never having been an alternative. He did not much care for Jacques, regarding him as pompous and self-opinionated, but even so . . .

"The doom is already in train."

Jacques leapt down from his rock and stamped his foot. "You mean I've missed it?"

"That, no," said the traveller. He raised his staff and pointed across the twilight grey of the valley. "Do you not see, there by the gates, a certain number of persons making in this direction?"

"Why . . . yes, I believe I do." Jacques peered hard. "But from this distance I cannot discern who they are."

"I can," murmured the traveller. "They are those who are determined that Jacques the scrivener shall not be denied participation in the doom of Ys."

"What?" Turned sidewise in the gloaming, Jacques's face was ghastly pale. "Why me? What do they want with me?"

"A reckoning."

"But . . . !" Jacques shifted from foot to foot, as though minded to flee. "Explain! Pray explain!"

"So I will," the traveller conceded wearily, and took a comfortable grip to lean on his staff. "First you must understand that the would-be enchanters of Ys have succeeded beyond their wildest dreams, and—as they desired—have called back those who created the city and maintained it in times past. And they found, as was inevitable, that these ancestors were human beings, with human faults and failings, and not infrequently with remarkable outstanding faults, because this is the way with persons who are remarkable and outstanding in other areas of their lives."

"But—but I counselled against this foolishness!" stammered Jacques.

"No," corrected the one in black. "You did not counsel. You

said: you are pigheaded idiots not to see that I am absolutely and unalterably right while everybody else is wrong. And when they would not listen to such dogmatic bragging—as who would?—you washed your hands of them and wished them a dreadful doom."

"Did I wish them any more than they deserved?" Jacques was trying to keep up a front of bravado, but a whine had crept into his voice and he had to link his fingers to stop his hands from shaking.

"Debate the matter with those who are coming to find you," proposed the traveller sardonically. "Their conviction is at variance with yours. They hold that by making people disgusted with the views you subscribed to, you prevented rational thought from regaining its mastery of Ys. Where you should have reasoned, you flung insults; where you should have argued soberly and with purpose, you castigated honest men with doubts, calling them purblind fools. This is what they say. Whether your belief or theirs is closer to the truth, I leave for you and them to riddle out. I must, though, in all honesty observe that you're outnumbered."

Jacques stared again at the column of people winding this way from the city gate, and now could see them in detail. At the head of the line was a blacksmith with a hammer on his shoulder; behind him, a ditcher followed with a mattock, then a gardener with a sickle and two coopers with heavy barrel-staves. And those behind still bore each their handiest weapon, down to a red-handed goodwife wielding the stick from her butter-churn.

He glanced wildly around for a way of escape, teeth chattering. "I must run!" he blurted. "I must hide!"

"It would be of little help," the traveller said. "Those people yonder are determined; though you hid in the pit of Fegrim's volcano, they would still track you down."

"Oh, misery me!" moaned Jacques, burying his head in his hands. "Would that I had never come to this pass! Would that what I've done could be undone!"

"As you wish, so be it," said the traveller, and cheered up, for that put a very satisfactory end to this momentary aberration in the smooth progress of the cosmos. He tapped three times on the rock that had been Jacques's seat, and under his breath he said, "Laprivan! Laprivan of the Yellow Eyes!"

Jacques screamed.

Below in the valley, the column of determinedly advancing men and women bound to wreak vengeance on Jacques hesitated, halted, and broke ranks in disorder that increased to panic. For out of the side of the hill Laprivan was peering, and what was behind his eyes belonged to the age when chaos was the All.

Some small power remained to him so long as he survived, and he applied it to this single and unique purpose: to wipe clean the slate of yesterday.

So he looked down on Ys, and saw there what was to him an abomination, the shadow of the past given substance. He reached out one of his arms, and erased—and erased—and erased. . . .

Honorius, sowing contagious fever on the streets, was not.

Thirty sated children, smeared with blood on faces and fingers, were not.

Bardolus's mother, chuckling over the fate of her son, was not.

Shaping a noose from every rope in a cord-seller's shop, the first of the line of the Hautnoix was not.

Brandishing his brutal trophies, the adulterous d'Icque was not.

Three who had come forth from a vault were not.

Stripped of its food, its draperies, its gold and silver and precious works of art, the house of Meleagra was silent.

And those who had come to regulate accounts with the decadent lordling Vengis took their leave.

Also many who had come forth from graves and sepulchers, from hollow walls and wayside ditches, from dungeons and the beds of rivers and the depths of wells . . . were not.

"So!" said the traveller in black, when he had restored Laprivan to his captivity. "You have a reprieve, Jacques. Are you glad of that?"

The tawny-bearded man mouthed an affirmative.

"And will you learn a lesson from it?"

"I'll try—as heaven is my witness, I will try!"

"Fairly said," the traveller declared. "Go, then, to join those hiding in the valley. Approach them as a friend, not showing you're aware why they set forth bearing bludgeons. Say to them that the rule of chaos over Ys is ended, and so is Ys; they must return home for the last time and gather their belongings before they and all its people scatter to the corners of the world."

"But—but is this our world?" Jacques whimpered. "On the way to Barbizond I saw . . . and now here . . ."

"Ah, you'll suffer no more of that kind of thing. It belongs to yesterday, and with other traces of yesterday Laprivan has wiped it out." The traveller allowed himself a smile. "And do not lament excessively for Ys. For cities, as for men, there comes a time. . . . Besides, there is a prophecy: a prince shall seek a name for his new capital, and he'll be told of Ys, and out of envy for its greatness he will say, 'I name my city Parys, *equal to Ys!*'"

"I have little faith in prophecies as a rule," said Jacques, staring. "But in this extraordinary place . . . Well, no matter. Sir, I take my leave, and--and I thank you. You have held up an honest mirror to me, and I cannot resent it."

"Go now," the traveller adjured. "And be quick."

He waited long on the brow of the hill while the last daylight dwindled away and the stars wheeled gradually to the conformation marking midnight. It became more and more difficult to see Ys; the towers melted into mist, the walls and gates were shadow-dark among shadows. For a while torches glimmered; then even they failed to be discerned, and when dawn broke there was neither the city, nor the traveller in black, for anybody to behold.

THREE

The Wager Lost
by Winning

*What stake will you adventure on this
Game? (quoth Arundel).*

*Why, Sir, though I be naked and penniless,
yet stand I in possession of my Head (saith
Amalthea).*

*That prize I in no wise, quoth Arundel. I
had liefer win a Cooking Pot than such a
Numskull. Wager me in place of it that
Treasure, which though you lose it to me
shall be yours again when I have done.*

—Fortunes and Misfortunes of Amalthea

I

DOWN THE SLOPE of a pleasant vale an army marched in good order: colors at the head fluttering in the warm summer breeze, drummers beating a lively stroke for the men behind perspiring in their brass-plated cuirasses and high-thonged boots. Each of the footmen wore a baldric with an axe and a shortsword in leather frogs, and carried a spear and a wide square shield. Each of the officers rode a horse draped in fine light mail, wore a shirt and breeches of velvet sewn with little steel plates, and carried a longsword in a decorated sheath. Sunlight glinted on pommels bright with enamel and gilt.

Leaning on his staff, the traveller in black stood in the shade of a chestnut tree and contemplated them as they filed by. Directly he clapped eyes on them, the banners had told him whence they hailed; no city but Teq employed those three special hues in its flag—gold, and silver, and the red of new-spilled blood. They symbolized the moral of a proverb which the traveller knew well, and held barbarous, to the effect that anything worth owning must be bought by the expenditure of human life.

In accordance with that precept, the lords of Teq, before they inherited their fathers' estates, must kill all challengers, and did so by any means to hand, whether cleanly by the sword or subtly by drugs and venom. Consequently some persons had come to rule in Teq who were less than fit—great only in their commitment to greed.

"That," said the traveller to the leaves on the chestnut tree, "is a highly disturbing spectacle!"

Nonetheless he stood as and where he was, neither concealed nor conspicuous, and as ever allowed events to pursue their natural course. Few of the rank-and-file soldiery noticed him as they strode along, being preoccupied with the warmth of the day and the weight of their equipment, but two or three of the officers favored him with inquisitive glances. However, they paid no special attention to the sight of this little man in a black cloak, and likely, a mile or two beyond, the recollection of him would be dismissed altogether from their minds.

That was customary, and to be expected. Few folk recognized the traveller in black nowadays, unless they were enchanters of great skill and could detect the uniqueness of one who had many names but a single nature, or perhaps if they were learned in curious arts and aware of the significance of the conjunction of the four planets presently ornamenting the southern sky in a highly specific pattern.

But there had been changes, and those who recognized him now were exceptional.

The journeys the traveller had made had long surpassed the possibility of being counted. Most of them, moreover, were indistinguishable—not because the same events transpired during each or all, but because they were so unalike as to be similar. A little by a little earnests of his eventual triumph were being borne upon him. Perhaps the loss of Ryovora into time had marked the pivotal moment; however that might be, the fact was incontestable. Soon, as the black-garbed traveller counted soonness, all things would have but one nature. He would be unique no more, and time would have a stop. Whereupon . . .

Release.

Watching the purposeful progress of the army, the traveller considered that notion with faint surprise. It had never previously crossed his mind. But, clearly, it would be a wise and kindly provision by the One who had assigned him his mission if his single nature should include the capacity of growing weary, so that in his instant of accomplishment he might surrender to oblivion with good grace.

That climax, though, still needed to be worked towards. He waited while the rear-guard of the army passed, slow commissary wagons drawn by mules, bumping on the rough track;

then, when the drumbeats died in the distance, their last faint reverberation given back by the hills like the failing pulse of a sick giant, he stirred himself to continue on his way.

It was not until he came, somewhat later, to Erminvale that he realized, weary or no, he must yet contend with vastly subtle forces ranged against him.

For a little while, indeed, he could almost convince himself that this was to be the last of his journeys, and that his next return would find the places he had known tight in the clutch of time. The borderland between rationality and chaos seemed to be shrinking apace as the harsh constraint of logic settled on this corner of the All. Reason is the stepchild of memory, and memory exists in time, not the arbitrary randomness of eternity.

Thus, beyond Leppersley the folk remembered Farchgrind, and that being's chiefest attribute had been that no one should recall his deceits, but fall prey to them again and again. Yet where once there had been a monstrous pile of follies, each a memento to some new-hatched prank—"Build thus and worship me, and I will give you more wealth than you can carry!" or: "Build thus and worship me, and I will restore you the health and vigor of a man of twenty!" (the wealth of course being ore by the ton load and the health that of a paralyzed cripple)—there were sober families in small neat timber houses, framed with beams pilfered from the ancient temples, who said, "Yes, we hear Farchgrind if he speaks to us, but we recall what became of Grandfather when he believed what he was told, and we carry on about our daily business."

The traveller talked with Farchgrind almost in sorrow, mentioning this skepticism that had overtaken humankind, and accepted without contradiction the retort.

"You too," said the elemental, "are part of the way things are, and I—I am only part of the way things were!"

Similarly, though there were hoofmarks on the road which Jorkas had patrolled, they were not his; some common cart-horse had indented them, and rain tonight or tomorrow would make the mud a palimpsest for another horse to print anew. Moreover, at black Acromel that tall tower like a pillar of onyx crowned with agate where once dukes had made sacrifice to the Quadruple God was broken off short, snapped like a dry stick. In among the ruins fools made ineffectual attempts to revive a dying cult, but their folly was footling compared to the grand insanities of the enchanter Manuus who once had taken a hand in the affairs of this city, or even of the petty tyrant Vengis, whose laziness and greed brought doom on his fellows and himself.

"Ah, if only I could find the key to this mystery!" said one of them, who had bidden the traveller to share the warmth of a fire fed with leather-bound manuscripts from the ducal library. "Then should I have men come to me and bow the knee, offer fine robes to bar the cold instead of shabby rags, savory dishes instead of this spitted rat I'm toasting on a twig, and nubile virgins from the grandest families to pleasure me, instead of that old hag I was stupid enough to take to wife!"

"As you wish, so be it," said the traveller, and knocked his staff on the altar-slab the fool was using as a hearth.

In the chill dawn that followed, his wife went running to her neighbors to report a miracle: her husband was struck to stone, unmoving yet undead. And, because no other comparable wonder had occurred since the departure of the Quadruple God, all transpired as he had wished. His companions set him up on the stump of the great black tower and wrapped their smartest robes about him; they burned expensive delicacies on a brazier, that the scent might waft to his nostrils; and sought beautiful girls that their throats might be cut and their corpses hung before him on chain-stranded gallows—all this in strict conformance with most ancient custom.

But after a while, when their adulation failed to bring about the favors which they begged, they forgot him and left him helpless to watch the robes fade and the fire die in ashes and the girls' bodies feed the maggots until nothing was left save bare white bones.

Likewise, a packman met at Gander's Well complained in the shade of brooding Yorbeth whose taproot fed his branches with marvellous sap from that unseen spring, and said, "Oh, but my lot is cruel hard! See you, each year when the snows melt, I come hither and with the proper precautions contrive to pluck leaves and fruit from these long boughs. Such growths no sun ever shone upon before! See here, a fuzzy ball that cries in a faint voice when you close your hands on it! And here too: a leaf transparent as crystal, that shows when you peer through it a scene no man can swear to identifying! Things of this nature are in great demand by wealthy enchanters.

"But what irks me"—and he leaned forward, grimacing— "is a matter of simple injustice. Do those enchanters plod the rocky road to Gander's Well? Do they risk death or worse to garner the contents of a heavy pack? Why, no! That's left to me! And what I get I must dispose of for a pittance to strangers who doubtless half the time botch the conjurations they plan to build on what I bring them! Would that I knew beyond a peradventure what marvels can be wrought by using the means that I make marketable!"

"As you wish," sighed the traveller, "so be it." He knocked with his staff on the coping of the well, and went aside to speak to Yorbeth of release—that release which he himself was coming unexpectedly to envy. For there was one sole way to comprehend the applications of what grew on this tall tree, and that was to take Yorbeth's place within its trunk.

Where, trapped and furious, the packman shortly found himself, possessed of all the secret lore he had suspected, down to the use that might be made of a shred of the bark when luring Ogram-Vanvit from his lair . . . and powerless to exploit the knowledge for his gain.

Yorbeth, naturally, ceased to be. Heavyhearted, the traveller went on.

II

IN THE MOUNTAINOUS LAND called Eyneran, where folk were above all proud of their fine sheep and goats, he had once incarcerated the chilly elemental Karth, thanks to whose small remaining power one strange valley stayed frozen beneath a mask of ice when all around the summer flowers grew bright and jangly music clanged from the bellwethers of the grazing flocks. Here the traveller came upon a fellow who with flint and steel was seeking to ignite the ice, grim-visaged and half blue with cold.

"Why," inquired the traveller, "do you lavish so much effort on this unprofitable pastime?"

"Oh, you're a simpleton like all the rest!" cried the man, frenziedly striking spark after spark. "Is it not the nature of ice to melt when hot sun falls on it? Since what is in this valley does not melt, it can't be ice. Certainly, moreover, it's not stone. It differs in significant respects from rock-crystal, quartz, adamant and fluorspar. Therefore it must be of an amberous nature, QED. And amber is congealed resin, and resin burns well, as any drudge can say who has lit a stove with pine-knots. Accordingly this so-called ice must burn. Sooner or later," he concluded in a more dispirited tone, and wiped his brow. The gesture entailed a little crackling noise, for so bitter was the wind in this peculiar valley that the sweat of his exertion turned at once to a layer of verglas on his skin.

The traveller thought sadly of Jacques of Ys, who also had been persuaded that he alone of all the world was perfectly right, and suppressed his opinion of the would-be ice-burner's logic. Sensing disagreement nonetheless, the fellow gave him a harsh and hostile glare.

"I'm sick of being mocked by everyone!" he exclaimed. "Would that the true nature of this substance could become clear for you and all to see!"

"As you wish, so be it," said the traveller, realizing that the time of release had come also to Karth. With the cessation of his dwindled ancient power, sunlight thawed the glacier and warm zephyrs fathered water from its edge.

The man looked, and touched, and tasted, and paddled his hands in it, and cried out in dismay.

"If this is water, that must have been ice—but that was not ice, therefore this is not water!"

Spray lashed him; rivulets formed around his ankles.

"It is not water," he declared, and stood his ground. But when the pent-up floods broke loose they swept him with his flint and steel far down the hillside and dashed him to death on a rock that was deaf to his entreaties.

Aloof on a promontory, the black-clad traveller watched the whirling torrent, thinking that he, so aged there was not means to measure his duration, knew now what it meant to say: "I am old."

So too in Gryte, a fair city and a rich, there was a lady who could have had her choice of fifty husbands, but kept her heart whole, as she claimed, for one man who would not look at her, though he had wooed and conquered maids for leagues around.

"Why does he scorn me so?" she cried. "He must be hunting for a wife who will give him surcease from his endless philandering! Can he not come to me, who hunger for him?"

"As you wish, so be it," said the traveller, and next day the man she dreamed of came a-courting. She pictured all her hopes fulfilled and made him free of her household and her body. And the day after he treated her like all the rest: rose from her couch where he had taken his pleasure, not sparing a kind look or a kiss, and left her to wring hands and moan she was undone.

* * *

Likewise there stood a tombstone in the cemetery at Barbizond, under the arch of rainbow signalling the presence of the bright being Sardhin. Grass by it flourished in the gentle never-ceasing rain. The traveller visited it because he owed a particular debt to the man beneath, who full of years and honor had gone to his repose.

Turning away from Eadwil's grave, he was addressed by a person in a cape of leaves who might have passed at a glance for seven years of age, either boy or girl.

"Good morrow, sir!" this person chirruped in a treble voice. "Think you to brace yourself for death by contemplating all these tombs—or have you cause to wish it may overtake some other sooner than yourself?"

"In the latter case, what?" inquired the traveller.

"Why, then"—slyly—"I could be of service. For thirty-one years I have been as you see me: dwarfed, sexless, and agile. What better end could I turn such a gift to, than to become the finest assassin ever known in Barbizond? You stand surrounded by testimonials to my skill: here a miserly old ruffian whose daughter paid me half his cofferload, there an elder son who blocked his brother's way to an inheritance!"

"You speak openly of this foul trade?"

"Why, sir, no one is around to hear me save yourself, and would not folk think you deranged were you to claim a child had boasted of such matters to you?"

"In truth, your childish form is a deep disguise," the traveller conceded. "But tell me: do you address me merely to solicit new custom, or because that disguise grows oppressively efficient?"

The person scowled. "Why, I must confess that now and then the very secrecy which benefits my calling does gall my self-esteem. I gain my living in a unique manner, but no one knows I'm the ultimate expert in my trade save those whom I have served, who dare not admit they know the truth. Would I might be famed far and wide as a past master in my profession!"

"As you wish, so be it," said the traveller, and struck his staff against the side of Eadwil's tomb. That very evening rumors took their rise in Barbizond, and everyone who had lost a relative in suspicious circumstances, to a poison subtler than a hired enchanter could detect, or a silent noose, or a knife hissing out of shadow, nodded their heads and remarked how marvellously well the appearance of a child of tender years might mask a killer.

The traveller passed the body next morning, sprawled on a dungheap by the road to Teq.

Will it be now? The question haunted the traveller as he went his way. With half his being he was apprehensive, for all he had ever known throughout innumerable aeons was the task allotted to him; with the balance, he yearned for it. Karth gone, Yorbeth gone, Jorkas gone—would there shortly also be an end for Laprivan? And if for them, what of the Four Great Ones: Tuprid and Caschalanva, Quorril and Lry, whom he had contrived at best to banish, not to whelm?

On impulse, when he came to the grove of ash trees at Segrimond which was one of the places where such processes were possible, he constrained Wolpec to enter the customary candle, but when he tried to smoke a piece of glass over its flame and read the three truths therefrom, the glass cracked. With resignation he concluded that this was not for him to learn, and went his way.

In Kanish-Kulya the wall that had once divided Kanishmen from Kulyamen, decked along its top with skulls, had crumbled until it was barely more than a bank enshrouded with ivy and convolvulus, and roads pierced it along which went the gay carts of pedlars and the tall horses of adventure-seeking knights. Yet in the minds of certain men it was as though the old barrier still stood.

"Not only," groused a portly Kanish merchant to the traveller, "does my eldest daughter decline to accept her proper fate, and be sacrificed in traditional manner to Fegrim! She adds insult to injury, and proposes to wed a Kulyan brave!"

The traveller, who knew much about the elemental Fegrim, including his indifference to sacrifices, held his peace.

"This I pledge on my life!" the merchant fumed. "If my daughter carries on the way she's going, I shall never want to speak to her again—nor shall I let her in my house!"

"As you wish, so be it," said the traveller, and from that moment the merchant uttered never a word. Dumb, he stood by to watch the fine procession in which the girl went to claim her bridegroom, and before she returned an apoplexy killed him, so that the house was no more his.

But nothing in this was remarkable. Greed, hate, jealousy—these were commonplace, and it was not to be questioned that they should defeat themselves.

Onward again, therefore, and now at last to Erminvale.

III

IN THAT LAND of pleasant rolling downs and copses of birch and maple, there stood the village Wantwich, of small white farms parted by tidy hedgerows, radiating out from a central green where of a summer evening the young people would gather with a fiddler and a harpist to dance and court in bright costumes ornamented with pheasant-feathers and fantastical jingling bangles. At one side of this green was a pond of sweet water which the traveller in black had consigned to the charge of the being Horimos, for whom he had conceived a peculiar affection on discovering that this one alone among all known elementals was too lazy to be harmful, desiring chiefly to be left in peace. While others older than themselves danced, the village children would splash in the pond with delighted cries, or paint their bare bodies with streaks of red and blue clay from the bank, proudly writing one another's names if they knew how. In winter, moreover, it served for them to skate on, and well wrapped in the whole hides of goats they slid across it with double wooden runners strapped to their feet.

Good things were plentiful in Erminvale: creamy milk, fat cheeses, turnips so firm and sweet you might carve a slice raw and eat it with a dressing of salt, berries and nuts of every description, and bearded barley for nutritious bread. Also they brewed fine beer, and on a festival day they would bear onto the green three vast barrels from which anybody, resident or visitor, might swig at will, the first mug always being poured of course to Horimos. Content with that small token of esteem, he slumbered at the bottom of his mud.

All this was what the girl named Viola had known since a child, and it made her well satisfied to have been born in Wantwich. Where else offered you a better life? By report, great cities were crowded and full of smoke and stinks; moreover, they had more demanding patrons than Horimos, like Hnua-Threl of Barbizond, black with the dried blood of those who had duelled at his altar, or that blind Lady Luck who smiled randomly on the folk of Teq and might tomorrow turn her back for good on the one she had favored yesterday.

She had heard about Teq from a finely clad rider who had come, a while ago, on a tall roan stallion, twirling long fair mustachios and spilling gold from his scrip like sand.

He had arrived on the first fine evening of spring, when Viola and her betrothed man Leluak joined all the other young people in a giddy whirling dance around the green, and because it behooved one to be courteous to a stranger—even a stranger who complained about the narrowness of his room at their only inn, and passed unflattering remarks concerning Wantwich beer as against the wines of home—and also, she admitted to herself, because all the other girls would be envious, she had complied with his request to join him in demonstrating some newly fashionable steps from Teq. Instruction took a moment only; she was a skillful dancer, light on slender legs that not even the bleaching of winter had worn to paleness from last summer's tan. After dancing they talked.

She learned that his name was Achoreus, and that he served one of the great lords of Teq. She learned further that he thought her beautiful, which she granted, since everyone had always said the same: she had long sleek tresses, large eyes that shifted color ceaselessly like opals, and skin of the smoothness of satin.

He declared next that such loveliness was wasted in a backwater hamlet and should be displayed to the nobility and gentry of a great city—meaning Teq. She thanked him for his compliments but explained she was already spoken for. Thereupon he proved that for all his elegant airs he lacked common civility, for without asking her leave he tried to fondle her inside her bodice, at which she marched away.

Had he acted decently, invited her to stroll in the woods and find a couch of moss, she would naturally have consented; it was the custom of Wantwich to receive all strangers as one would one's friends. But as things were—so she told Leluak when bidding him good night—he seemed to expect that the mere sight of him would make her forget the boy she had grown up with all her life. What foolishness!

Accordingly, all plans for her marriage went ahead in the ancient manner, until at sunset the day before the ceremony her father, her mother, her two sisters, and her aunt equipped her in the prescribed fashion for a night she had to pass alone, during which she must visit each in turn of five high peaks enclosing Erminvale and there plant five seeds: an apple, a sloe, a cob, an acorn and a grain of barley.

With a leather wallet containing bread and cheese, a flask of water, and a torch of sweet-scented juniper, and followed by the cries of well-wishers, she set forth into the gathering dusk.

The tramp was a long one, and tricky in the dark, but she had wandered around Erminvale since she was old enough to be allowed out of sight of her mother, and though she must clamber up rocky slopes and thread her way through thickets where nightbirds hooted and chattered, she gained each peak in turn with no worse injury than thorn-scratches on her calves. As dawn began to pale the sky she set in place the final seed, the barley-grain, and watered it from her body to give it a healthy start in life. Then, weary but excited, she turned back singing on the road to home. By about noon she would be safe in Leluak's embrace, and the feasting and merrymaking would begin.

Still a mile off, however, she started to sense that something was amiss. Smoke drifted to her on the breeze, but it lacked the rich scent of baking which she had expected. A little closer, and she wondered why there was no shrill music audible, for no one had ever been able to prevent Fiddler Jarge from striking up directly his instrument was tuned, whether or no the bride had come back from the hills.

Worst of all, at the Meeting Rock that marked the last bend in the road, the huge granite slab by which the groom traditionally took the hand of his bride to lead her into Wantwich, there was no sign of Leluak.

She broke into a run, terrified, and rounded the rock. Instantly she saw the furthest outlying house, that of the Remban family, which she remembered seeing built when she was a toddler, and almost fainted with the shock. Its fine clean walls were smeared with a grime of smoke, its gate was broken, and the Rembans' finest plough-ox lay bellowing in a pool of blood.

And there beyond: the Harring house afire—source of the smoke she'd smelled! Her own home with the shutters ripped off their hinges, the front door battered down with an axe from the kindling-pile! Leluak's, unmarked, but with the door ajar, and no one inside to answer when she shouted through!

Wildly she raced onward to the village green, and there was Jarge's fiddle broken on the ground. The beer barrels set out for the wedding had been drained. Near them was a patch of scorched grass she could not account for, and all the water of the pond was fouled with the blood of the ducks which daily had quacked there.

Crouched in her chair, from which for longer than Viola could recall she had watched and grinned at the weddings she had witnessed: the only remaining villager of Wantwich, Granny Anderland, who was in fact a great-great-grandmother, toothless and senile.

"Granny!" shrieked Viola. "What happened?"

But all that Granny Anderland could do—all that she had ever been able to do since Viola was a baby—was to expose her gums in a silly grin and rock back and forth on her chair.

Helpless, Viola screamed Leluak's name till she was hoarse, but eventually she collapsed from exhaustion and horror, and that was how the traveller found her when he chanced that way.

IV

HE BARELY CHECKED HIS PACE as he entered Wantwich, along another road than that which Viola had followed on her return from the five peaks. But his expression grew sterner with every step he took, until when finally he could survey the full measure of the calamity from the center of the green his brow was dark as thunderclouds.

His footsteps were too soft upon the sward for the weeping girl to hear them through her sobs, and it was plain that the old woman near her either had been so shocked as to have lost her reason, or was too senile to understand the world. Accordingly he addressed the girl first.

At the sound of his voice she cringed away, her tear-wet face a mask of terror. But there was little in the appearance of this small man leaning on a staff to suggest he might have connection with the rape of Wantwich. And, for all that he looked furious beyond description, it did not seem that anger was directed at herself.

"Who are you, child?" the traveller inquired.

"My—my name is Viola, sir," the girl forced out.

"And what has happened here today?"

"I don't know, I don't know!" Wringing her hands, Viola rose. "Why should anybody want to do this to us? Monsters of some kind must have done it—devils!"

"There are few such creatures left hereabouts," the traveller murmured. "More likely it will have been men, if one can dignify them with that name. Were you away from the village?"

"I was to be married today," Viola choked.

"Ah. So you were walking the five peaks."

"You're—you're acquainted with our customs, sir?" Viola was regaining control of herself, able to mop away her blinding tears and look more clearly at the newcomer. "Yet I don't remember that I saw you here before."

"This is not the first time that I've been at Wantwich," said the traveller, refraining from any reference to the number or date of his earlier visits. "But, to pursue the important matter: did this old lady witness what occurred?"

"If she did, she won't be able to describe it," Viola said dully. "She has been as you see her for many years. She likes to be talked to, and nods and sometimes giggles, but beyond that . . ." She gave a hopeless shrug.

"I see. In that case we must resort to other means in order to determine what went on. Girl, are you capable of being brave?"

She stared at him doubtfully. "Sir," she said at length, "if you can do anything to help get back my man, and right the wrong that has been done to these good people, I'll be as brave as you require of me."

"Then come with me," said the traveller, and took her hand. He led her across the green, past the patch of grass scorched black—at which she cast a puzzled glance—to the rim of the pond.

"Stand firm," he commanded. "Do not be afraid of what you see."

"I don't understand!"

"Better for you that you should not," the traveller murmured, and thrust his staff into the water. He dissolved one of the forces bonding the light of which it was composed, and a shaft of brilliance lanced downward to the bottom.

"Horimos!" he cried. "Horimos!"

The girl's eyes grew round with wonder, and then her mouth also, with dismay. For the water heaved and bubbled sluggishly as pitch, and from the plopping explosions a thick voice seemed to take form, uttering words.

"*Le-e-eave me-e a-a-lo-o-one . . . !*"

"Horimos!" barked the traveller. "Stir yourself! You've slumbered centuries in that soft bed of mud, but you have not forgotten how! Shall I remove you to Kanish-Kulya, make you share the pit of his volcano with Fegrim?"

A noise between a grumble and a scream.

"Yes, he'd be a restless companion, wouldn't he?" the traveller rasped. "Up! Up! I desire speech with you!"

Beside him Viola had fallen to her knees, all color vanished from her cheeks. Too petrified even to blink, she saw the water where she had so often bathed rise in tumult—yet absurdly slowly, as though time had been stretched out to double length. More bubbles burst, and she could watch their surface part; waves and ripples crossed the pond so slothfully one would have thought to push them into new directions without wetting one's palm.

And ultimately . . .

"You may prefer to close your eyes now," the traveller said didactically, and added, "Horimos! Speak! And be quick—the sooner you tell me what I want to know, the sooner you may sink back to your ooze. What's become of all the people from this village?"

"Been taken away," Horimos mumbled. It was not exactly a mouth he used to shape the words—but then, like all elementals, his physical form was somewhat arbitrary.

"How and by whom?" The traveller rapped the bank impatiently with his staff.

"Army marched in this morning," Horimos sighed. "Went around the village, drove everybody to the green. Most of them were there already, anyhow. Set up a forge there where the grass is blackened, brought a chain, and welded fetters to it for each person. Killed some ducks and hens for their dinner, drank the beer, herded the villagers away. Good riddance, too, say I. Never had a moment's peace since you put me here, what with fiddling and dancing and swimming and skating and all the rest of it!"

"Whose was the army? What colors did they fly?"

"Should I know who bears a flag of silver, red, and gold?"

The traveller clamped his fingers tighter on his staff.

"And you made no attempt to intervene?"

"Told you—glad to see the back of them." Horimos made the whole surface of the pond yawn in a colossal expression of weariness. "And but for you I'd have enjoyed a decent sleep for a while, now I'm alone!"

"For your idleness," said the traveller softly, "I decree that until the folk of Wantwich are restored to their homes, you shall itch so much you can enjoy no rest. Begone with you. Hope that the matter is speedily set to rights."

"But—!"

"You argue with me?"

Horimos declined. When once again he had subsided to the bottom of his pond, the water was no longer pellucid and still as before, but roiled continually without a breeze to stir it.

"Who are you?" Viola whispered. "I'd always thought Horimos was . . . was . . ."

"Was imaginary?" The traveller chuckled. "Not exactly. But his worst fault is mere laziness, and compared to what faults one finds elsewhere it's far from the grossest of shortcomings. . . . As for my own identity, you may call me what you will. I have many names, and only one nature."

He waited to see whether the information, which he gave only to those who directly demanded it, meant anything to her. Interestingly, he discovered that it did, for on the instant a blend of hope and awe transfigured her pretty face.

"Is it true, then," she cried fiercely, "that I may require of you my heart's desire?"

"Think well if you do so!" warned the traveller, raising his staff. "Only you can know what's in your secret mind! Reflect and ponder!"

"I don't have to," she said with terrible certitude. "I want to be reunited with my man!"

The traveller sighed, but as always was resigned to the inexorable course of events. "As you wish, so be it," he replied.

"What shall I do?" Viola whispered, suddenly overcome with a sense of the finality of her request.

"Wait."

"No more than wait? Wait here?" She turned frantically, surveying the ravished homes, the slaughtered livestock, the smoke that still drifted over the burning house. "But—"

And when she looked again for the traveller in black, he was gone.

* * *

A little after, when the sun was still high in the sky, there were clopping noises on the road by which the army had arrived, and she roused from her torpor and made to flee. But the horseman easily ran her down, bowing from his saddle to sweep her off her feet and mount her on the withers of his steed, laughing at her vain attempts to break away.

"I missed you when they rounded up the rest of them," said Achoreus of Teq. "I couldn't forget a lovely face like yours. Even less can I forget an insult like the one you offered me when first I came here. So I dawdled, thinking you'd be back eventually, and here you are. Not for long, though! You're going to rejoin your family and friends, and that country bumpkin you preferred to me!"

He set spurs to his horse, and away they galloped in the wake of the miserable gang of captives strung with chains.

V

LAUGHTER RANG loud and shrill under the gorgeous canopy that shaded Lord Fellian of Teq from the naked rays of the sun. The canopy was of pleated dragon-hide, bought at the cost of a man's life in a distant land where chaos and reason had once been less evenly matched, so that strange improbable beasts went about with lion's claws and eagle's beaks and wings of resounding bronze. Report held that there were no more such creatures to be found; even their bones had been rejected by reality.

"But I have my canopy!" Lord Fellian would say.

Its shade fell on a floor of patterned stone: marble was the most commonplace of the minerals composing it, outnumbered by chalcedony, jasper, sardonyx, chrysoberyl, and others yet so rare that they had no name save "one of the tiles in Lord Fellian's gallery." This was on the very apex of the grand high tower from which Fellian might survey his domain: lands from here to the skyline and beyond which bled their wealth into his coffers.

But on the houseward side there was a high wall, so that when he sat upon his throne of state—made from the ribs of a creature of which the enchanters declared no more than one could ever have existed, translucent as water but harder than steel—not even an absentminded glance over his shoulder might reveal to him the sole building in Teq which outreached his tower. Atop that mighty edifice presided the figure of Lady Luck, the goddess blind in one eye and masked over the other, whose smile dictated the fortunes of those who ruled in Teq.

It was not the custom to look on her. It was said that those who secretly attempted to, in order to discover whither her gaze was bent, would die a fearful death. And indeed the agents of Lords Fellian, Yuckin and Nusk did occasionally deposit in the chief market-square the bodies of men and women who had clearly undergone repulsive torture, and the common folk interpreted these as an awful caution. More often than not, these corpses belonged to persons who had boasted of their favor with the Lady. It was taken for granted that the others belonged to those who had not even enjoyed the brief pleasure of making such a boast.

To look on Lady Luck was the one gamble no lord of Teq would risk. Why should he? Was not affluence itself proof that the Lady bent her enigmatic smile continually on the person who possessed it?

Lord Fellian, on his chair of inexplicable bones cramped with pure gold, robed in satin dyed with the purple of the veritable murex, shod with sandals of the softest kidskin on which had been stamped, again in gold, a series of runes to guide him in the most prosperous of paths; his foppish locks entwined with green ribbons, his nails painted with ground pearls, his weak eyes aided with lenses not of rock-crystal such as his rivals must make do with but of diamond, his lobes hung with amber, his girdle glittering with sapphires: he, Lord Fellian, the greatest winner among all the past and present lords of Teq, laughed, and laughed and laughed again.

His mirth drowned out the soft rattling from the table on which a trained monkey, tethered by a velvet leash, kept spilling and gathering up a set of ivory dice, their values after each throw being recorded by a slave on sheets of parchment; likewise, the humming of a gaming-wheel turned by an idiot— both these, with bias eliminated, to determine whether after fifty thousand throws or spins there would be some subtle preference revealed, that he might exploit in his ceaseless rivalry with Lords Yuckin and Nusk. Furthermore his hilarity drowned the chirrup of two gorgeous songbirds in a gilded cage which he had won last week from Nusk in a bout at shen fu, and the drone of musicians playing on a suite of instruments he had won—along with their players—from Yuckin a year or more past. Those instruments were of eggshells, ebony, and silver, and their tone was agonizingly sweet.

Facing the chair of bones, Achoreus—who had committed himself to the service of Lord Fellian when he was but seventeen and keep complimenting himself on his farsightedness— grinned from ear to ear at the brilliant inspiration of his master.

"Before those fools learn that winning from me costs me nothing," Fellian declared, "I shall have taken the very roofs from over their heads! They will be shamed if they refuse to match my stakes, and I may climb as high as I wish, while they—poor fools!—struggle to clamber after me. Oh, how I look forward to seeing Yuckin's face when tonight I bet him a hundred skillful servants, including girls fit for a royal bed! You've done well, Achoreus. Torquaida, come you here!"

From among the gaggle of retainers who by day and night attended Fellian, subservient to his slightest whim, there shuffled forward the elderly treasurer whose mind encompassed, so he bragged, even such detail as how many of the copper coins in store had been clipped around the edge, instead of honestly worn, and were therefore reserved to pay off tradesmen.

In no small part, Fellian acknowledged, his victories in the endless betting matches with his peers were due to Torquaida instructing him what they could or could not stake to correspond with his own wagers. He had rewarded the old man suitably, while those who served his rivals in like office were more often punished for letting go irreplaceable wonders on lost bets, and grew daily bitterer by consequence.

"Young Achoreus here," the lord declared, "has performed a signal service. Thanks to him, we now have one hundred or more extra servants, surplus to the needs of the household, and additionally many children who can doubtless be trained up in a useful skill. How, say you, should this service be repaid?"

"This is difficult to estimate," mused Torquaida. His ancient voice quavered; Fellian scowled the musicians into silence that he might hear the better. "There are two aspects of the matter to be considered. First, that he has brought a hundred servants —that is easy. Let him have dirhans to increase his stake in the wager he has made with Captain Ospilo of Lord Yuckin's train; our privy intelligence states that bet is won on odds of nine to four, whereas Ospilo is yet in ignorance of the result. Thereby the winnings may be much enlarged. I'd say: one coin for every healthy servant."

Fellian slapped his thigh and chortled at the ingenuity of the deceit, while Achoreus preened his mustachios and basked in the envy of those around.

"Beyond that, however," Torquaida continued in his reedy tones, "it remains to be established what the true value of these servants is. As one should not wager on a horse without inspecting both it and its competition, thus too one must begin by looking over the captives."

"Let them be brought, then!" Fellian cried. "Clear a space sufficient for them to parade!"

"Sir," ventured Achoreus, "there were not a few among them who resented the—ah—the invitation I extended to enter your lordship's service. It will be best to make space also for the escort I detailed to accompany them."

"What?" Fellian leaned forward, scowling. "Say you that a man on whom Lady Luck smiles so long and so often is to be injured by some stupid peasant, by some village boor? Or is it that you neglected to disarm them?"

Seeing his newfound fortune vanishing any second, Achoreus replied placatingly, "My lord! There was hardly a weapon in the whole of Wantwich, save rustic implements whose names I scarcely know, not having truck with country matters—scythes, perhaps, or hatchets . . . Which, naturally, we deprived them of! But all of those we brought are able-bodied, and hence remain possessed of feet and fists."

"Hmm!" Fellian rubbed his chin. "Yes, I remember well a gladiator whom Lord Yuckin set against a champion of mine in years gone by, who lost both net and trident and still won the bout, by some such underhand trick as clawing out his opponent's vitals with his nails." He gave an embarrassed cough; he hated to refer to any wager he had lost. "Well, then, bring them up, but keep a guard around them, as you say."

Relieved, Achoreus turned to issue the necessary orders. Accordingly, in a little while, to the music of their clanking fetters, a sorry train of captives wended its way out of the grand courtyard of the palace, up the lower slopes of the ramp leading to the gallery—which were of common granite—and stage by stage to the higher levels, where the parapets were of garnets in their natural matrix, and the floor of cat's-eye, peridot, and tourmaline.

Refused food on the long trudge from Erminvale to Teq to discourage the energy needed for escape, granted barely enough water to moisten their lips, they found the gradual incline almost too much for them, and their escorts had to prod them forward with the butts of spears.

At last, however, they were ranged along the gallery, out of the shade of the dragon-hide awning, blinking against sunlight at their new and unlooked-for master. At one end of the line was Leluak, his left eye swollen shut from a blow and testifying to his vain resistance; as far distant from him as possible, Viola, nearly naked, for her struggle against Achoreus had caused much ripping of her clothes. And between them, every villager from Wantwich barring Granny Anderland, from grey-pated patriarchs to babes in arms.

Accompanied by the proud Achoreus, Torquaida passed along the line peering into face after face, occasionally poking to test the hardness of a muscle or the flab of a belly. He halted before one bluff middle-aged fellow in a red jerkin, who looked unutterably weary.

"Who are you?" he croaked.

"Uh . . ." The man licked his lips. "Well, my name's Harring."

"Say 'so please you'!" Achoreus rasped, and made a threatening gesture towards his sword.

Harring muttered the false civility.

"And what can you do?" Torquaida pursued.

"I'm a brewer." And, reluctantly after a brief mental debate: "Sir!"

"You learn swiftly," Achoreus said with mocking approval, and accompanied Torquaida onward. "You?"

"I'm a baker—sir."

"I? Oh, a sempstress!"

"And I'm a bodger, turner, and mender of ploughs."

The answers came pat upon the questions, as though in naming their trades the captives could reassure themselves they still retained some dignity by virtue of their skill. At Torquaida's direction a clerk made lists of all the names and crafts, leaving aside the children under twelve, and finally presented them with a flourish to Lord Fellian.

Scrutinizing them through his diamond lenses, the lord addressed Achoreus.

"And of what standard in their callings are these louts? Competent? Shoddy?"

"As far as I could judge, sir," Achoreus answered, "they might be termed competent. Of course, their criteria fall far short of our own; still, their houses seemed sturdy, they kept their fences mended, and their byres and folds were sound enough to keep their livestock in."

"I see." Fellian scratched the tip of his nose with the facets of a gemstone ringed to his left middle finger. "Then there might be something to be said for keeping them instead of staking them. We have no brewer in the palace that I know of. Some scullery drab or turnspit would be less useful than that man—what's his peasant's name? Harring? Therefore do thus, Torquaida: take away their brats and put them to nurse or be apprenticed, then sort the rest and for each one you judge worth adding to my staff select one servant we already have, who's lazy or sullen or deformed, and set him at my disposal to be staked tonight. Hah! Was this not an inspiration that I had?" He rubbed his hands and gave a gleeful chuckle.

"Oh, how I long to see the faces of those dunderheads when I wager fifty servants against each of them! I simply cannot fail to gain by this affair! If they win, which Lady Luck forfend, they will merely clutter up their households with extra mouths to feed, while I have acquired new useful tradesmen, and should I win—which I don't doubt I shall—I'll have plenty of spare overseers to cope with the servants those two stake! Ho-ho! We must do this again, Achoreus."

Achoreus bowed low, and once more stroked his mustachios.

"Take them away," Fellian commanded, and leaned back in his throne, reaching with fat pale fingers for the mouthpiece of a jade huqqah nearby on a lacquered table. An alert slave darted forward and set a piece of glowing charcoal on the pile of scented herbs its bowl contained.

Frightened and angry, but too weak to resist, the folk of Wantwich turned under the goading of the soldiers and filed back to the courtyard. Fellian watched them. As the tail of the line drew level with him, he snapped his fingers and all glanced expectantly towards him.

"That girl at the end," he murmured. "She's not unhandsome in a rustic way. Set her apart, bathe, perfume and dress her, and let her attend me in my chamber."

"But—!" Achoreus took a pace forward.

"You wish to comment?" Fellian purred dangerously.

Achoreus hesitated, and at last shook his head.

"Let it be done, then." Fellian smiled, and sucked his huqqah with every appearance of contentment.

VI

FURIOUS, ACHOREUS TURNED to superintend the final clearance
of the captives from the gallery, and thought the task was done,
but when he glanced around there was one stranger remaining,
who certainly was neither a household officer nor a slave: a
man in a black cloak leaning on a staff.

"Achoreus!" Fellian rasped. "Why have you not taken that
fellow with the rest?"

Staring, Achoreus confessed, "I have not seen him before!
He was not with the villagers when we assembled them— Ah,
but I *have* seen him, not at Wantwich. Now I recall that when
we were on the outward leg from Teq he stood beneath a tree
to watch our army pass, having that same staff in his hand."

"And he's come to join the captives of his own accord?"
Fellian suggested with a laugh. An answering ripple of amusement at what passed for his brilliant wit echoed from his
sycophants. "Well, then, we shall not deny him the privilege
he craves!"

Faces brightened everywhere. Fellian was a capricious
master, but when he spoke in this jovial fashion it was probable
that he was about to distribute favors and gifts at random,
saying it was to impress on his retinue the supreme authority
of luck.

"So, old man!" he continued. "What brings you hither, if
not the long chain linking those who have been here a moment back?"

"A need to know," said the traveller in black, advancing
across the multicolored floor.

123

"To know what? When the gaming-wheel of life will spin to a halt for you against the dire dark pointer of death? Why, you may ask that face to face of Lady Luck, and she will tell you instanter!"

At that, certain of his attendants blanched. It was not good taste—or wise—to joke about the Lady.

"To know," the traveller responded unperturbed, "why you sent armed raiders to the village Wantwich."

"Ah, yes," Fellian said ironically. "I can see how a stranger might put a question of that order, lacking proper comprehension of the priorities in life. Many think that all they need ever do is act reasonably, meet obligations, pay their debts . . . and then some random power intrudes on their silly calm existence, perhaps with a lash, perhaps with a sword, and all their reasoning is set at naught. That then is their opportunity to learn the truth. Not sense but luck is what rules the cosmos, do you hear me? *Luck!*"

He leaned forward, uttering the last word with such intensity that a spray of spittle danced down to the floor.

"See you that idiot who turns a gaming-wheel for me? Ho, you! Bring the creature here!"

Retainers rushed to obey. Fellian peeled rings from his fingers, decorated with stones that might bring the price of a small farm or vineyard, and flung them on the soiled hem of the idiot's robe.

"Turn her free! Luck has smiled her way today!"

"Not so," contradicted the traveller.

"What? You gainsay me—you gainsay *Fellian*?" The lord was popeyed with horror.

"Say rather I see two sides of this good fortune," the other murmured. "Is it not great luck for an idiot to be fed, housed, and clothed by a rich lord? Is this not worth more to her than to be given some pretty baubles and left to fend alone? Where is the benefit if next week she starves?"

Fellian began to redden as the validity of the point sank in, and he glared fiercely at someone to his right whom he suspected of being about to giggle.

"You chop logic, do you?" he grunted. "You're a schoolman,

no doubt, of the kind we take to gaze on Lady Luck, who thereupon die horribly!"

"Which event," the traveller remarked mildly, "puts a term to the possibility of persuading them to share your views. The dead are not the easiest persons to convert; their attitudes tend to be somewhat rigid. . . ." He shifted his staff from one hand to the other, and continued.

"Let me see if I understand these views of yours. You maintain, I believe, that life is one long gamble?"

"Of course it is!" barked Fellian.

"In that case, why should one wish to make more wagers? Is not any other, compared to the wager that embraces the whole of life, too trivial to be worth attention?"

"On the contrary. It is the gamble of life that must prove ultimately trivial, since none of us can win at it forever. . . ." Fellian sounded uncomfortable at making the admission, and proceeded rapidly to a more agreeable aspect of the subject. "What lends spice to the period of awaiting the inevitable is winning other wagers. And in myself I constitute an irrefutable proof of the correctness of my opinion. You see me sitting here—is it not plain by that token that I'm as much a winner in the game of life as anyone can hope to be? I staked my very survival on the right to be a Lord of Teq, and my present eminence proves that the Lady on the tower smiles my way!"

The traveller cocked his head sardonically. He said, "Call yourself a great gambler, a great winner, whatever you like. But I can name a bet you'll not accept."

"What?" Fellian howled, and all around there were cries of shocked dismay. "You think you can insult a Lord of Teq with impunity? Guards, seize and bind him! He has offered me a mortal affront, and he must pay for it."

"How have I affronted you—how? To say that I can name a bet you will not accept is not to insult you, unless you can but will not match my stakes!" The traveller fixed Fellian with a piercing stare.

"Am I to bet with a nobody? I bet only against my peers! It takes uncounted wealth to bet with me!" Fellian snorted. "Why, were I to treat you seriously, any bumpkin could come to me and say, 'I wager my rags and clogs, all I possess, against all that you possess—and that's a match!'"

"But there is one thing any man may bet against any other," said the traveller. "For no man can have more than one of it."

There was silence for the space of several heartbeats. "My lord," Torquaida said at last in a rusty voice, "he means life."

Fellian went pale and licked his lips. He blustered, "Even so! A life that may have fifty years to run, like mine, against one which may snuff out tomorrow, or next week?"

"Regrettably," Torquaida creaked, "that is fair stakes. However"—and he gave a tiny dry smile and wheezing chuckle—"it's over-soon to name the stakes before one knows the bet, is it not?"

Fellian flashed him a grateful grin; this was the outlet he had failed to spot himself. He said loudly, "Yes, a crucial point! What bet is this that you seek to make with me, old man?"

"I bet you," said the traveller amid a general hush, "that the face of Lady Luck is turned away from your throne."

There was an instant of appalled shock. But with great effort Fellian forced a booming laugh.

"Why, that wager's lost already!" he exclaimed. "I've said as much already: it's proof of the Lady's favor that I enjoy unparalleled riches."

"They are what you awoke to today," the traveller said. "Tomorrow is yet to eventuate."

"Why stop at tomorrow?" Fellian countered. "Next week, next month, next year if you like, when I have won still more bets against Yuckin and Nusk, we'll hoist you on a tall pole that you may look on the Lady directly and see that she does smile towards me. Meantime, enjoy the hospitality of my dungeons. Ho, guards!"

"Thank you, I am in no need of lodging," said the traveller. "Moreover, a week is too long. Less than a day will suffice. I will see you again tomorrow; let us say at dawn. For now, farewell."

"Seize him!" Fellian bellowed, and two soldiers who had remained behind, on Achoreus's signal, when the party of captives was led away, darted in the direction of the traveller.

But they went crashing against one another, as though they had sought to arrest an armful of air.

VII

IN THE GREAT CAVELIKE KITCHENS of the palace, a cook sweated with ladle and tongs at a cauldron of half a hogshead capacity. The fire roaring beneath scorched his skin, the smoke blinded his eyes with tears.

From the dark corner of the hearth a voice inquired for whom the savory-smelling broth was being prepared.

"Why, for Lord Fellian," sighed the cook.

"But no man can engulf such a deal of soup. Will he have guests?"

"Yes, so he will." The cook grimaced. "They'll eat two ladlefuls apiece, or maybe three."

"And you then will enjoy what is left over?"

"I, sir?"—with a rueful chuckle. "No, on my soul, I wouldn't dare. What my lord leaves in the dish goes to his hounds! Tonight as ever I shall sup off a dry crust, with cheese or moldy bacon-rind. Still, hounds have no taste for wine, so if I'm quick I may claim the goblet-dregs from the high table, and liquor will soothe my grumbling belly long enough to let me sleep."

Among the fierce ammonia stench of guano, a falconer worked by an unglazed window, tooling with gnarled yet delicate hands a design of rhythmical gold leaf on the hood and jesses of a peregrine.

"This leather is beautiful," said a soft voice from over his shoulder. "But doubtless you put on far finer array when you sally forth of an evening to enjoy yourself at a tavern?"

"I, sir?" grunted the falconer, not turning around; the light was wasting, and he was forbidden the extravagance of lamps or candles. "Why, no. I'm in the service of Lord Fellian, and have no time to amuse myself. And had I time, I'd be constrained to wear what you see upon me now—old canvas breeches bound with fraying rope. Besides, with what would I purchase a mug of ale? A scoop of fewmets?"

In the stables, a groom passed a soft cloth caressingly over the fitments of a stall; they were of ivory and jacinth, while the manger was filled with new sweet hay, fine oats fit to have baked bread, and warm-scented bran.

"Palatial," said a voice from behind the partition. "This is truly for a horse?"

"Aye," muttered the groom, declining to be distracted from his work. "For Western Wind, Lord Fellian's favourite steed."

"By comparison, then, I judge you must take your repose on high pillows stuffed with swansdown, beneath a coverlet of silk, or furs for winter."

"I sleep on straw, sir—do not jest with me! And if I have time to gather clay to stop the chinks in my hovel against the cold of night, I count myself well off."

Beside a marble bath, which ran scented water from a gargoyle's mouth, a slender girl measured out grains of rare restorative spices onto a sponge, a loofah, and the bristles of a brush made from the hide of a wild boar.

"With such precautions," a voice said from beyond a curl of rising steam, "your beauty will surely be preserved far past the ordinary span."

"Think you I'd dare to waste one speck of this precious essence on my own skin?" the girl retorted, tossing back a tress of hair within which—though she could be at most aged twenty —there glinted a betraying thread of silver. "I'd be lucky, when they detected me, to be thrown over the sill of that window! Beneath it there is at least a kitchen midden to afford me a soft landing. No, my entire fortune is my youth, and it takes the powers of an elemental and the imagination of a genius to spread youth thin enough to satisfy Lord Fellian from spring to autumn."

"Why then do you continue in his service?"

"Because he is a winner in the game of life."

"And how do you know that?"

"Why," sighed the girl, "everyone says so."

In the high-vaulted banquet-hall, as the sun went down, the rival lords Yuckin and Nusk came to feast with their respective retinues at the expense of the current greatest winner prior to the onset of the night's gambling. They had come to his palace too often of late; there was no friendly chat between them. Gloomily—though displaying fair appetite, because their own kitchens did not furnish such delicacies—they sat apart, growing angrier and angrier as platters of gold succeeded those of silver, goblets of crystal replaced those of enamelled pottery . . . and often recognizing items they had owned and lost.

Lord Fellian should have been in high spirits at the downcast mood of his adversaries. Instead, he too appeared depressed and anxious, and the talk at his long table was all of the strange intruder in a black cloak who had proposed so disturbing a bet.

"It's nonsense!" roundly declared Achoreus, who was seated beside Fellian as a mark of special favor. "As you rightly said, sir, it's absurd to expect someone of your standing to wager with a penniless nobody. Moreover, the bet he named is by definition incapable of settlement!"

But his brow was pearled with sweat, and when he had repeated his assertion for the third time his voice was harsh with a hoarseness no amount of wine could allay.

"And how say you, Torquaida?" demanded Fellian, hungry for reassurance—though not for food; course after course was being removed from his place untouched.

"There is no need to worry," the elderly treasurer wheezed. "Like you or dislike you, Lords Yuckin and Nusk would have to concede the propriety of declining such a wager. Short of compelling someone to look directly at the statue, there's no way of deciding the matter—and anyone we chose might lie when he reported."

"Is that not precisely what I've just been saying?" crowed Achoreus.

Even that, however, did not ease Fellian's mind. "Would I might know the outcome anyway," he grumbled. "No matter how right I was when I declined the fellow's terms!"

At that the black-clad traveller, standing apart in the dark of an embrasure, gave a sad and secret smile.

"As you wish," he murmured, "so be it. Indeed you chose aright when gambling against me, Fellian—and there are and have been few in all the cosmos who can make that claim. Yet in the very instant when you won, you lost beyond all hope."

The question settled now, he went away.

Shortly, they cleared the dishes from the hall, bringing in their place the hand-carved dominoes required for the game shen fu, the lacquered plaques destined for match-me-mine and mark-me-well, the tumbling gilded cages full of colored balls known as the Lady's Knucklebones, the gaming-wheels— those with four, those with nine, and those with thirty-three divisions —blind songbirds trained to pick out one among three disparately dyed grains of corn, jumping beans, silver-harnessed fleas, baby toads steeped in strong liquor, and all the other appurtenances on which the lords of Teq were accustomed to place their bets. Additionally, from among their respective trains they marshalled their current champions at wrestling, boxing with cestae, and gladiatorial combat, not to mention tumblers, leapers, imbeciles armed with brushes full of paint, dice-throwing monkeys, and whatever else they had lately stumbled across upon the outcome of whose acts a wager might be made.

It was the practice for one of the challengers to name the first game, and of the challenged to declare the stakes. Thus, in strict accordance with protocol, Lord Yuckin as the last to lose to Lord Fellian cleared his throat and began with a single hand of shen fu, to which Fellian consented, and won a basket of desert-hoppers—a typical low stake for the early hours.

Then Lord Nusk bet on a jumping toad, and won a purse of coins from Barbizond, to which Lord Fellian replied with a spin of the four-part wheel and won a bag of sapphires. He nudged his companions and whispered that the old fool on the gallery must have been wrong.

Thus too he won the next five bouts, on toads again, on fleas, on two hands of shen fu, and lastly on the pecking birds. After that he lost a spin on the nine-part wheel and had to concede to Yuckin a chased and jewelled sword that Torquaida dismissed as pretty but not practical, its blade being inferior: no great loss.

"Now, I think," murmured the pleased Lord Fellian, and on Lord Nusk naming shen fu as the next bout, declared his stake: fifty male servants on this single hand.

The impact was all he could have wished. Though they might scornfully disclaim involvement with such mundane matters, none knew better than the lords of Teq how many were kept employed to ensure their affluence, through what different and varied skills. To bet one servant was occasionally a gesture of last resort after a bad night; to risk fifty at one go was unprecedented.

Captain Achoreus chortled at the dismay that overcame the visiting lords, and nudged Torquaida in his skinny ribs. "The greatest winner!" he murmured, and signalled for another mug of wine.

Yet, when the dominoes were dealt, the Star of Eve fell to Lord Nusk, and only the Inmost Planet to Lord Fellian.

Nusk, who was a fat man with a round bald pate fringed with black, grinned enormously and rubbed his paunch. Scowling, Fellian trembled and made challenge to Lord Yuckin at the same game.

Yuckin, old and gaunt, eyes blank behind lenses of grey crystal, named as much gold as a particular man might carry, and won, and challenged back, and Lord Fellian staked the other fifty servants.

Whereupon he displayed the chief prize of shen fu, the Crown of Stars, and mocked Lord Yuckin's petty deal of Planets Conjoined.

A few minutes later, on a hopping toad, he won back from Lord Nusk the former fifty servants, and again from Yuckin a fresh batch, including three skilled armorers that lord could ill afford to lose, and beyond that a farm in the Dale of Vezby, and a whole year's vintage of sparkling wine, and three trade-galleys with their crews; and then from Nusk the High Manor of Coper's Tor, with the right to make a celebrated ewe's-milk cheese according to a secret recipe; then lost for five short minutes the Marches of Gowth with all four fortresses and the Shrine of Fire, but won them back on a spin of the four-part wheel and along with them the Estate of Brywood, the Peak of Brend, and the territory from Haggler's Mound to Cape Dismay.

Securely positioned now, he commenced the calculated process of attrition that he had long dreamed of, the process which ultimately would reduce his rivals to penury: a cook who knew how to make sorbets without ice, a gardener who could raise strawberries in winter, a boy skilled at charming game from barren ground by playing a whistle, an eight-foot-tall swordsman, champion of the last public games . . .

Torquaida might have been forgiven for growing harried trying to keep track of the winnings and match what was in hand against what remained to the rival lords. By a supreme effort he stayed in control, always remembering to send a clerk to warn Lord Fellian when a stake was unworthy, to say for example that this concubine was scarred from the smallpox, or that guardsman had a palsy and his shield-arm shook, or a certain chest of coins bore a geas, and touched without the proper spell would turn to pebbles.

Lord Fellian granted him free of feoff the Estate of Brywood as reward for his valuable support, and laughed joyously night-long at the discomfiture of his opponents.

VIII

FAR BELOW THE BANQUET-HALL, cast back by its high and vaulted roof, that ringing laughter reached the ears of those miserable deportees from Wantwich who were still awake. Some were asleep—on straw if they were lucky, on hard flags if they were not . . . but at least asleep.

One who was wakeful even on a mattress of eider feathers, draped in a diaphanous gown of finest lawn embroidered with seed pearls, was the girl Viola, surrounded by other female pleasure-objects destined for Lord Fellian's delight. At a footstep on the floor beside her couch, she started and peered into obscurity, seeing only a black form outlined on greater blackness.

"Is someone there?" she whimpered.

"I," said the traveller.

"How—how did you get in?" Viola sat up. "I tried the doors, and the windows too, and all are locked!"

The traveller forbore to explain.

After a moment, Viola began to weep. "Go away!" she commanded. "I never want to see you again! You did this awful thing to me, and I hate you!"

"On the contrary. You did it to yourself."

"I never asked to be locked up here, waiting for some gross old lecher!"

"Ah, but you've been reunited with your man Leluak, and that's what you said you wanted. You are both under the same roof; when Lord Fellian tires of you, you will be cast forth together to share the same dank alleyway and the same fevers, chills, and pestilences. This in essence constitutes reunion."

133

"I should have thought longer before choosing," Viola said after a pause for reflection. The traveller nodded. At least, then, this cruel experience had battered some sense into her pretty head.

"You had, I believe," he said, "encountered Achoreus before the attack he supervised on Wantwich."

"I did so. I companioned him when he joined us for the spring dance."

"Out of courtesy?"

"Of course." In the dark, the girl bridled.

"Or was it because he was a stranger, and good-looking, and every other girl in the village would have changed places with you?"

"A little of that too," she admitted meekly.

"And is it not true, my child, that you were more concerned to regain the handsomest, most eligible bachelor in Wantwich, for whom you had competed against all the other girls less attractive than yourself, than you were to right the wrong done to your family and friends upon the day of your projected wedding?"

"I must have been!" Viola moaned. "Would that overhasty wish of mine could be undone!"

"The second time a person calls on me," said the traveller, "I may choose whether or not to grant the request. In this case, I choose not."

"Have pity!" she cried, and caught his arm.

"Do you truly wish to find yourself once more upon the green at Wantwich—alone except for dotard Granny Anderland?"

There was an awful silence, which she eventually broke with a sob.

"However," the traveller resumed, when he judged she had suffered long enough to imprint the moral on her memory, "you may rest easy. All is due to reach a satisfactory outcome. Though if I were to tell you the name of your savior, you'd not believe it. . . ."

He tapped his staff against the bed she sat on, and concluded, "Sleep, child. Wake at dawn."

*   *   *

Dazed with elation, when the returning sun began to gild the turrets of Teq with the promise of a new day, Lord Fellian struggled to the high gallery of his tower in order to witness the departure of his defeated rivals. On their own! No one in the history of the city had won so fantastic a victory in a single night! Stripped even of their closest body-slaves, Lords Yuckin and Nusk were creeping into the morning twilight like whipped dogs. It had been more by grace than necessity that they had been permitted to keep clothing.

Fellian leaned drunkenly over the parapet and whooped like a falconer sighting quarry; when the cowed face of Lord Yuckin tilted upward to see what the noise was, he spilled on it the contents of his latest beaker of wine.

"So much for that old fool who wanted to bet that Lady Luck's visage was turned away from me!" he bellowed, and laughed until the racket of his boasting was reflected from the nearby rooftops.

"Are you sure?"

To the edge of his politely voiced question the traveller appended the faint swish of his cloak as he advanced across the inlaid floor.

"Why, you . . . !" Lord Fellian gasped and made to draw back, but the parapet was hard against his spine and there was no way to retreat save over its top and into air. "Guards! Guards!"

"None of them has followed you up here," said the traveller gravely. "They are persuaded that upon a winner like yourself—if there has ever been one—Lady Luck smiles so long and so favorably that no harm can possibly assail you."

"Ah-hah!" Fellian began to recover his composure. "I conclude from that statement that you admit you would have lost your bet with me, had I been fool enough to take it on!"

"Why, no," said the traveller, and his expression showed regret, for it had always seemed a shame to him that a person of intelligence—and Fellian was far from stupid—should be seduced into a self-defeating course of action. "I would have won."

"What? You're insane!" gasped Fellian. "Prove your claim!"

"I shall," said the traveller, and with his staff he smote the wall that screened this gallery from sight of the tallest tower in Teq. A slice fell away like a wedge cut from a cheese. Beyond, there where Fellian's reflex gaze darted before he could check himself, Lady Luck's pinnacle loomed on the easterly blueness of the dawn.

A scream died stillborn in his throat. He stared and stared, and after a while he said, "But . . . but there's only a stump!"

And it was true: against the sky, instead of the celebrated statue, nothing but a jagged pediment upreared.

He began to giggle. "Why, you'd have lost after all! Your wager was not that Lady Luck had ceased to smile on me, which would be a fair victory. You said her face was turned away from my throne!"

"True."

"How can you utter such nonsense?"

The traveller gestured with his staff. "Go nearer; examine the chunks of stone I have broken from the wall."

Hesitant, yet ashamed to appear frightened, Fellian obeyed. His fingertips fumbled across rough plaster while he coughed at the dust he was stirring up, and found smooth chased stones not conformable to the flat surface of the broken wall. A knot of hair-ribbon interpreted in sculpture; the slope of a gown, petrified, slanting over shoulder blades of granite . . .

"There was a storm," said the traveller didactically. "You will recall the one because it brought part of your wall down. During it, lightning-struck, the figure tumbled and landed in the street. It has always been the custom, has it not, that anyone who looked on Lady Luck should die? Save the breath you'd waste for an answer; I know your agents dump those whom you dislike in the market-square, claiming it was for that reason they expired.

"Accordingly, none recognized the fragments. When you commanded masons to repair your wall, which as I said had also suffered in the storm, they gathered up whatever they could find, and into the gap they set the broken pieces of the statue, in such fashion that the back of its head was just behind your throne."

"But that's not fair!" shrieked Fellian. "You knew this all the time, didn't you?"

"Who are you to talk of 'fair' and 'unfair'?" snapped the traveller. "Did not I hear you yesterday promising to reward Achoreus by increasing his stake on a bet that your privy intelligence informed you he had won already? Be silent! I am not here to argue, but to inflict on you your just deserts! Now look upon the face, at last, of Lady Luck!"

He reached out with his staff. As effortlessly as though he rolled an empty wine-jar, he turned the stone head over, and before Fellian could snatch his gaze away he saw what he had most dreaded all his life.

With one eye socket vacant and the other masked, she was not smiling. Not on him and not on anyone. She was grinning, and in that look he read inconceivable malevolence.

"Your long-vanished ancestors who carved her image," said the traveller, "understood the nature of luck better than you ever did or will. No wonder your masons felt this face was safer hidden in a solid wall."

Fellian tried to answer. He could not. In compliance with the most ancient custom of his city, hands clawing at the air as though he could cram it by fistfuls into his choking lungs, the greatest winner among all the lords of Teq departed into nowhere.

Sighing, more than a little sorrowful, the traveller went his way.

A while later, when they came upon the corpse, those who had pledged themselves to Fellian's service began to quarrel about partitioning what he had left behind: in sum, the total wealth of Teq and its environs.

"I will have the treasury!" Torquaida cried. "It's no more than my due!" But a young and vigorous clerk from the counting-house struck him down with a gold candlestick. His old pate cracked four ways, like the shell of an egg.

"If I can have nothing more, I'll take the booty Lord Fellian cheated me of!" vowed Achoreus, and set off in search of the girl Viola. But he tripped on a slippery marble step at the entrance of the women's quarters, and by the time he recovered from his bang on the head she was awake and away.

By contrast, though, on learning that after all his lord had been a loser in the game of life, the groom who tended Western Wind made haste to saddle up his charge.

"At least this recompense is due to me," he sighed, opening the door of the stable. Outside he found the girl whose hair was turning grey at twenty, pleading for a chance of escape. He hoisted her to his saddlebow and let the stallion prove his mettle on the open road.

Later, in Barbizond, they offered him to cover mares in heat, and from the foals which resulted built up a livery stable of their own.

Likewise the falconer, on being told the news, gathered his prize merlin and went out into the countryside to get what living he could. He lost the merlin by flying her at an eagle that was trying to steal a baby, a match the eagle was foredoomed to win. But the child, who survived unhurt, was the only son of a wealthy landowner, and in gratitude he made the falconer bailiff of his estates.

Also the cook gathered up a brand from beneath his cauldron and went forth by a secret tunnel leading from the back of his ox-roasting hearth. There he turned his ankle on a square object lying in the dust of the passageway, and the light of the brand showed that it was the lost Book of Knightly Vigor, from which — legend claimed — the Count of Hyfel, founder of Teq, had gained the amorous skill to woo and wed his twenty-seven brides. With recipes from it he opened a cookshop, and defeated lovers from a score of cities trudged over hill and dale to sample his unique concoctions.

Amid all this coming and going, however, the captives from Wantwich were content to find their way to freedom in the morning sun.

IX

ON RETURNING HOME, the villagers were a trifle puzzled to discover that the pond beside the green, which for as long as anybody could recall had been placid, now roiled unaccountably. However, as their repairs proceeded—new roofs and shutters, new gates and fences, to replace those broken by the troops from Teq—that disturbance ceased. Before the new beer was brewed, before new barrels were coopered, before a new fiddle had been made and strung for Jarge, the water had resumed its normal state.

And on the day when, belatedly, Leluak led out his bride to start the dancing proper to a marriage, a person in a black cloak stood with a benign smile in the shelter of a sycamore.

"Was it not clever, Horimos?" he said under his breath to the imprisoned elemental. "Was it not ingenious to pervert the thinking of rational men into the courses of a gambler, who lacks even the dangerous knowledge of an enchanter when he tampers with the forces of chaos?"

Unnoticed except by the traveller, the pond gave off a bubble full of foul marshy gas, which might have been intended for an answer.

"*Shu-ut—brr'p—brr'up!*"

"By all means, Horimos," the traveller murmured, and drained the mug of Brewer Harring's good beer which he, like all passers-by on a festival day, had been offered. He set the vessel on a handy stump, and the music rose to a frantic gay crescendo.

When, a little diffidently, Viola came to greet him and ask if he would like to take his turn at partnering her in the dance, there was no trace of his presence save the empty mug.

FOUR

The Things That Are Gods

Lo how smothe and curvit ben these rockes
that in the creacioun weren jaggit, for that
they haf ben straikit by myriades of
thickheidit folk hither ycommen in
peregrinage, beggarlie criand after Miracula.
And I say one at the leste wis granted em.
Was't not a marveil and a wonder, passand
credence, that they helden dull ston for more
puissaunt than your quicke man, the which
mought brethe and dreme and soffre and
fede wormes?

—A Lytel Boke Againste Folie

I

TIPPING BACK THE HOOD of his black cloak, leaning on his staff of curdled light, the traveller paused beneath the midnight sky, wherein the conjunction of four significant planets was manifest to those learned in such study, and contemplated the land where he had incarcerated the elemental called Litorgos. That being loathed both salt and silt; accordingly, here had been a most appropriate choice.

Half a day's walk from the edge of the sea the ground reared up to form a monstrous irregular battlemented cliff twenty times the height of a tall man, notched where a river cascaded over the rim of the plateau above. Thence it spilled across a wedge-shaped plain of its own making and developed into a narrow delta, following sometimes this and sometimes that main channel. In principle such land should have been fertile. Opposite the river's multiple mouths, however, a dragon-backed island created a swinge, such that at spring tide ocean-water flooded ankle-deep over the soil, permeating it with salt. Therefore only hardy and resistant crops could be grown here, and in a bad year might be overtaken once too often by the saline inundation before they were ready to harvest.

This had not prevented the establishment of cities. One had been founded close to the waterfall, and flourished awhile on trade with the plateau above. A crude staircase had been carved out of the living rock, up which slaves daily toiled bearing salt, dried fish, and baskets of edible seaweed, to return with grain and fruit and sunflower oil. Then the elemental slumbering below stretched to test the firmness of his intangible

143

bonds; they held him, but the staircase crumbled and the city disappeared.

More recently a port had been built at the mouth of the main channel; it stood on wooden piles brought from the island opposite, which had been thickly forested. With the clearance of the woodland, marble was discovered. Cutting and polishing it, exporting it on rafts poled along the coastal shallows, the citizens grew rich enough to deck their own homes with marble and colorful tiles in patterns each of which constituted a charm against ill fortune. But now the marble was exhausted, and so was most of the timber, and the city Stanguray which had once been famous was reduced to a village. Its present inhabitants lived in the attics and lofts of the old town, and as they lay down to sleep could listen to the chuckle of water rippling within the lower portion of their homes. To pass from one surviving building to another even toddlers deftly walked along flimsy rope bridges, while the needs of the elderly and better-off—for there were still rich and poor in Stanguray—were met by the bearers of reed-mat palanquins, adept at striding down the waterways and across the mudflats on stilts taller than themselves. This mode of transport had no counterpart elsewhere.

And it was entirely fitting, the traveller reflected, that there should be one thing at least unique about this place. For once the river which here met the ocean had run beside the ramparts of Acromel, and was known as Metamorphia. No longer did it instantly change whatever fell or swam in its waters, it having been decreed that after a certain span of amending the nature of other things, it must alter its own. Yet and still a trace of what had gone before remained, and would forever in the work of all rivers: they would erode mountains, create plains, cause the foundation and destruction of uncounted cities.

Moreover, in all the settlements along it, including those on the plateau around Lake Taxhling—the first earnest of the inevitable change in the river's nature, inasmuch as there it spread out and grew sluggish and reed-fringed before it ultimately spilled over the cliff and became the opposite, fast and violent and sparkling—the residual magic of Metamorphia had led to schools of enchantment. Of no very great import, admittedly, nothing to compare with the traditions of Ryovora or Barbizond or the Notorious Magisters of Alken Cromlech, but dowered nonetheless with a certain potency.

Such matters being of the keenest interest to him, the traveller set onward along riverside paths towards this paradoxical village of marble columns and tiled pilasters. Dawn was breaking before he reached it; clouds in the east were flushing scarlet and rose and vermilion, and fisherfolk were chanting melodiously as they carried their night's catch ashore in baskets of osier and spilled them into marble troughs, once destined for the watering of nobles' horses, where women and children swiftly gutted them. The smell of blood was acute in the traveller's nostrils when he was still a quarter-hour's walk distant.

And then it occurred to him that there was no wind to carry it. What slight breeze there was, was at his back: blowing off the land, towards the sea.

Moreover he perceived of a sudden that it was not just the light of dawn which was tinting pink the water in the channels either side of the crude causeway he was following.

There must have been an astonishing slaughter.

The traveller sighed. Last time he had seen a river literally running red in this manner, it had been because of a battle: one of dozens, all indecisive, in the constant wars of Kanish-Kulya. But matters there had been regulated pretty well to his satisfaction, and in any case this was not human blood.

If it were a precedented event, the inhabitants of Stanguray would presumably be able to inform him concerning this tainting of the flow. The ground being impregnate with salt, one could not sink a sweet-water well; rainfall, besides, was exiguous and seasonal hereabouts. Consequently folk were much dependent on the river's cleanliness.

More perturbed by the situation than seemed reasonable, the traveller lengthened his strides.

II

WHEN THE FISH-GUTS had been thrown to the gulls the people of Stanguray went their various ways: the poorest to the beach, where over scraps of driftwood barely dry enough to burn they scorched a few of the smaller fish, sardines and pilchards, and gobbled them bones and all with a smear of oil and a crust of bread left over from yesterday's baking; the most prosperous, including naturally all of those who owned an entire fishing-smack with a reliable charm on it, to their homes where a more substantial breakfast awaited them; and the middling sort to the town's only cookshop, where they handed over a coin or a portion of their catch against the privilege of having their repast prepared on the public fire. Fuel was very short in Stanguray.

The said cookshop was the upper part of what had formerly been a temple, extended under the sky by a platform of creaky scantlings, water-worn and boreworm-pierced, salvaged from a wreck or a building long submerged.

Here a thin-faced, sharp-nosed, sharp-tongued young woman in a russet gown and a long apron supervised a fire on a block of slate whose visible sides were engraved with curlicues and runes. It would have been the altar when the temple's cult still throve. Presiding over it like any priestess, as well as cooking fish she deigned to dispense hunks of grid-dle cake and char or stew vegetables brought by those lucky enough to own a farmable patch of ground. Meantime a hunch-backed boy who never moved fast enough to please her meted out rations of sliced onion, vinegar and verjuice to add a quicker relish to the simple food.

A public fire, plainly, was a profitable operation, for everything about the shop was better appointed than one might have predicted. Though the external platform was fragile, though the variety of the menu was wholly dependent on who brought what, nonetheless the woman's gown was of excellent quality, and the walls were ornamented with numerous precious relics such as one would rather have expected to find in the homes of wealthy boat-owners. Also, at least for those who paid in money, not only beer but even wine was to be had. The hunchback, lashed on by the woman's shouted orders, rushed them by the mugful to the customers.

It was clear that at least one more waiter was not only affordable, but urgently needed.

However, that—to the traveller's way of thinking—was not the most curious aspect of this cookshop.

Having sated their bellies, the homeless poor plodded up from the beach carrying clay jars which they had filled at the point where the estuarial water turned from brackish to drinkable . . . or should have done. Not long after, a string of children also assembled, bearing by ones and twos full leathern buckets. Some could scarcely stand under the load.

For a long while the woman in charge seemed not to notice them. The delay grated on the patience of one girl, some twelve or thirteen years old, and finally she called out.

"Crancina, it's a foul-water day!"

"What of it?" the woman retorted, rescuing a roasted turnip from the flames, not quite in time.

"We had salt eels this morning, and we're clemmed!"

"Tell your mother she ought to know better," was the brusque reply, and Crancina went on serving her other customers.

Finally, several minutes having elapsed, she stood back from the hearth and dusted her hands. Instantly the people waiting rushed towards her. The poorer got there first, being adult and desperate—despite which they contrived to offer at least a copper coin, which she took, bit, and dropped in the pocket of her apron, while pronouncing a cantrip over their water-jugs.

Forced to the rear by those larger and stronger, the children from wealthier homes had no lack of cash, but they tasted the water cautiously after the spell had been spoken, as though fearing that much repetition might weaken it. All satisfied, they took their leave.

"Are you curious concerning what you see, sir?" a thin voice said at the traveller's elbow. He had taken pains, as ever, not to be conspicuous, but it was time now for direct inquiries.

Turning, he found the hunchback boy perched on a table, for all the world like a giant frog about to make a leap. His sly dark eyes peered from under a fringe of black hair.

"I own I'm intrigued," the traveller said.

"I thought you would be, seeing as I don't recall noticing you before. A pilgrim, are you? Cast ashore by some rascally sea-captain because contrary winds made it too expensive to carry you all the way to the shrine you booked your passage for?" The boy grinned hugely, making his face as well as his body resemble a frog's.

"Do you receive many castaway pilgrims here, then?"

A crooked shrug. "None, to my knowledge! But even that would vary the monotony of my existence. Every day is more or less the same for all of us. Why otherwise would this enchanting of water be remarkable?"

"Ah: so magic is at work."

"What else? Crancina has a sweet-water spell from Granny, all she left us when she died, and so whenever the river pinkens they all come here. It's making her a nice little pile."

"She charges everybody?"

"Indeed yes! She claims that performing the rite tires her out, so she must be recompensed."

"What of those—for there must be some such—who have not even a worn copper to buy her services?"

"Why, she says they may wait for rain!" The boy essayed a laugh, which emerged as more of a croak.

"I deduce you are Crancina's brother," the traveller said after a pause.

"How so?" The boy blinked.

"You spoke of what Granny left to 'us,' as though you shared her."

A grimace. "In fact, half-brother. I often wonder whether it was Granny's curse that twisted me, for I know she disapproved of Mother's second marriage . . . However that may be!" His tone took on a sudden urgency. "Will you not instruct me to deliver you something, if only a hunk of bread? For I should by now have served her the choicest of last night's catch, rich with oil and fragrant with herbs, and grilled to perfection on the most odoriferous of our scant supply of logs. Any moment she will tongue-lash me until it stings like a physical castigation—at which, I may say, she is equally adept! Would you inspect my bruises?"

"There seems to be little love lost between you," the traveller observed.

"Love?" The hunchback cackled. "She wouldn't know the meaning of the word! So long as my father survived, and before our mother became bedridden, I made the most of life despite my deformity. Now she's my sole commander, mine's a weary lot! I wish with all my heart that someday I may find means to break free of her tyranny and make my own way in the world, against all odds!"

Prompt to his prediction Crancina shouted, "Jospil, why have you not set my breakfast on the embers? Costly wood is going up in smoke and all the customers are served!"

Her shrill reprimand drowned out the traveller's reflexive murmur: "As you wish, so be it."

Cringing, the boy regained the floor and scurried towards her. "Not so, sister!" he pleaded. "One remains unfed, and I did but inquire what he would order."

Abruptly noticing the traveller, Crancina changed her tone to one of wheedling deference. "Sir, what's your pleasure? Boy, make him room and bring clean dishes and a mug—at once!"

"Oh, I'll not trouble you to cook for me," the traveller answered. "Your brother has explained how casting your spell fatigues you, and you must need sustenance yourself. I'll take a bit of fish from pickle, bread, and beer."

"You're courteous, sir," Crancina sighed, sinking on a nearby bench. "Yes, in truth these foul-water days do take it out of me. In sum, they're a cursed nuisance! Over and over I've proposed that a band of well-armed men be sent out, to trace the trouble to its source, but it's on the high plateau, and these fainthearts hold that to be a place of sorcerers none can oppose. Monsters too, if you believe them."

"Maybe it's the one slaughtering the other," Jospil offered as he set mug and platter before the traveller. "There must come an end of that, when all expire!"

"It's not a joking matter!" snapped Crancina, raising her fist—and then reluctantly unballing it, as though belatedly aware she was being watched by a stranger. But she continued, "By all the powers, I wish I knew what use there is in spilling so much blood! Maybe then I could turn it to my own account for a change, instead of having to pander to the wants of these cajoling idiots, fool enough—*you* heard the girl, sir, I'll warrant! —fool enough to eat salt eels for breakfast when their noses must advise 'em there'll be nothing sweet to quench their thirst. Would you not imagine they could keep a day or two's supply that's fit to drink? If they can't afford a coopered barrel, surely there are enough old marble urns to be had for the trouble of dragging them to the surface. But they can't or won't be bothered. They're so accustomed to leaning out the window and dipping in the stream—and sending their ordures the same way, to the discomfort of us who live the closest to the sea— they regard it as a cycle in the natural order, never to be resisted, which if it does come right one day will do so of itself."

"They pay you for performing your spell," the traveller said, munching a mouthful of the pickled fish and finding it savory. "There's a compensation."

"I admit it," said Crancina. "In time I may grow rich, as wealth is counted in this miserable place. Already two widowers and a middle-aged bachelor are suing for my hand, plus, of course, half a share in this cookshop. . . . But that is not what I want!"—with sudden fierceness. "I'm accustomed to being in charge, and I want that with all my heart and soul, and I'm seeking a way of securing my fate whether or not this dismal half-ruined town crumbles into the sea!"

So long ago there was not means to measure it, the traveller had accepted obligations pertaining to his sundry and various journeys through the land.

The enforced granting of certain wishes formed an essential element of the conditions circumscribing him . . . though it was true that the consequences of former wishes were gradually limiting the previous total of possibilities. Some now were categorically unimplementable.

But even as he muttered formal confirmation—"As you wish, so be it!"—he knew one thing beyond a peradventure.

This was not one of those.

III

ONCE IT HAD BEEN PERMITTED him to hasten the seasons of the year and even alter their sequence. But that power belonged to the ages when the elementals roamed at large, their random frenzy entraining far worse divagations from the course of nature. Tamed and pent—like Litorgos under the delta of the river that no longer merited the name of Metamorphia—they were little able to affect the world. Events were tending, in the prescribed manner, towards that end which Manuus the enchanter had once defined as "desirable, perhaps, but appallingly dull." The day would break when all things would have but one nature, and time would have a stop, for the last vestige of the chaos existing in eternity would have been eliminated.

To make way for a new beginning? Possibly. If not, then—in the very strictest sense—*no matter, never mind* . . .

Until then, however, the elementals did still exist and fretted away with their enfeebled force, like Fegrim vainly beating at the cap of cold lava which closed the crater of his now-extinct volcano. Not a few had discovered that human practitioners of magic were, without having chosen to be, their allies. But there was a penalty attached to such collaboration, and the most minor of them had paid it long ago; they were reduced to activating hearth-charms. No doubt this was the fate that had overtaken Litorgos—no doubt it was he who drew the blood from the foul water, though he was in no position to benefit thereby. Blood had its place in magic, but it could never free an elemental.

But the traveller did not want so much as to think about Litorgos, or Stanguray, until the remainder of his business was completed. Nonetheless he did wish—and withal wished he could grant himself that wish, as he must grant those of others—that he could whirl the planets around to the conformation which would mark the conclusion of his journey, and thereby enable a return to that place which, with every pace he took, seemed more and more likely to become the focus of terrible and inexplicable events.

Making haste was pointless, though. The orderly succession of time which he himself had been responsible for, as river-silt had created land at Stanguray, now held him tight in its grip. Some relief from his apprehension might be obtained, however, by overoccupying himself. Accordingly on this journey he made a point of visiting not only those places familiar to him from aforetime—and sometimes from before time—but also newer locations.

One such was in the forest near to Clurm. Here in the shadow of great oaks a former petty lord, who held his birthright to have been usurped, planned with a group of fanatical followers to establish such a city as would lure anyone to remove thither at its mere description. Now they shivered in tents and ate wild game, half raw, and nuts and mushrooms; but this new city was to have towers that combed the clouds, and streets wide enough for a hundred to march abreast, and brothels with the fairest of women to attract spirited youths, and a treasury overflowing with gold and gems to pay their fee, and an army would be forged from them to overthrow the usurper, and magicians would be hired to render them unquestioningly loyal, and all in the upshot would be as this wild dreamer pictured it.

Except that after a year of exile his little band had not erected so much as a log cabin, deeming manual labor beneath their dignity.

"But the new Clurm will be of such magnificence!" asserted the lordling, seated as ever closest to the warmth of their tiny camp-fire; they dared not build a larger one, for fear of being spotted by the usurper's forces, who roved free in the country-side while they hid among trees, being less beloved of the common folk. "It will be . . . it will be . . . Oh, I can see it now in my mind's eye! Would you too could see its wonders! Would I could make you believe in its existence!"

Standing apart among underbrush, and leaning on his staff, the traveller said, "As you wish, so be it."

Next morning the inevitable happened. The band awoke convinced that their city was real, for they imagined they saw it all about them. Joyful, bent on their leader's errand, they set out towards all points of the compass and, just as he had predicted, returned with many eager young recruits.

Who thereupon, not finding any city grand or otherwise, set about those who had enticed them hither, beat them with cudgels, bound them hand and foot, and committed them for lunatics. The lordling was not exempted from this treatment.

But the traveller, departing, found himself unable to avoid thinking about Stanguray.

Therefore he turned aside from the road which led to Wocra-hin, and made his way to a green thicket in the midst of a perfectly circular expanse of hard clay, which neither rain nor thawing after snow could turn to mud. Here was imprisoned Tarambole, with sway over dryness, as Karth formerly over cold in the land called Eyneran: a being to whom had not been imparted the gift of telling lies.

Within the thicket, concealed from sight of passers-by— which was as well, since lately the people of the region had taken much against magic—the traveller resigned himself to the performance of a ceremony none but he and Tarambole recalled. His actions gained him the answer to a single question, and it was not what he had looked forward to.

No, it was not, so Tarambole declared, a powerful and un-suspected elemental that drew his mind back, and back, and back again to thoughts of Stanguray.

"Would that I might consult with Wolpec," sighed the trav-eller. But he knew not where that strange coy harmless spirit bided now; he had yielded too early to the blandishments of humans, and by his own volition had wasted his power to the point where it was needless to imprison him. He chose his own captivity. Much the same might be said for Farchgrind, who once or twice had provided intelligence for the traveller, and indeed for countless others.

There remained, of course, those whom he had only banished: Tuprid and Caschalanva, Quorril and Lry. . . . Oh, indubitably they would know what was happening! It was not out of the question that they themselves had set this train of events in motion. But to summon them, the most ancient and powerful of his enemies, when he was in this plight, weakened by puzzlement . . .

Had they set out to undermine him, knowing they could not match him in fair fight?

Yet Tarambole who could not lie had said: his disquiet was not due to the opposition of an elemental.

The gravely disturbing suspicion burgeoned in the traveller's mind that for the first (and the next word might be taken liter-ally in both its senses) *time* a new enemy had arrayed against him.

New.

Not an opponent such as he had vanquished over and over, but something original, foreign to his vast experience. And if it were not the Four Great Ones who had contrived so potent a device . . .

Then only one explanation seemed conceivable, and if it were correct, then he was doomed.

But his nature remained single, and it was not in him to rail against necessity. Necessarily he must continue on his way. He retrieved his staff and with its tip scattered the somewhat repulsive residue of what he had been obliged to use in con-juring Tarambole, and headed once more towards Wocrahin.

* * *

Where, in a tumbledown alley, a smith whose forge blazed and roared and stank yelled curses at his neighbors as he hammered bar iron into complex shapes. His only audience was his son, a boy aged ten, stepping on and off the treadle of the huge leather bellows that blew his fire.

"Hah! They want me out of here because they don't like the noise, they don't like the smell, they don't like me— That's what it boils down to, they don't like me because my occupation's not genteel! But my father lived here, and my grandad too, and I have clear title to the house. And they buy my wares, don't they? Boy, answer when you're spoken to!"

But the boy had been at his work three years, and the racket had made him deaf and inhalation of foul smokes had harmed his brain, so he could only nod or shake his head by way of reply. This his father had failed to register, being taken up with grievances as much imaginary as real.

Fortuitously this time the boy did the proper thing: he nodded. Thus assuaged, the smith resumed his complaining.

"If they don't care to live hard by a forge, let 'em buy new homes outside the town—or, better yet, let 'em club together and buy me a house in the country, with a stream beside to lift and drop a trip-hammer! Let 'em turn their hands to helping me, as I do them! After all, a forge must be sited somewhere, right? They should see what it's like to live without iron, shouldn't they, boy?"

This time, by alternation, the youngster shook his head. Infuriated, the smith flung down his tools and bunched his fists.

"I'll teach you and the rest of 'em to make mock of me!" he roared. "Oh that they and you and everyone could see what life is like when you lack strong black iron!"

"As you wish," the traveller said from a smoky corner, "so be it."

Whereat all iron in the smithy turned to crumbling rust: the anvil, the hammerheads, the tongs, the chisels and the nails, the cramps that held the massy wooden lever of the bellows, even the blank horseshoes waiting in a pile. The smith let out a great cry, and the neighbors came running. Such was their laughter that shortly the phrase "like a smith without iron" entered the common parlance of Wocrahin. Indeed, he taught them to make mock. . . .

But the traveller was ill pleased. This was not like his customary regulation of affairs. It was clumsy. It was more like the rough-and-ready improvisations of the times before Time.

And he could not cure himself of thinking about Stanguray.

In Teq they still gambled to the point of insanity, and might supplanted right among its decadent people.

"No, you may not waste time making mud pies!" a woman scolded her toddler son, dragging him back from a puddle where a score of children were amusing themselves. "You're to be the greatest winner since Fellian, and support me in my old age. Ah, would I knew how to make you understand my plans for your future!"

"As you wish," sighed the traveller, who had taken station in the square into which the lightning-struck image of Lady Luck had tumbled—where now greedy unscrupulous landlords sold lodging by the night in squalid hovels to those who imagined sleeping here would bring good fortune.

The boy's eyes grew round and a look of horror spread across his face. He sank his teeth in his mother's arm, deep enough to draw blood, and took screaming to his heels, to scrape a living as best he could among the other outcasts of this now dismal city. Given the schemes his mother had in mind, he was the better for his freedom.

Yet that also struck the traveller as unbefitting, and still he could not rid his mind of thoughts of Stanguray.

In Segrimond the folk no longer tended a grove of ash trees. They had been felled to make a fence and grandstand around an arena of pounded rocks, where for the entertainment of the wealthy savage beasts were matched with one another and against condemned criminals, armed or unarmed according to the gravity of their offense and the certainty of the jury which had heard the evidence. Today the arena had witnessed the demise of a girl who had charged her respectable uncle with rape.

"Now this," said the traveller under his breath, "is not as it should be. It smacks more of chaos, this indecision, than of the proper unfolding of time. When all things have but a single nature, there will be no room for the doubt which calls for resolution in this random manner."

He waited. In a little the dead girl's uncle, resplendent in satin trimmed with fur, came weeping from the vantage point reserved for privileged onlookers. "Ah, if you but knew," he cried to fawning hangers-on, "how much it cost me to accuse my darling niece!"

"So be it," said the traveller, and by nightfall the people did indeed know what it had cost him, in bribes to perjured witnesses. On the morrow he was kicked to death by a wild onager.

Yet and still the traveller felt himself infect with the foulness of the world, and could not release his mind from thinking about Stanguray.

Like Teq, Gryte was no longer rich. On the marches of its land a new town had grown up called Amberlode, a name commemorative of the reason for its founding. To it had removed the more enterprising of the old rich families of Gryte; against it the less enterprising were mouthing curses.

But the powers on which they called were petty compared for instance to those which had carried Ys—albeit briefly—back to eternity across the frontier of time, so their impact on Amberlode was minimal. Realizing this, a man who hated his younger brother for seizing an opportunity he had rejected cried aloud, and said, "Would it were I rather than he who enjoyed that fine new house in the new city!"

"As you wish," murmured the traveller, who had accepted the hospitality this man accorded grudgingly to travellers in order to acquire virtue against some misty hereafter.

At once the situation was reversed . . . but because the younger brother under whatsoever circumstances was the more intelligent and talented of the two, when it came his turn to utter curses his spells were genuinely efficacious, and the fine new house collapsed, to the vast discomfiture of its then occupants.

* * *

And that was wrong!

The realization brought the traveller up short. There should have lain neither blame nor suffering on whichever brother chose aright and made the move to Amberlode, yet here it came, and with brutal force. From as far back as he could recall it had been the traveller's intention that the literal interpretation he placed on the wishes he granted should be a means of ensuring justice. If penalties ensued, they should be confined to those who had deserved them. What was awry?

The constellations had not yet wheeled to the configuration marking the conclusion of his journey. By rights he should have continued in prescribed sequence from one stage of it to the next, to the next, to the next . . .

But he found he could not. If it were true that some hitherto unencountered foe, neither human nor elemental, now ranged against him, that implied a fundamental shift in the nature of all the realities. Beyond which, it hinted at something so appalling that he might as well abandon his task at once. He had believed his assignment binding, forever and forever, within and outside time. But it must necessarily lie within the power of the One for Whom all things were neither possible nor impossible, to—

He cancelled that thought on the instant. Completion of it would of itself wipe him from the record of what was, what might be, and what was as though it had never been. His status was, as he well knew, at best precarious.

Which made him think of the rope-walking children at Stanguray.

Which made him take the most direct route thither, and immediately.

Which taught him the most painful lesson of his existence.

IV

SO FAR AS human habitation went, initially around Lake Taxhling there had been only reed huts wherein dwelt fisherfolk who well understood how to charm their way across its waters, and distinguish by simple conjuration those natural fishes that were safe to eat from those which had been transformed by the river Metamorphia and on which a geas lay.

Certain onerous duties bought them this privilege, but by and large they regarded their prime deity Frah Frah as being, if exigent, not unkind.

Time, though, wore on, and by degrees they quit performance of the rituals that had purchased their livelihood; in particular, they no longer ceremonially burned down and rebuilt their homes twice annually.

By then it was no longer so essential to judge the nature of one's catch; the river's power was waning. Now and then someone died through carelessness, generally a child or an oldster, but the survivors shrugged it off.

Then, as the river's magic diminished further, certain nomads followed it downstream: traders, and pilgrims, and people who had so ill-used their former farms that the topsoil blew away; and criminal fugitives as well. Finding that on the seaward side of Lake Taxhling there was a sheer enormous drop, they decided to remain, and the original inhabitants—being peaceable—suffered them to settle.

Henceforward the reed huts were not burned, because there were none. The newcomers preferred substantial homes of timber, clay and stone. Henceforward the shrines dedicated to Frah Frah were increasingly neglected. Henceforward meat figured largely in the local diet, as fish had formerly; herds of swine were established in the nearby woodlands, and grew fat in autumn on acorns and beechmast, while sheep and goats were let loose on the more distant slopes, though the grazing was too poor for cattle. The way of life around Lake Taxhling was transformed.

There followed a succession of three relatively gentle invasions, by ambitious conquerors, each of which endowed the area with a new religion not excessively dissimilar from the old one. It was a reason for children to form gangs and stage mock battles on summer evenings, rather than a cause for adult strife, that some families adhered to Yelb the Comforter and others to Ts-graeb the Everlasting or Honest Blunk. They coexisted with fair mutual tolerance.

Altogether, even for someone like Orrish whose stock was unalloyed pre-conquest, and whose parents maintained a dignified pride in their seniority of residence, life on the banks of Taxhling was not unpleasant.

Or rather, it had not been so until lately. Oh, in his teens— he had just turned twenty—he had been mocked because he confessed to believing in the fables told to children about a town below the waterfall with which there had once been trade. But he was strong and supple and could prove his point by scaling the ruined stairs both ways, using creepers to bridge the sections where the carven steps had crumbled, thereby demonstrating that the idea was not wholly absurd.

That, therefore, was endurable. So too was the military service imposed by the region's current overlord, Count Lashgar, on all males between eighteen and twenty-one. It was a nuisance, but it was imperative if one wished to marry, and it enabled youngsters to break free of their parents, which could not be bad. Because the count had no territorial ambitions, and spent his time poring over ancient tomes, the most dangerous duties he assigned his troops consisted in keeping track of goats on hilly pastures, and the most unpleasant in the monthly shambles. There were too many people now for fish to feed them all, so the latest invader, Count Lashgar's grandfather, had exhibited a neat sense of household economy by decreeing that the slaughter of animals should henceforth be an army monopoly, thereby tidily combining weapons training (they were killed with sword and spear) with tax collection (there was a fixed charge based on weight and species, which might be commuted by ceding one sheep of six, one goat of seven, and one hog of eight), with religious duty (the hearts were saved to be offered on the altar of his preferred deity, Ts-graeb the Everlasting), and with—as he naïvely imagined—an increase in the fish supply. It struck him as reasonable to assume that by establishing a shambles in the shallows of the lake one could contrive to give aquatic creatures extra nourishment, thanks to its waste.

The lake being sluggish, however, the stench grew appalling; moreover, it was the only source of drinking and cooking water. His son peremptorily removed the shambles to the very edge of the plateau, and for a long while his grandson Lashgar saw no grounds for disturbing this arrangement. Now and then in the old days one had seen, on the delta below, people shaking fists and shouting insults, but they were too far away to be heard, and none of the lowlanders had the temerity to climb the ancient stairs and argue. Not since before Orrish was born had it been deemed advisable to maintain double guards along the rim of the cliffs.

Maybe if that old custom had been kept up . . .

Perhaps, yes, things would not have taken such a horrifying turn around Taxhling. He would naturally not have been able to do what he was doing—deserting his post by night—without silencing his co-sentry or persuading him to come along; on the other hand, the necessity would not have arisen. . . .

Too late for speculation. Here he was, scrambling down the cliff, repeating under cover of darkness his climb of five years ago, wincing at every pebble he dislodged, for the steps rocked and tilted and some had vanished for five or ten feet together, and he had had no chance to assess which of the nearby creepers were most securely rooted. His muscles ached abominably, and though the night was frosty rivulets of perspiration made him itch all over. However, there was no turning back. He must gain the safety of the level ground below. He must let the people of Stanguray know what enormities one of their number was perpetrating, rouse them to anger and to action!

Under his cold-numbed feet a ledge of friable rock abruptly crumbled. Against his will he cried out as he tumbled into blackness. His memory of the climb he had made when he was fifteen was not so exact that he knew how high he was, though he guessed he fell no more than twenty feet.

But he landed on a heap of boulders, frost-fractured from the cliff, and felt sinews tearing like wet rags.

How now was he to bear a warning to Stanguray?

And if not he, then who?

There was nothing else for it. Despite his agony, he must crawl onward. Even though the witch Crancina had been spawned among them, the folk of Stanguray did not deserve the fate she planned. They had at least, presumably, had the sense to drive her out, instead of—like that damned fool Count Lashgar!—welcoming her and giving in to every one of her foul demands.

V

AUTUMN HAD BEGUN TO BITE when the traveller returned to Stanguray. It was a clear though moonless night. Mist writhed over the marshes. The mud was stiff with cold, and here and there a shallow puddle was sufficiently free from salt to form a skim of ice.

Despite the chill, blood-reek was dense in the air.

But in the village of marble pillars and gaudy tilework there was no sign of life, save for suspicious birds and rats.

Unable at first to credit that the place was totally deserted, the traveller slacked the grip of the forces that held together his staff of curdled light. A radiance bright as the full moon's revealed it was only too true. Everywhere doors and shutters stood ajar. No chimney, not even on the wealthiest homes, uttered smoke. From the quay all the boats were gone, and some few poor household items lay on its flags, abandoned.

Yet this did not smack of, say, a pirate raid. There was no hint of violence—no fires had been started, no dead bodies lay untidy on the ground. This had been a planned and voluntary departure.

Moreover, as he abruptly realized, something else was amiss. He was immune to the night's freezing air, but not to the chill of dismay which the discovery evoked in him.

Litorgos was no longer penned between salt and silt. The elemental too was absent from this place.

Until this moment the traveller had believed that in all of space and all of time none save he had been granted power to bind and loose the elemental spirits. Could it be that to another the mirror of his gift had been assigned? Surely the One Who—

But if that were so, then Tarambole had lied. And if *that* were so, then the universe would become like the pieces on a gameboard, to be tipped back in their box and redeployed with different rules. There was no sign of such a catastrophe: no comets, no eruptions, no dancing stars . . .

A new enemy.

More at a loss than ever before, he pondered and reviewed his knowledge, standing so immobile that hoarfrost formed on the hem of his cloak. With all his powers of reasoning he was still far from an answer when he heard a thin cry, weak as a child's but far too baritone.

"Help! Help! I can go no further!"

Half in, half out, of a muddy channel, some three or four hundred paces towards the escarpment, he came upon the one who had shouted: a young man in leather jerkin, breeches and boots, whimpering for the pain of torn leg-ligaments.

"Who are you?" the traveller challenged.

"Orrish of Taxhling," came the faint reply.

"And your mission here below the plateau?"

"To warn the folk of Stanguray what doom's upon them! I never dreamed such horrors could be hatched in a human brain, but— Ow, ow! Curses on my injured leg! But for it, I'd have been there long ere now!"

"To small avail," the traveller said, extending his staff so that Orrish might use it to haul himself clear of the icy water. "They're gone. All of them."

"Then my errand of mercy would have been in vain?" said Orrish blankly as he gained the bank. Of a sudden he began to laugh hysterically.

"Not so," the traveller returned, probing with his staff along the painful leg. At every contact a light shone forth, the color of which humans have no name for. "There, how does that feel? Has the pain gone?"

Orrish rose incredulously to his feet, testing the damaged limb. "Why, it's a miracle!" he whispered. "Who are you, that can work such magic?"

"I have many names, but a single nature. If that means aught to you, so be it; if not, and increasingly I find it doesn't, well and good, for either way it is the truth. . . . With a name like Orrish, I take you to be of ancient Taxhling stock."

"You know our people?"

"I dare say I've known them since before you were born," the traveller admitted. "What's amiss, that sent you on your desperate mission?"

"They've gone insane! A witch has come among us, dedicated to the service of Ts-graeb—or so she says!—claiming to know how to make our lord Count Lashgar live forever! Now me, I hold no brief against the worshippers of Ts-graeb, or anyone else, although in truth . . ." Orrish's tongue faltered.

With a hint of his customary dry humor the traveller said, "In truth you adhere to the cult of Frah Frah, and you wear his amulet in the prescribed invariable place, and because your belt has come adrift from your breeches the fact is plainly discernible. I am pleased to learn that Frah Frah is not wholly devoid of followers; his ceremonies were often very funny in a coarse sort of way, and among his favorite offerings was a hearty laugh. Am I not right?"

Frantically making good the deficiencies in his garb, Orrish said in awe, "But that was in my grandfather's day!"

"More like your three-times-great-grandfather's day," the traveller responded matter-of-factly. "Now gather your wits, if you please. I need to know precisely why you were so desperate to bear a warning to the folk of Stanguray."

Piecemeal, then, he extracted the whole story, and from what he was told was able to deduce that Tarambole, while of course he could not lie, did have access to the gift of ambiguity.

That discovery was a vast relief. But it still left an unprecedented situation to resolve.

"The witch is called Crancina," Orrish said. "She came among us recently—last spring—and brought with her a familiar in the guise of a hunchbacked boy. They said they hailed from Stanguray, and at once everybody was prepared to accept them as marvel-workers, for in living memory none save I ever attempted to scale the face of yon escarpment. . . . And," he added bitterly, "my schoolfellows whom I shamed by making both the descent and the ascent when they said it was impossible now deny I ever made the climb! How flimsy memory must grow in five short years!"

The traveller prompted Orrish with a gentle cough.

"Ah . . . yes! We'd always regarded Count Lashgar as a harmless, bookish fellow. In shops and taverns one might hear the people say with nods and winks, 'You could do worse than endure such an overlord!' Confessedly, I've often said the same.

"Little did we guess that he was plotting with his books and incantations to find a means of adding our lives to his own, so as to outlive us all! But *she* did, the witch Crancina, and she came to Lashgar and said she knew a use for the blood spilled from the beasts we kill each month at the dark of the moon. She told him to move the shambles back to their old site, because only if there were *enough* blood in the water of the lake— Sir, are you well?"

For the traveller had fallen silent and stock-still, gazing into the past.

In a little he roused himself enough to answer, "No! No, my friend, I am not well, nor is anything well! But at least I now comprehend what is the nature of my unprecedented enemy."

"Explain, then!" pleaded Orrish.

"First tell me this. Crancina made out that once enough blood was in the water, it would become an elixir of long life: is that the case?"

"Why, yes! Moreover, she asserted it would be ample for us all to drink, giving us each an extra span of years!"

"In that she lied," the traveller declared, flat-voiced.

"I have suspected so." Orrish bit his lip. "I won't presume to ask how you know. That you're a strange and powerful personage, my well-healed leg declares. . . . Would, though, I might give the witch the lie direct, on your authority! For what they propose up yonder, in my name, is so ghastly, so horrid, so disgusting . . . !"

"You speak of what drove you to desert your post?"

The young man gave a miserable nod. "Indeed, indeed. For, lacking as much blood as she claimed was requisite, folk began to say, 'Are there not those who bleed at Stanguray? And must not human blood be more effective? Let us set forth and capture them, and drag them hither, and cut their throats to make the magic work!'"

"And what said Count Lashgar to this mad idea?"

"Unless Crancina's rites succeed today, he'll give his soldiers orders for the mission."

"Hmm! Who's making rope?"

The question took Orrish aback for a second; then he caught on and burst out laughing, not as before—halfway to hysteria—but with honest mirth, making as it were an offering to Frah Frah.

"Why, I'm as dumb and blind as they! Surely it will call for miles of rope to drag hundreds of unwilling captives over level ground, let alone haul them up the cliff!"

"Such work is not in hand?"

"Why, no! Drunk on promises, the people care only for

butchery. Now it's reached such a stage, those who set snares by night are ordered to bring their catch, still living, to be included in the daily sacrifice. And woe betide those whose rabbits, hares and badgers are already dead!"

"I understand," the traveller said somberly, and thought on an ancient ceremony, practiced when the forces of chaos were more biddable than now. Then, one had taken a shallow bowl, ideally of silver, incised with the character harst, midmost of those in the Yuvallian script, and filled it with water, and laid therein the germ of a homunculus, and pricked one's finger and let fall three drops, whereupon the homunculus set forth to do one's bidding. Kingdoms had been overthrown that way.

What would transpire when the ceremony was expanded to a whole wide lake?

And, particularly and essentially: this lake of all . . . !

"Sir," Orrish ventured anxiously, "you spoke just now about an enemy. Is it the witch? Is your enemy the same as ours? May we count you as an ally?"

The traveller parried the question. "What drove you to climb down the cliff by night? Fear that you, not worshipping Ts-graeb, would be excluded from the universal benefit of immortality?"

"No—no, I swear on my father's honor!" Orrish was sweating; the faint light of the false dawn glistened on his forehead. "But—well, in the cult of the god I have been raised to worship, it is said that pleasure bought at the cost of another's suffering is no pleasure at all. So it seems to me with this pretended immortality—even given that this is the goal of those cruel ceremonies, which you contest. How can a life worth living be purchased at the expense of so much brutality?"

"Then let us return together to Taxhling," the traveller said with decision. "Your wish is granted. You shall give the witch the lie direct."

"But *is* she your enemy?" Orrish persisted.

"If you asked her—assuming she has not forgotten my existence—she might very well say that, on the contrary, she has good reason to be grateful to me."

"Then—who?"

Because the question was posed with an honest need to know, the traveller was constrained to answer, after long reluctance.

"That which is against me is within me."

"You speak in riddles!"

"So be it! I had rather not let it be noised abroad that I overlooked so crude a truth: this is my fault. For the first time, I set forth to fight *myself*."

VI

BLESSEDLY WARM in the room assigned to her at Count Lashgar's residence—here on the plateau they could afford to be prodigal with fuel, and a log fire had burned all night two steps from her bed—Crancina woke with a sense of excitement such as she had only felt once before: back in the spring, when it dawned on her what use could be made of all that blood fouling Stanguray's river.

A serving-maid drowsed on a stool in the chimney corner. Shouting to rouse her, Crancina threw aside her coverlet.

Today, yes, today, her efforts were sure to be rewarded! Then let that slimy count go whistle for his dreamed-of immortality! He was on all fours with the greedy men who had sought her hand in marriage when what they wanted was not her, but the profits of her cookshop and her sweet-water spell.

Today would teach him, and tomorrow would teach the world, a lesson never to be forgotten.

Humming a merry tune, she wrapped herself snug in a sheepskin cape against the early-morning chill outside.

* * *

"My lord! My lord, wake up!" whispered the valet whose
duty it was to rouse Lord Lashgar. "Mistress Crancina is certain
of success today, and sent her girl to tell me so!"

Muzzily peering from among high-piled pillows, the count
demanded, "What's worked the trick, then? The extra animals
I ordered to be brought from snares and gins?"

"My lord, I'm not party to your high councils," was the
reproachful answer. "But surely in one of your books the
secret's explained?"

"If that were so," Lashgar sighed, forcing himself to sit up,
"I'd not have waited this long for the fulfillment of my lifelong
dreams."

Through the mists that haunted the edges of the lake a band
of shivering soldiers marched with drums and gongs, and on
hearing them people turned out enthusiastically, forgoing
breakfast save for a hasty crust and a mouthful of strong liquor.
In the old days the morning of a shambles was one to be
avoided; now, amazingly, it had been transformed into the
signal event of the month . . . today more than ever, for the
rumors had already taken rise.

"Today's the day! Crancina told the count—it's bound to
work today! Just think! Maybe some of us, maybe all of us,
will be deathless by tonight!"

Only a few cynical souls were heard to wonder aloud what
would happen if it proved there was power enough in the
bloody water to make one person live forever, and no more.
Who would benefit, if not the witch?

But those were generally of the aboriginal lakeside stock,
whose ancestors had had their fill of magic long ago. Those
who worshipped Ts-graeb the Everlasting, as Lashgar did—
and his adorers had grown vastly more numerous since the
witch arrived—clamored loudly for the favor of their deity, and
arrived at the lakeshore singing and clapping their hands.

They raised a tremendous cheer when Lashgar and Crancina
appeared, preceded by the image of Ts-graeb in the guise of
an old bearded wiseacre, which was borne on the shoulders
of six men-at-arms. The procession was flanked by the priests
and priestess of Yelb the Comforter, portrayed as having nipples

all over her naked bulk from toes to hairline, and also the handful who still adhered to Honest Blunk, whose image and sym-
bol was a plain white sphere. No professors of Frah Frah were
bold enough to parade their creed, and indeed only a handful
remained.

But, bringing up the very tail, here came a hunchbacked boy
in jester's garb, with bells on hat and heels, capering and
grimacing as he feigned to strike the onlookers with his wand
of office: a pig's bladder on a rod tied with gaudy ribbons. Even
the followers of Honest Blunk were glad to crack a smile at
the sight of his antics, for a bitter wind soughed over the
plateau.

"And where," the traveller murmured as he contrived to fall
in beside Jospil, "did you obtain that particolored finery?"

"It's not stolen, if that's what you're thinking," came the
sharp reply. "It belonged to the jester whom Count Lashgar's
father kept, and I received it from the mistress of the palace
wardrobe. Who are you that you put such a question to me — ?
Why, I recall *you*, and only too well." At once the boy ceased
his awkward parody of a dance. "It was the very day after you
spoke with her that my sister took this crazy notion into her
head, and forced me hither up the cliffs! More than once I
thought I would die, but my deformity has luckily left my torso
light enough for my arms to bear its weight, so where she
almost fell I could cling on for us both. . . . But often I feel I'd
rather have let her fall than be condemned to my present lot!"

"Is it no better than at Stanguray?"

"Perhaps by a whisker, now I've acquired these clothes and
wand." Jospil struck the traveller with the latter, scowling. "But
they made me out to be Crancina's familiar at first, and wanted
to feed me on hot coals and aqua regia. Besides, they have no
sense of humor, these people. If they did, would they not long
ago have laughed Crancina out of countenance?"

"You are absolutely correct," the traveller agreed solemnly.
"And therein lies the key to fulfillment of a wish you made in
my hearing. Do you recall it?"

The hunchback gave a crooked shrug. "It would have been

the same as what I say to everybody, except of course my sister: that one day I should find a means of freeing myself from her."

"And making your way in the world against all odds."

"I've said that over and over, and doubtless to you."

"Meaning it?"

Jospil's eyes flashed fire. "Every word!"

"Today, then, is your chance to make the most of your jester's role and achieve your ambition simultaneously."

Jospil blinked. "You speak so strangely," he muttered. "Yet you came to the cookshop like anybody, and you were politer to my sister than she deserved, and—yes, it was precisely from the morning of your visit that she took these crazy notions into her head, and . . . I don't know what to make of you, I swear I don't."

"Count yourself fortunate," the traveller said dryly, "that you are not called on so to do. But remember that there is magic abroad today, if not the kind Count Lashgar is expecting, and that you are a crux and focus of it. Sir Jester, I bid you good morning!"

And with a deep-dipping bow, and an inclination of his staff, and a great flapping swirl of his black cape, the traveller was gone about his business.

VII

How IT WAS that he was back at his guardpost in time to reclaim his spear and shield and greet his dawn relief before his absence was noted, Orrish could afterwards never quite recall— nor what had become of his mysterious companion once they were on the plateau.

But he did remember one thing with perfect clarity. He had been promised the chance to give the witch the lie direct. Anxious, he awaited his opportunity. There seemed small chance of it happening today, though, for immediately on returning to barracks he had been cornered by a sergeant with a squad lacking one man, and sent to collect the night's trapped animals and bring them to the lakeside to have their life's blood let. In all their various tones they squeaked and growled and whimpered, and their cries made a hideous cacophony along with the bleating and grunting of the few remaining domestic animals, pent in folds of hurdles within scent of the bloody water. At this rate of slaughter, though there would be more pickled meat than they had barrels to hold, and more smoked meat than hooks to hang it on, which would see the community through the winter, there would be no breeding stock to start anew next summer. Orrish shook his head dolefully, detesting the assignment he had been given almost as much as he loathed the notion of kidnapping and killing the folk of Stanguray.

That at least, if the traveller in black was to be trusted, was no longer a possibility.

But where was the traveller? Orrish scanned the vicinity with worried eyes. Like all those who came of the ancient Taxhling stock, he had been raised to distrust magic and its practitioners, and the way his leg had been healed left no room for doubt that the man in the black cloak trafficked in such arts. Was he— like the witch Crancina—deceitful and self-serving . . . ?

Orrish started a little. How did he know the witch was defrauding the people? Why, because the traveller had told him so. Maybe he should believe what the rest of his people believed, rather than taking the word of a stranger?

Biting his lip in terrible confusion, he was distracted by a shout from the sergeant, calling the soldiers to attention at the appearance of Count Lashgar. Numbly obeying, Orrish wished desperately that the traveller would come back; everything had seemed so simple in his company.

Along with the other young conscripts, he awaited the order to butcher the pitiable beasts.

* * *

There were obligatory cheers and shouts; they did not last long, however, because everybody was too eager to hear what Crancina proposed to do today. Graciously bowing from side to side as he took station on a grassy promontory at the waterside, Lashgar addressed his subjects in a surprisingly powerful voice for so slim and short a man.

"We are promised marvels!" he declared. "You want to see them as much as I do! Therefore I'll waste no time on speechifying, but let Mistress Crancina have her way!"

Everybody brightened at the brevity of his introduction. And then quietened, and shivered. Even while Lashgar was speaking, Crancina had thrown aside her sheepskin cape and begun to make passes in the air, muttering to herself the while. The words could not be made out even at close quarters, yet there was such a resonance to them that if one caught their slightest echo it could send a tremor down the spine.

Now and then she felt in a pouch hung at her girdle and tossed a pinch of powder into the water, rather as though she were seasoning a soup.

Along with all the rest, the traveller was mightily impressed. This was the first occasion, in more of his visits to this world than he cared to try and count, when he had witnessed a genuinely new magic rite. Even though the change might be classed as more quantitative than qualitative, the purpose Crancina was putting her work to was radically different from anything he could recall.

Now and then in the past he had wondered whether cookery, where the practitioner might begin with something not only unpalatable but actually poisonous, and conclude with something not only digestible but delicious, might not be the ultimate destiny of temperaments which in earlier ages would have been tempted to meddle in magic. He made a firm resolve to keep a careful eye on cooks in future.

For this recipe, at least, was working fine.

Much like milk being curdled by rennet, the water of Lake Taxhling was solidifying. Instead of the random patterns due to wind and wave, shapes were discernible on the surface, and though they jostled and shifted, they did not break up any longer. The onlookers oohed and aahed, while Count Lashgar, barely disguising his incredulity, tried not to jump up and down for joy.

The shapes were not altogether comfortable to look on; however, they were visible, and little by little they were beginning to stand up above the surface, first as shallowly as ripples, then with more and more protuberance. Also they enlarged. Somewhat separated from each other, they numbered a thousand or two, and their forms were strange beyond description. If this one was reminiscent of a claw-tipped fern-frond, its neighbor hinted at a dishmop with a crown of flexing tentacles; if another called to mind a hog's skull with extra holes in it, the next resembled a giant mouse with twenty legs.

The only thing they had in common, bar their present almost stillness, was their coloration. They were the grey of common pumice stone, and bobbed on the now-oily surface of the lake, which had congealed to form them, with a motion as sluggish as though time for them had slowed to a twentieth of its regular rate.

"Magic!" murmured the crowd, delighted. "Magic indeed!"

"But she is a liar—she *is*!" came a sudden cry from the direction of the stock-pens, where soldiers were dutifully readying the last of the animals to be killed. "*The witch Crancina is a liar!*"

Everyone reacted, especially Lashgar and Crancina herself. The count shouted an order to a sergeant to quiet the man who had called out, while she shot one nervous glance in that direction and kept on with her recital of cantrips, faster and faster. The images forming on the lake wavered, but grew firm again.

"Silence that man!" the sergeant bellowed, and two of his companions tried to pinion Orrish by the arms. He shoved his shield in the face of one, breaking his nose, and winded the other with the butt end of his spear, on his way to the nearest point of vantage, the shambles stone—formerly at the far end of the lake near the waterfall, but lately brought back to this spot in the interests of conserving the spilled blood. It was a block of basalt with runnels cut in the upper face for the blood to drain down. Taking stance on it, Orrish waved his spear aloft.

"How did she expect to get away with it?" he roared. "We know what these apparitions are!"

They wavered again, but remained solid, and now were stock-still, as rigid as glass, and as brittle.

Suddenly, tentatively, a few of the watchers—mostly elderly—nodded. Realizing they were not alone, they drew themselves proudly upright and did it again more vigorously.

"And *we* know they have nothing to do with immortality!" Orrish yelled at the top of his lungs. "*Get* away!"—kicking out at the sergeant who was trying to snare him by the ankles. "I don't mean *you*, or your blockhead of a master, the count! I mean *us*, whose families have lived here long enough not to be cheated by the witch! Look at her! Look! Can't you read fear and terror in her face?"

Crancina was shouting wildly, but the wind had risen in the past minute or two, and her words were carried away. Beside her, paling, Count Lashgar was signalling his bodyguard to close in; the priests of Blunk and Yelb and Ts-graeb were like-wise huddling together for comfort.

Meantime the images formed from the lake remained un-moving.

"And for the benefit of those of you who weren't lucky enough to be brought up like me in a household where they still know about this kind of thing," Orrish blasted, "I'll explain! In the distant and barbaric past our superstitious ancestors imagined that the weird objects which drifted down the river—those which had been of a sinking nature floated, obviously!—all these objects were divine and deserving of worship. So they set up shrines, and made offerings, and called on them when reciting hearth-spells, and the rest of it. There were even fights over the respective merits of this, that or the other idol.

"But at last a teacher arose among us, endowed with better sense, who asked why we had so many petty deities when we could devise one with all their best attributes and none of their worst. The people marvelled and wondered and agreed, and that was how we came to worship Frah Frah! And when everybody had consented to the change, the old gods were carried to the lake and thrown back in, to lie on the bottom until the end of the world. And so they would have done, but for Crancina! Now ask her what they have to do with immortality for us, or even her and Lashgar!"

"This is all falsehood!" Crancina gasped. "I know nothing of your city's former gods!"

"But do you know anything of immortality?" demanded Lashgar. Seizing a sword from the nearest of his guardsmen, he levelled its point at her breast.

"Of course she doesn't!" came a crowing voice. "She's fit to run a cookshop, and no more, and that's what she used to do in Stanguray. Hee-hee-hee-hee-hee-*haw*!"

And Jospil in his jester's guise frog-hopped towards his halfsister with a donkey-loud bray of laughter.

Startled, about to launch another broadside of invective, Orrish high on the slaughter stone checked, and glanced at Jospil, and against all best intentions had to grin. The grin turned to a chuckle; the chuckle became a roar of merriment, and he had to lean on his spear for support as he rocked back and forth with tears streaming from his eyes. So contagious was his hilarity that, without knowing what was funny, small children echoed it; tending them, their parents could not help but giggle, at the least, and that also spread. While Lashgar and Crancina and the more pompous of the attendant priests— of whichever denomination—looked scandalized and shouted orders which went disregarded by their subordinates, the entire crowd was caught up in a monstrous eruption of mirth. The eldest of the onlookers, hobbling and toothless, who were as much at a loss about the proceedings as the babes in arms, cackled along with the rest, until the welkin threatened to ring with the sound.

And it did.

Echoed, re-echoed, amplified, the laughter started to resonate. A sort of buzzing filled the air, making it feel denser than normal. The vibrations fed on one another; they became painful to the ears; they set the teeth on edge; they shrilled and rasped and ground. Here and there amid the throng people looked frightened and cast about for a way to escape. But there was none. The whole huge bowl-like plateau round Lake

Taxhling had become a valley of echoes, where sound instead of dying away increased in volume, and intensity, and harshness.

Meantime the accidental creations of the river once known as Metamorphia, conjured back to the surface after so many centuries, remained utterly still . . . until they began to tremble under the impact of the noise.

Suddenly a thing like a walrus with a flower for a head cracked sharply across. A sprinkling of fine powder wafted into the air, dancing in time with the vibrations.

Then a curiously convoluted object, half slender and half bulky, as though a giant dragonfly had miscegenated with a carthorse, shattered into tiny fragments. At once there was a rush into the vacancy from either side. Something not unlike a monstrous fist, with lamellar excrescences, collided with a great hollow structure and reduced it to tinkling shards.

The laughter took on a rhythmical pattern. Now it could be discerned that whenever it reached a certain pitch of intensity another of the objects Crancina had conjured forth broke apart; each such breaking entailed another, and then others. The watchers, who for a moment had been frightened, found this also very amusing, and their mirth redoubled until all were gasping for breath.

Into dust vanished the last relics of articles cast long ago from the citadel of Acromel; into sparkling crystals and jagged fragments dissolved what had once been sacrifices, and weapons, and the bodies of sad drunken fools, and those of condemned criminals, and the carcasses of careless animals, and the husks of insects, and luck offerings, and deodands, and stolen treasure abandoned by its thieves, and fish which had swum from higher reaches of the river, and all sorts of casual rubbish, and leaves and twigs and branches tossed into the water by children at their play, and accidental conformations created by the perversity of the river itself out of lumps of mud that tumbled from its banks.

Instead of a horde of weird fantastical solid objects there was for a moment a silvery shimmering expanse. Precisely then the laughter reached its peak, and the final gust was like a blow from a gigantic hammer, descending so fast that the very air grew solid at the impact.

So powerful was the impact, it made the plateau split.

Those who were closest to the cliff-edge fled from it, shouting, all thought of merriment forgotten. The earth trembled underfoot, and a jagged cleft appeared across the bed of the lake, beginning where the waterfall tumbled down the escarpment.

In one—two—three violent shifts of colossal mass, Lake Taxhling disappeared: first in a torrent, carving a gash down the face of the steep rocks a dozen times as wide as formerly; then in a steady flood as more and more of the cliff-rim fell away and the water could spill over as from a tilted basin; lastly as a dribbling ooze, which bared the mud of its bottom. . . .

And in the middle of the new flat bare expanse, a statue: a little awry from the vertical, and draped moreover with garlands of grey-green weed, but the solitary item not affected by the pounding laughter that had smashed all of Crancina's evocations into rubble, and intact enough after its long submersion to be instantly identifiable.

The first to recognize it was Orrish, regaining his feet after being knocked down by the earth-tremors. For a long moment he gazed at it in disbelief. Then, in sudden frantic haste, he clawed open the belt holding up his leather breeches, and produced the amulet he secretly wore.

Holding it aloft, he shouted, "Frah Frah! Have we not at last given you the offering you most desire? Laughter has been scant since you departed! And there's a bigger joke than all the rest!"

Raising his spear, he pointed at Lashgar and Crancina and those who had taken station nearest them. The pattern of the rifts breaching the lake floor was such that the little promontory they stood upon was isolated between two crevasses. As though the spear had been a magic wand, the promontory's surface tipped, and with a sighing noise subsided. The count, and the witch, and the priests, and the idols, and all their hangers-on, were abruptly floundering waist-deep in the foulest possible kind of muck. With every desperate attempt to scramble free they sprayed more of it over themselves and one another, until they were all unrecognizable.

* * *

"A satisfactory outcome after all," the traveller said, putting by the staff that had dislodged the promontory. "But it was a narrow squeak. Still, this time the amusement I hear is unforced."

There had been one person agile enough to escape the general muddying of the count's party, and now in his gaudy garb of red and yellow he was leaping up and down on safe dry land, waving his bladder-tipped stick as to conduct the chorus of laughter emanating from the crowd.

One final touch . . .

The traveller waited for precisely the correct instant; then, with a tap of his staff on the ground, he ensured that just as Jospil pointed towards it, the statue of Frah Frah tilted forward, overbalanced, fell smack on its face, and disappeared into the yielding mud, over which already the clear stream of the river was coursing in search of its future channel.

At that, which might be seen as ominous, the laughter faded, but the people dispersed good-humoredly enough despite the problem—to be solved on the morrow—of what those formerly dependent on the lake would do to earn their living now. A few daring boys hurled lumps of mud at Lashgar and Crancina and the priests, but the pastime staled rapidly and they too made off.

Apart from those stuck in the mud, after a few minutes the only ones left were Jospil and Orrish. Unaccountably despondent, gripped by a sense of anticlimax, they sat side by side on a rock, shivering in the bitter wind, watching those who were entrapped and wondering why their struggles did not seem so funny anymore.

Shortly they grew aware of a third.

VIII

"IT IS NOT GIVEN to many to enjoy their heart's desire," murmured the traveller. "Did you enjoy it?"

"I . . ." Not knowing quite whether he was speaking, nor whether he was speaking to somebody, Orrish licked his lips. "I guess I'm glad to have made the proper offering to Frah Frah. But as for what tomorrow will bring . . ." He shrugged. "All I know is, things can never be the same."

"Interesting," said the traveller. "One might say the same about chaos—not that anyone existing in it would think it worth making so trite an observation—yet here we are at a point where its forces wane so much mere laughter serves to defeat them. . . . If it's any comfort, in times to come you will be remembered, and even honored, as the one who gave the witch the lie direct. As for you, Jospil, even though you are not likely to be revered, you may henceforth pride yourself on having broken free of Crancina's tyranny, to make your own way in the world against all odds."

"If that be so," answered the hunchback curtly, "I reckon little of it. How much of a witch was my sister before you came to Stanguray?"

The traveller was discreetly silent for a while, then said at last, "I should like you to know: it is an earnest of the fulfillment of my task that you relish my aid so much less than what you have accomplished on your own."

"I am not one to ponder riddles," Jospil sighed. "I care only for straight answers to straight questions. What happened

180

to Crancina, that she made me quit our home in search of employment with Count Lashgar?"

"She had made a wish, and I was bound to grant it."

"A wish?" Jospil's eyes grew round. "Of course! I'd nearly forgotten! To know what use might be made of all the blood being spilled up here!"

"Your recollection is exact."

"And she discovered, or worked out, that it could be used to revive those strange and antique idols from the lakebed. . . . How?"

"Yes, how?" chimed in Orrish. "And to what end?"

"Jospil knows the answer to half that question," said the traveller with a wry smile.

"You mean . . . ?" The hunchback bit his thumb, puzzled. "Ah! We only spoke of part of her wish. Her greater ambition was to be in charge."

"As you say."

"But if part was granted, why was the other part not? Why is she not in charge completely and of everything, which I'm sure would be ideally to her taste?"

"Because you also made a wish. And, as it so happens, when I'm obliged to grant two wishes that conflict, the outcome tends to be biased in favor of whichever party cares less for himself, or herself."

He added sternly, "But in your case, boy, it was a close call!"

Jospil gave his sly frog's grin. "Well, at least I have a trade now"—he slapped the traveller with his bauble—"and there will be great dispersion from Taxhling, in all directions. From Lashgar's wardrobe mistress I've learned that a comedian at court may be a personage of influence; certainly my involuntary benefactor was, who served Count Lashgar's father till he was beheaded."

"You're prepared to run that risk?" Orrish demanded, aghast.

"Why not?" Jospil said, spreading his hands. "It's better than some dangers that we take for granted. They say a moment of glory may redeem an age of suffering. . . . But one more thing, sir, if I may trespass on your patience. What did my sister hope to achieve, if not to make herself immortal?"

"To re-enact on a far grander scale a certain ceremony involving a homunculus."

Jospil blinked. "That means nothing to me!" he objected. "Nor would it have done to her when you called at our cookshop. But for your intrusion, we might still be there and —"

"And she would still be pronouncing her sweet-water cantrip at every dark of the moon."

"Exactly!" Jospil rose awkwardly to his feet. "Sir, I hold you entirely to blame for the plight we're all cast into!"

"Even though you so much desired to be rid of your halfsister's tyranny, and you are?"

"Yes — yes!"

"Ah, well" — with a sigh. "I deserve these reproaches, I admit. Since but for me Crancina would never have known how reviving the strange creations of Metamorphia and imbuing them with blood could make her mistress of the world."

Orrish's jaw dropped; a second later Jospil clutched the hem of the traveller's cloak.

"She could have done *that*?"

"Beyond a peradventure. What magic is left nowadays is by and large residual, but the bed of Lake Taxhling was the repository of an enchantment such as few contemporary wizards would dare risk."

"I could have been half-brother to the ruler of the world?" Jospil whispered, having paid no attention to the previous remark.

"Indeed you could," the traveller said calmly, "if you had genuinely believed that 'a moment of glory redeems an age of suffering' — and, I assure you, had she achieved her aim she would have understood how to cause suffering."

Frowning terribly, Jospil fell silent to reflect on lost opportunities, and Orrish ventured, "Sir, will you stay with us to rectify the consequences of your actions?"

There was a long dead pause; the traveller hunched gradually further and further into the concealment of his hood and cloak.

Finally he said, as from a vast distance, "The consequences of my actions? Yes!

"But never the consequences of yours."

* * *

There followed a sudden sense of absence, and in a while Jospil and Orrish felt impelled to join the rest of the people, shoring up houses rendered unstable by the earthquake.

Which, of course, was all that had really happened . . . wasn't it?

IX

"LITORGOS!" said the traveller in the privacy of his mind, as he stood on a rocky outcrop overlooking the salt-and-silt delta being transformed by the outgush of water from on high. Already the pillars of Stanguray were tilting at mad angles; marble slabs and tiled façades were splashing into the swollen river. "Litorgos, you came closer to deceiving me than any elemental in uncounted aeons!"

Faint as wind soughing in dry branches, the answer came as though from far away.

"But you knew. You knew very well."

And that was true. Silent awhile, the traveller reflected on the charge. Yes indeed: he had known, though he had not paid attention to the knowledge, that when he granted Crancina her wish he was opening the bonds which held Litorgos. For the sole and unique fashion in which the blood spilled into Lake Taxhling might be turned to the purpose Crancina had in view was through the intervention of an elemental. So much blood had been spilled the world over, another few thousand gallons of it was trivial, except . . .

And therefore Tarambole had told the truth. It was not an

elemental working against the traveller that called him back to Stanguray.

It was an elemental working *with* him.

For otherwise the wish could never have been granted.

"There was a time," the traveller said in this confessional, "when I was ready to believe that the One Who—"

"She does not change Her mind," came the sharp retort.

"She has not done so," the traveller corrected. "But as the One to Whom all things are neither impossible nor possible . . ."

"Then if that may prove to be the case, reward me right away, before the unthinkable occurs!"

"Reward you? For deceiving me?"

"For working *with* you, instead of against you!"

The traveller considered for a little; then he said, "I find that while I am not constrained to grant the wish of an elemental, I have done it in the past and am therefore not debarred from doing so. Besides, I am inclined to favor you, inasmuch as you foresaw the need for the citizens of Stanguray to evacuate their homes and contrived that they should do so before the flood came pouring down from Taxhling. I will not ask what horrid apparitions you employed to drive them out. . . . What, then, is your wish?"

"I would cease!"

The fury behind the message made the plateau tremble one more time, and people striving with ropes and beams to buttress half-wrecked houses redoubled their efforts.

"Once I and all my kind were free and had the cosmos for a playground! Once we could roam at large, tossing stars about as humans toss a ball, breaking the chain of time or making it crack like a whip! Then we were caught and bound, and pent as you pent me, and I know, in the very core and center of my being, that this imprisonment will never cease.

"So let *me* cease!"

For a long, long moment the traveller remained impassive, marvelling at what a change Litorgos had just wrought. Now the balance had been tipped; now the triumph he looked forward to was certain—always excepting the intervention of the Four Great Ones whom he could only banish, and who might return.

But who would be insane enough to open a road for Tuprid and Caschalanva, Quorril and Lry? Even if anyone remembered their existence?

With a great sigh of contentment the traveller declared aloud, "In eternity the vagaries of chaos permit even death to be reversed. In time the certainties of reason insist that even elementals may be—*dead*."

For another hour the flood continued to wash away both salt and silt from the area where Litorgos had been and was no longer.

Later, the settlements which had surrounded Lake Taxhling were overthrown by further earth-movements, and at last there was a vast slumping of the escarpment, such that half the old delta was hidden under scree and mud.

And in due time, when new folk came and settled thereabouts, ignorant of what cities had stood on the same site before—though not wholly the same, for the coastline also changed—it was held to be a pleasant and fortunate ground, where generations prospered who knew nothing about magic, or elemental spirits, or rivers running stinking-red with blood.

FIVE

Dread Empire

Lo! thy dread empire, Chaos, is restored;
Light dies before thy uncreating word . . .

—Pope: *The Dunciad*

I

"GOOD MORROW, SIR," the folk said civilly to the person in black who stood leaning on a staff—of unusual substance—watching them fetch and carry water from Gander's Well. He answered in turn, but absently, preoccupied, and none of them marked him so closely as to recognize him again. It was plain he was concerned with private thoughts.

Indeed, so absorbed was he that the sun dipped down and the boys and goodwives whose chore it was to collect water had gone home to their well-earned supper before he stirred a pace from where he had wasted the day. Then it was to address a man, muffled up against the evening cool, who came to scrape flakes of punk from a rotten tree-stump not a great distance from the wellmouth, and dropped them as he gathered them into a pottery jar.

Seeing him then spark and apply a fizzling wick of braided withes, taken from a pouch slung to a baldric that also supported a torch of rushes soaked in tar, the traveller said, "You go a journey, sir, I take it!"

"Why, yes," the man said, glancing up. "I'm called to see my sister, who's in labor with a nephew for me, or a niece. Her man's abroad, and someone answerable must be by to take her other bairns in charge."

"And this is what you'll use for tinder?" said the traveller, pointing at the tree-stump with his staff.

"None better can be found in this vicinity," the man replied. "All who must go a trip by night make use of it. It carries fire through most amazing storms. In fact, it's said"—but here he coughed, as though by way of apology for seeming to give credence to a superstition—"there's some bright spirit in it, that fosters sparks against all odds. If you, sir, whom I judge to be a stranger, think of continuing your walk by night, I counsel you should avail yourself of some. More than once friends of mine have been grateful for the means to light a torch, thinking to finish a journey in daylight and then coming on a washed-out bridge or flooded ford!"

"How far away, then, can your sister live? An hour or more remains till sunset, let alone full dark."

"Hmph!" said the man, straightening as he capped his tinder-jar and tossed aside his wick of withes, to sputter out on ground made wet by daylong spillage. " 'Tis plain you really are a stranger, sir! Although my sister lives a scant league from this spot, needs must I go by Cleftor Heights, and there the dark falls fast, believe you me. Indeed, if you'll forgive me, I must make haste, even with this to save me in the pitch black."

"One final question," said the traveller, and gestured with his staff. "I've seen folk tramping weary miles from town to fill yoked pails of water at this well. Is it regarded as especially sweet?"

The man chuckled. "Why, sir," he returned, "as to drinking straight, not especially. But, see you, the season's on us to brew ale and beer, and—for what reason I know not—if you brew with water from Gander's Well, you remain lively and jolly all evening long, and the morning after your head's clear and your belly calm. Make sure that in the taverns of the town they offer you nothing worse; sometimes they'll try and palm off on a stranger what they will not drink themselves."

"Thanks for your counsel," said the traveller in black.

When he was alone, he sorrowfully shook his head. Once on this site Yorbeth had brooded in his guise of a tree, its longest taproot fed from a miraculous spring. Then that sad greedy fool of a packman . . .

But he was mortal, which the elemental had not been, and what was left? This stump, yielding tinder for overnight way-farers, and a well whose chief renown was for the brewing of beer!

* * *

Yet it was not entirely to be wondered at. The news was of a piece with all the rest of what he'd learned during this latest of so many journeys undertaken in accordance with the obligations that bound him. Latest? Not impossibly, he was beginning to believe, the *last*.

Long ago it had made small difference that this journey was *this* journey, not the one before or after. In chaos, randomness was so extreme that the very contrasts made for a sense of uniformity. Now there were actual changes: the vanishing of Yorbeth not the greatest.

Back beyond Leppersley, for instance, Farchgrind was a household pet! The people heard him still, but conjured him to entertain their friends, and scoffed when he made his wheedling promises. Laprivan of the Yellow Eyes had spent his substance, whatever the nature of it might have been, and wearied of his struggle against the past. Footprints left by those who plodded up his hill endured until the next high wind or fall of rain.

And Barbizond had followed Ryovora, despite Sardhin. The advance of rationality had worn him down—that bright being in his rainbow-gleaming cloud. It was still claimed that a knife from Barbizond would keep its edge forever, but the only person who had mentioned the belief to the traveller this trip had been a sober landholder in Kanish-Kulya, and he'd employed the same diffident tone as the man just departed, the one who'd been embarrassed at reference to a spirit in the punk which carried fire so well.

That farmer was an earthy man leading a placid life, a little puzzled now and then when one of his fat and cheery plough-boys brought some improbable growth to show him: a bunch of grapes that shone like polished metal, a turnip which, split apart, revealed the chambers of a human heart . . .

But his wine was plentiful and sweet, and there was never a lack of roasts to grace the spit in his kitchen, so he bothered his head not at all with traces of another age. Even the ancestry of his daughter-in-law was a source of kindly jokes around his table. Time was when any good Kanish family like his would have banished Kulyan girls to the goose-run, be they never so beautiful—or perhaps honored their good looks by gang rape, if there were drunken men about.

Now, regal in a gown of peach-colored silk, a Kulyan lady nightly shared his dinners, his heir fondly touching her goblet with his own to drink toast after toast to their three handsome boys asleep upstairs. With grandchildren growing apace, who should care when the blade of a harrow caught in the eye socket of some moldering skull? That war was over; the armistice continued.

Likewise in Teq they made a mock of Lady Luck; her offering was a gobbet of spittle, launched at the floor when one of the company voiced hopes for an overbold project.

Yet the rule bound him, and the traveller's nature was not such that he should complain. Forth he went on paths grown unfamiliar, and spoke with many people in many places, as for example in Wocrahin, where once—

Memory! Memory! He had never foreseen that that intangible, binding the fluid nature of eternity into the sequential tidiness of time, would also hamper the will like age itself. Almost, he began to envy those who could die. . . .

No matter. In Wocrahin a man sat gobbling lamprey pie in a splendid banquet hall: gross in a purple velvet suit ornate with gravy-stains. Chomping words around a mouthful of the fish and crust, he forced out, "'Fonly w'were freah y'muzzer!"

"Ah, yes!" sighed his wife, accustomed to interpreting such talk: fat as a prize breeding-sow, though childless, her vast bosom exposed almost to the bulging nipples above a gown encrusted with seed pearls, her head seeming to be depressed into her neck by the weight of the gem-crusted tiara she had put on, though they had no company at dinner apart from thirty scrag-lean servants ranged around the hall.

"If only we were free of my mother!" she assented when she had rinsed her gullet with a swig of wine. "Ah, how finely we would live were we rid of her! The old bag eats us out of house and home!"

"Sh'yeats zazouter 'ousernome!" concurred the man.

The tall windows of the banquet-hall stood open to the

warm spring night. Beyond them, watching the line of men-dicants who daily came—more from habit than from hope—to beg the cook for scraps, the traveller in black both heard the exchange and also saw the lady's mother, in draggled rags, pleading for a share of the beggars' crumbs at the barred grille of the cellar where she was shut up.

He tapped his staff on the wall.

"As you wish, so be it," he decreed, and went away. The ceiling of the banquet-hall creaked behind him, repairs to its hammer-beam roof having been too long neglected; its fall freed the greedy pair within a minute from all burdens, life itself not excluded.

Likewise in Medham, a city noted for its lovely girls, a man sat in a tavern who had enjoyed—or so he claimed—more than a score of them, and bragged of his expertise in the art of seduction.

"Ah, if I had a mug of ale for every one, I'd hardly be sober again in this life!" he hinted to his listeners, turning over his purse and finding it void of coin. "Why, did not the lady Fretcha come to me on hands and knees, saying I had ruined her? Haw-haw! Begged me, on my oath—literally *begged* me—to make an 'honest woman' of her! Haw-haw-haw! And then there was the lady Brismalet; she did the same—what impu-dence! And the lady Thespie, and then Padovine . . . Ho! As I say, did I but have a pint of ale for each—"

"As you wish, so be it," said his neighbor, a person clad in black with an unusual staff, and rose. No one noticed him depart. All were too taken aback at the spectacle of the boastful philanderer, belly distended like a hogshead, vomiting disgust-ingly because, gross as he was, he could not hold ale exceeding twenty-seven pints.

"You stupid brute!" cried a carter in a hamlet hard by the site of Acromel, and lashed his horse across the hindquarters with a steel-barbed whip. Violent though the blow was, it barely drew blood; he had employed the lash so often, the horse's back and legs were cicatrized with impermeable scars.

Nonetheless the poor beast whinnied and cringed. Therefore he beat it again, and harder still.

"Ho, that you were blessed with better sense!" he roared. "Would that you could learn how not to spill my load crossing a rut!"

Still grumbling about his horse's lack of wit, he went to the back of the cart to retrieve an ill-stowed sack of grain that had tumbled off.

"As you wish, so be it," said the traveller, and the horse reared up, tipping the whole ton-weight of bags on the stooping carter. Then it chewed intelligently through the traces and took its leave, to enjoy lush upland grasses and roam free.

"By your favor, sir," said a boy of ten or twelve years, hunting a hedgerow near the village Wyve, "are such plants poisonous or wholesome?"

Offering for inspection a glabrous brown fungus.

"Wholesome," replied the traveller. "They may be fried."

With a moue the boy tossed the toadstool aside.

"Are you not glad to have learned that it's edible?" asked the traveller. "I took it you were gathering food."

"No, sir," said the boy. His voice and eyes were older than his years. "I seek a poison to give to my mother. She rules me unkindly, and will not let me have my way in anything."

He sighed enormously. "Ah, that I might recognize instanter what may be relied on to entrain death!"

"As you wish, so be it," said the traveller, and went on, leaving the boy weeping because he realized: no matter what diet is chosen, sooner or later death ensues.

Thus, pretty much as might have been expected, the way of the traveller wound on, until that night deeper than other nights which overtook him on the flank of Rotten Tor, in which he discovered why the honest workingman at Gander's Well had carefully sought tinder to bear on his journey of a single league when it still lacked an hour or more to sundown.

And why the tinder had to be of a tree that once had drunk a wondrous spring far underground.

And also one thing far more important: why, when all about

him he saw the triumph of the homely everyday virtues, the prevalence only of commonplace vices such as laziness and greed—earnest, if any were to be had, of the impending conclusion of his task—he first should learn the flavor of the new and bitter tang that apprehension can acquire, which turns it into something cruder.

Fear.

II

TRULY THIS WAS NOT like an ordinary night! Though she was wrapped in a good plaid shawl, and had moreover mittens to her hands, the woman was dismayed by the solidity of the blackness, by the chill that bit from it through garments be they never so well woven, to the ultimate marrow. Behind her the child Nelva, whom she had not dared to leave at home, was too weary—or too cold—even to whimper.

At least, however, far ahead, there gleamed one spark: the pole-hung lamp that marked her destination.

Though going back . . .

She shivered so violently her teeth chattered. It was something to be faced, the return, and could not be helped. Bowing her head, though there was no apparent wind, she clutched her daughter's hand and hurried on.

Whoever had suffered by the coming of these unseasonable black nights to the Cleftor Fells, it wasn't Master Buldebrime, who dealt in lamps. He had doubled his production, and his sales.

Within his shop, lamps were ranked by the score—on the

adze-shapen counter facing the door that admitted clients from
the street, and on all the pale pine planks doing the duty of
shelves that lined the room wherever there was solid wall.
There was even a lamp hung on that other door, of boards
nailed to a saltire frame, which gave access to the living-quarters
of the house.

And such had been his profit recently that, even though the
shop was vacant at the moment, more than a dozen of the
lamps were shedding light.

A couple of them burned candles of good wax and tallow,
and rather more of rank stale fat. Others burned wicks float-
ing in sweet oil, but these were few, and none at all were alight
from his most expensive range, those that fed on exotic distil-
lations and dispersed into the air not only a luminance slightly
tinged with sapphire blue but also a delightful perfume. These
last had reservoirs to match their content, fine-wrought in
alabaster, amethyst, and orichalcum, and were never lighted
save for the wealthiest of customers, those apt to sniff the scent
and wave a hand and say, "I'll take as many as you have in
stock."

Cold on the road it might be, but shutters had boarded in
the shop's two streetward windows long before, so well sealed
at their edges by strips of wetted leather that the air within
was past being only warm. Now the room was hot from those
flames entrapped by clear glass chimneys, tinted crystal globes,
or shields of thin-pared horn. The air was growing rancid with
vaporized fat; on their rich diet, the flames appeared almost
starved.

Nonetheless, even now, their glimmering made the coarse
roof of overarching beams look like a mine of dismal coal illu-
mined unexpectedly by an irrupting river, that had washed a
shaft of sunshine underground and shown that there were also
jewels in the rock.

On the counter a tall time-candle, of bright red wax crossed
at thumb-joint intervals by bands of black, told that the hours
of trading for today were nearly done.

Abruptly and in unison the flames bowed, like heads of barley in a field assaulted by a storm, as the outside door slammed
open and shut. In dived the woman, her clogs announcing her

arrival on the floor flags. Forgetful on the instant of her weariness and chill, the toddler Nelva at her skirts exclaimed with ooh! and aah! at this small wonderland, so warm, so full of light. A rush of burnt-fat stink took to the outdoors like a dying man's gasp, and there was a cry from beyond the inner wall: "I come apace!"

Snuffer in hand ready to douse the time-candle and the rest, the owner of the shop appeared in a tallow-stiff smock. Shaven, his red jowls glistened as though he sweated the very fabric of his wares. He was poised to fawn, expecting one of the gentry who came hither by ordinary late in the evening, they being readier than the common sort to brave the dark, what with their covered carriages and palanquins.

But that lasted a mere eyeblink. Here was only some non-descript poor woman, likely hoping to trade some useless odds and ends against a lamp instead of purchasing one with honest currency.

"What is it you want?" he demanded.

She was not, however, quite the person he had thought her, for she snapped back in a tone as sharp as his, "What would anybody come here for except a lamp?" And added from the corner of her mouth, "Be silent, Nelva!"

The little girl complied, but her eyes remained enormously round as her gaze flicked from one to the other of the shining lights.

"Here!" the woman went on, slapping coins on the counter. "Three good coppers, as you see—what's more, the rims aren't clipped, or even worn! I need a lamp so I may go abroad by night. We keep some bees, and now and then we kill a sheep, so we have no lack of wax and fat for casting candles, and we contrive our own wicks out of rush-pith. But my man Yarn is sick, and in the dark and cold must huddle by the fire, where smoke so stings his eyes he salts his supper-dish with tears. . . . Sell me a lamp that I can carry to the field to find stray lambs or gather eggs mislaid in hedgerow roots. For the sake of my sick husband and my bairn, give me the best you can!"

Arms akimbo, she stood back. Taking up the coins, Master Buldebrime inspected them. As claimed, they were properly round and gave back to the time-candle the proper reddish

sheen. He bit each in turn, shrugged, and turned to a shelf
of his next-to-cheapest lamps. Selecting one with a thin glass
chimney, he said, "This is the best I can offer. Take it or leave it."

The woman looked it over cannily. She said, "But there's
a short candle in it, that's been lit—and Nelva and I have to
make out our homeward path!"

"Then have a brand-new candle, and my blessings," the
shopkeeper snorted, catching one up at random from a stack
and throwing the shortened one to be remelted. "For three
coppers that's the best that I can spare. I wouldn't part with
so much but that yon's a pretty child." Leaning forward on
the counter, he eyed Nelva lasciviously. "Hmm! Yes! In three-
four years you should return here. I'll prentice her to the lamp-
maker's trade. There's men aplenty who'd wed a wife with
such a profitable skill."

"None hereabout!" the woman retorted harshly. "We know
how ill you brook rivalry in your business! And we hear tales
about your apprentices, even where we live hard by Rotten
Tor. So you like girls, do you, as well as little boys?"

The shopkeeper's face darkened below the saddest ruby of
any of his lamps.

"Get out!" he rasped, and made as though to hurl his brazen
snuffer.

Though the hand that clutched the coins stayed safely on
the counter.

Once more the flames quavered as, faced with the prospect
of returning to that dreadful black and cold, Nelva objected
to the prospect of departure; shortly, however, her mother
dragged her over the threshold and the door banged shut.

Buldebrime remained for a long moment fuming as foully
as his cheapest candles, then mastered his rage and went to
bar the entrance. He made the rounds with his snuffer, and
resorted at last to his cozy living room, leaving the shop lit
only—through a skylight—by the far-off gleam of four crucial
conjunct planets wheeling downward from the zenithal line.

III

NOT RIGHT, the traveller decided—not right at all!

He stood and pondered on the flank of Rotten Tor, a louring crest so friable not even goats might climb it safely, staring in what long familiarity assured him must be the direction of Cleftor Vale. Granted that the entire valley lay in the daytime shadow of the heights, should it not now be lit at least by starshine? Come to that, was not the moon inclining towards its full?

Yet here was such blackness as only a shout might penetrate —or a scream! Like the one that had just echoed to him, in two parts: beginning with the cry of a child, continuing in a tone louder, deeper, and more heartfelt.

"Ho, that we were safe at home! Help, if there's anybody there!"

The traveller did not need to hide his smile; the blackness performed that function for him. Tapping his way with his staff, he skirted the brink of the rocky torrent which here assured the summertime vegetation of its moisture. Shortly his approach was detected by the woman who had called out.

"Ah! Friend, whoever you may be!" She caught blindly at his arm. "Save me and my daughter—take us in!"

"*I* have no lodging hereabout," the traveller said. "But you do, surely."

"What?" The woman seemed bewildered; then of a sudden recovered herself. "Why, what a fool I must be!" She went forward, groping, and in a moment was heard to knock her fists upon resounding planks. "Home!" she cried. "Oh, praise be!"

199

A door creaked on awkward hinges, and a gleam of firelight showed the outline of a cottage originally built of sturdy logs and four-square boards, that now was tilt-roofed and wore a melancholy garb of grey-green lichen. The child darted forward and threw her arms around a man who rose from a bed of coarse bags stuffed with bracken, discarding a blanket of threadbare woollen stuff, but could not speak in greeting for a cough that overcame him.

"My dear, you're safe!" he croaked when he recovered. "Oh, you should not have taken Nelva!"

"You were asleep," the woman said, embracing him. "And it's so rarely that you sleep quite sound. . . . Ah, but I'm forgetting! Yarn, this gentleman who stands at the door: he's my savior! Come in, sir—do come in!"

The traveller crossed the threshold at her bidding, with a bow.

"I was almost lost!" the woman babbled. "It was so dark—"

"But surely," Yarn began, and coughed still worse, and tried again. "But surely you went out to buy a lamp?"

"Indeed, indeed! To Master Buldebrime's—here, sir," she added to the stranger, bustling about in search of a stool while child and father sat down side by side on the crude bed, "do you make yourself comfortable, and welcome too! I'd have fallen in the gorge had you not chanced by, so completely was I lost at my own doorstep! Excuse the sparseness of our hospitality, but when I've mended the fire, if you fancy such poor fare we can offer a broth of greens, a morsel of bread with ewe-milk cheese, and—"

"But to buy a lamp, and come home in the dark!" Yarn forced that out in a single breath, before hacking into coughs anew.

"Hah!" The woman halted in the middle of the floor, where firelight showed her silhouette, and set her hands on her hips. "When I get back to town, shall I ever give Buldebrime a tongue-lashing? That lamp! That *lamp*! Here!"

She produced it from the folds of her shawl. "Why, did I not light it to see the path by when returning home? And did it not in the same moment smoke its chimney over, blacker than a barn door?"

She waved the defective item violently at her husband.

"Your pardon for my ill temper, sir," she added to the traveller. "But to be without a lamp these nights is more than a body can bear. It's as though the dark outside comes creeping in at the chinks of the wall, dulling the fireglow. Yet needs must I sometimes go about after sundown, and do I take a naked candle or a rush-dip torch the flame's light is sucked into nowhere, like drops of water on a bone-dry cloth. Now this is what to do, our neighbors say, Goodie Blanchett and Goodie Howkle and the rest: go to Master Buldebrime and buy a lamp, his are the best, we have our own and walk abroad secure at night thanks to their warm yellow shine. . . ." As she talked she was rubbing the smoked-over glass on a corner of her shawl. On the hearth damp logs sputtered a counterpoint to her words.

"I'll light it again, to prove my claim," she said, and bent to pick a splinter from the fire.

"What's worst of all," she added as she applied flame to the twisted wick, "he took coin from me for it, not a pailful of ewe's milk, or some trifle we could spare. . . . And it does this! Sir!"—rounding on the traveller—"do you not think it criminal, to take advantage of a poor soul thus?"

But the traveller was paying no attention. Gazing at the lamp-chimney, which as predicted was on the instant blearing over, he was uttering sad words within his head:

"Ah, Wolpec, Wolpec! Has it come to this?"

Once this pallid thing of grimy smoke had been an elemental he—even he—was now and then compelled to consult. There were conditions attached to such inquiry, by which he—even he—was forced to abide. Here, now, on the chimney of a common lamp, there writhed blurred characters such as formerly had expressed transcendent truths . . . but who alive could certify the meaning of such messages? Those tongues had been forgotten everywhere!

Reacting to the concentration of his gaze, the woman ventured, "Sir, you're not by any chance skilled in the repairing of lamps . . . ?"

Then, registering the fierceness of his expression, she lapsed into a puzzled silence.

Some of the old laws, it appeared, still stood, but the under-structure of them must have cracked, as after an earthquake a building may retain its general shape, yet lack huge plates of stucco from its façade and be unsafe to walk the stairways of. For this lamp was showing three truths in the ancient manner, without the ancient and obligatory rites. . . .

Of three, the first incomprehensible, in a variety of writing that creatures not quite manlike had employed to record dealings in imponderables. It had been hazarded that the records concerned a trade in souls, but that was barely an approximation. In any case, being an invention of chaos, the symbols had any value anyone cared to assign them.

And they were fading, and it was time to ask again.

"How come you to this pass?" the traveller thought.

Now, the truth debatable, in a single hieroglyph such as might have been seen on the high pillars of Etnum-Yuzup before that metropolis dissolved into dust with thunderclaps. The Grand Five Weavers had grown self-indulgent, and no longer observed the instructions they had issued to themselves in the days of the foundation of their city. This might be read plainly; the traveller read it.

One would cease.

Now for the final truth, the ineluctable . . . but the question must be aptly posed. Indeed, the traveller realized, it had better not be a question but a statement, a truth of comparable import. Within his head he framed it: "I have many names, but a single nature."

The weakening elemental understood, and on the glass appeared the characters of a poem by Shen-i-ya Eng-t'an Zwu, who sat for a thousand years beneath an elm while none could tell whether he lived or died, so perfectly was he attuned to the world around.

> *Smoke*
> *fades into the air*
> *is no more seen*

The candle-dousing winds of ages seemed to sough in the chimney of the cottage.

"Sir," the woman ventured anxiously, "you should not bother so much with our trifling problem."

"Is it not in fact a great matter for you, lacking a lamp?" The traveller did not raise his head.

The woman sighed. "Well, I must confess it is, sir. For the little one is yet too young to venture round our fields by touch, knowing the places where a hen may stray to roost or where a lamb may catch its fleece in thorns, and so dreadful is the cold once darkness falls that Yarn dare not set foot beyond the threshold lest his coughing make him tumble in a faint. . . . Yes, sir, it's true: I'd set my heart on owning a good bright clear new lamp!"

"As you wish," said the traveller, not without sorrow, "so be it."

He blew out the flame. When he cleaned the glass and lit the lamp anew, it shed a pure and grateful yellow light.

Wolpec was little, though wise; candles had sufficed to pen him. Fegrim was vast, and underlay a mountain. But the traveller had seen among the snag-toothed peaks of Kanish-Kulya how his volcano slumbered now beneath a cap of white, where once it had spluttered smoke a mile high. No ripples stirred the pool of Horimos; as for the river Metamorphia, no trace was left at all of anything whose nature had been changed by it. Housewives rinsed their laundry in the spring at Geirion, and the eldritch song that Jorkas had been used to sing was turned a lullaby with nonsense words to soothe asleep contented babes in wicker cradles. Yorbeth was gone—Litorgos—Tarambole . . . Even the names of the greatest ones: Tuprid and Caschalanva, Quorril and Lry—were one to speak them, folk would answer, "Who?"

They had retreated to fret powerless among the stars, and sometimes hurl futile spears of flame across the night . . . at which sight lovers, hand in hand, would cry, "Look, there's a star to wish on! Wish for early marriage and long happiness!" And kiss, and forget it in a moment.

Except here, and that was very strange. Disquieting! It was indeed in Cleftor country as had been described: as though the black of night could filter through the walls and dull the fire. Flames here were sullen red, and their heat was muted. This was not true of the new lamp, but there were good grounds for that.

It would be politic, the traveller reasoned, to behold the dawn.

Therefore, dissolving one of the forces that curdled the light-beams of his staff, he picked his way silently across the hut's floor, abandoning to Nelva the fleece he'd been allotted for a coverlet. Outside, the last hour of the night was oppressive with mephitic stench, as though every home in the valley had kept a fire ablaze nightlong against the mantle of blackness, and their smokes had come together in a foul miasma. Even the blade of light from his staff was foreshortened a pace or two ahead of his toes.

The trade of lamp-maker hereabouts must indeed be a profitable pursuit.

What this blackness was not was easy to define. It wasn't smoke, although much of that now mingled in it. It wasn't fog, clammy and opaque yet cleanly, being drops of water fine-divided. It wasn't cloud, which is of the same substance if more rarefied. It was—well, it was an inversion of brightness.

When dawn came, belatedly by the traveller's calculation, it behaved, moreover, in a peculiar fashion. Rather than thinning and being dispelled, as night ought to be by the rising sun, it drew in on itself, laying the countryside bare yard by yard from below, as though one could make thick tar flow uphill. And uphill was its direction, out of the vale and towards the ragged pinnacles of Cleftor Heights. There, at some point almost beyond the range of vision, it gathered itself as it were into a ball, into a spiralling cone, into a wisp . . . and nothing.

Yet it had left, over every inch of ground where it had lain, a brooding dismal aura of foreboding.

Going by ordinary ways, he later came on children turned out of the house to play, who were listlessly tossing pebbles at a target scratched on a tree-bole, and seemingly cared little whether they hit it or not; at least, none among them was keeping score.

"Who rules these lands?" the traveller inquired, and one among the children answered him.

"I think they call him Garch, sir. Would you that I run home and ask my mother? She would know."

"Thank you; the name's enough," the traveller said.

IV

AT THE FULL MOON Garch Thegn of Cleftor Heights adhered to certain customs that differed markedly from the common run of his daily business. One day before the plenilune he scarcely spoke, but locked himself away in private rooms to pore over thick tomes and crumbling scrolls; one day after, it was never sure — even to his chief counsellors and stewards, even to his sister Lady Scail — whether he would be fit to resume his normal court, in his great hall tiled with chrysoberyl slabs.

Yet and withal his was a domain envied far and wide, for by all criteria it was improbable. Though most of it was rocky and its soil was thin, its kine were famed for their fatness and the richness of their milk. Though their roots were shallow, often planted in mere crevices, never a hedge but yielded nuts, or fruit to be preserved by boiling down in honey. Though it was unpopulous, with villages few and far between, its folk were tall and strong and raised healthy children; what was more, garments elsewhere reserved to the grandest ladies might here be seen gracing a farmer's wife driving her trap to market, or her daughter on a high day bound for the wife-taking dance. Velvet and colored suede, satin and crimson plush, were donned as casually as homespun, and only at the very fringes of the Garch estates — as for example hard by Rotten Tor — did families lack for pewter spoons and china dishes to entertain the company at table.

Paradoxically, with all this the folk of the district were misliked. It was said they were overly cunning; it was said that doing business with them was like trying to stand an eel on its tail. It was further hinted that it was best not to let one's daughter marry thither, no matter how prosperous the man, for in a short while her only care for her family would be to take what advantage she could of them, and she'd have become like her neighbors, purse-mouthed, hard-eyed, and far too fond of coin.

Despite such talk, however, visitors came frequently to Garch's mansion, for purposes of trade. Notable among these, and arriving typically in the second quarter of the moon, were persons of a particular sort, who brought not conventional goods, but ideas, and treasures, and relics—it being at this specific time of the month that the thegn was readiest to receive them.

Few, nonetheless, passed the fierce initial scrutiny of his counsellors; penalties for wasting the thegn's time were severe, and all supplicants for audience must be grilled beforehand by these three. Each morning they assembled in an anteroom beside the great hall, with a scribe and a paymaster carrying a chest of coins, and confronted everyone who had come intending to trade. Often the business was quick and simple, concerning regular goods that might swiftly be bargained for, such as tapestry, or unguents, or fine handicrafts. Similarly, there were those who offered services, skill in carving or tailoring or cobblery, and were desirous to display the shield of warrant of their lord over their place of business; these were invariably permitted to undertake a trial venture for a small fixed fee—or, if they failed a first time, for no fee at all—then engaged on contract if their talents proved adequate. One of this class had, years ago, been Master Buldebrime, and now he supplied the lamps and candles for the mansion, toiling monthly uphill from the town with a selection of his choicest products.

In such cases the proceedings went slowly and involved
advance interrogation, and it was the hardiest and most venturesome of the visitors who survived such preliminaries. A
few aspirants, though, were invariably on hand.

Garch's trusted counsellors were three, as aforesaid. In a
high-backed chair of horse-bones pinned with bronze and
padded with bags of chicken-down, the old crone Roiga sat
to the left. To the right sat Garch's sister Scail, on lacquered
ivory made soft with sheep-fleece. And in the center, scorning luxury, presided one-eyed Runch on a common counting-
house stool. He wore green; Roiga, brown; the Lady Scail
affected purple. All else in the room was sterile grey, even the
table behind which they sat.

"Admit the first," said Runch in a barking voice, and alert
servants ushered in a man who wore the garb of the Shebyas,
itinerant traders whose ancestral home on the Isle of Sheb had
long gone back to yellow jungle; no one was certain why, but
enchantment was suspected. Doffing his cap, he placed on the
table an object in a small pink sack.

"Your honor, I bring a rare relic, from a city sunken in the
depths of Lake Taxhling. Had I but gold to finance such an
expedition, I'd hire divers—of whom there are as you are
doubtless aware a plenitude in that region where they gather
mussel pearls—and rake the bottom mud to haul up beyond
a peradventure many other potent articles." He coughed behind his hand and dropped his voice. "It would of course be
superfluous to mention that knowledge of an extraordinary
kind was available to the inhabitants of that city, which I'm
sure you will concede it's better not to name."

Runch looked over the relic, which was a corroded axe
blade. He said, pushing it aside, "You cannot name the city
because it isn't there and never was; Taxhling was ever bor-
dered by villages too small to deserve the epithet of town.
Besides, all magic departed from it following an earthquake
in the distant past. What you brought is part of the cargo of
a boat capsized by a storm. Go away."

"But, your honor—your grace—your highness!" the man

expostulated. The crone Roiga snapped bony fingers, and an attendant hurried him away.

"Next," she said in a voice like dry leaves rustling.

A man entered who swept the floor with a blue cloak as he bowed. "I, sir and ladies," he announced, "acquired a book at Pratchelberg. Lacking the skill to read the ancient language that it's couched in, I thought to bring it to your thegn, as being the most renowned, the most expert, the most—"

"Save your breath," murmured the Lady Scail, having turned a mere half dozen of the pages. "This text's corrupt—it looks as though the scribe was drunk—and anyway my brother has a better copy."

Protesting quite as loudly as his forerunner, the man in the blue cloak made a forced departure. To the music of his wails a third supplicant approached, offering a blue furry ball.

"This unique article," he declared, "speaks when it's gently squeezed, crying out in a small shrill voice. By repute it grew on the branches of Yorbeth, and I laid out half my lifetime savings so that it might be brought to your thegn."

Roiga accepted it and listened to its cry. She said as she cast it contemptuously to the floor, "Hah! Yes, indeed, it does cry out—by forcing air through twin taut reeds! And do you know what it says? It says, 'The man who bought me is a fool!' Now get you gone!"

"Will they never learn?" murmured the Lady Scail as this man also was frog-marched away. She had taken a tiny pad of emery and was buffing her nails, that were painted the same color as her gown. "Who remains—anyone?"

And there was a girl.

Suddenly the mild air stung their skins to rawness, like an infinity of tiny insects. Scail laid by her emery-pad, Roiga closed her thin old hands for reassurance on the table's solid edge, and Runch confirmed his balance on his stool. The newcomer stood before them in a broad hat and fur breeches and a black mail shirt that hung down to midthigh. For a long while there was utter silence.

Then, at length, she laid on the table a small packet wrapped in parchment and bound with a white ribbon. She said, "Spice."

The three counsellors inhaled as one, and it was Roiga who eventually said, "Vantcheen?"

"The best," said the girl. She was very thin, as though a skeleton had been dressed again in its skin without the underlying fat and muscle, and her eyes burned like a black fire.

"Then name your price!" cried Runch.

"Ah, yes. A price." The girl tapped one sharp front tooth with a nail even sharper. "Silver, then. Three ounces' weight. Cast in the shape of a hammerhead."

The three counsellors tensed. Lady Scail said, "As to the shaft—?"

The girl shook her head ever so slightly, and gave ever so slight a smile. She said, "I thank you for the offer, though I suspect your male companion might not"— at which Runch blanched and almost tumbled from his high stool. "But the shaft has already been—ah—ceded to me."

"Oh, but you're so young!" Roiga exclaimed. "And yet so skilled!"

"For that I would not claim the credit," the girl murmured, and turned to leave.

"Wait!" cried Lady Scail. "Do you not wish converse with my brother? It's long since one was here who proved so adept!"

"If the constellations are proper for our encounter, I shall meet the thegn," the girl replied composedly, and took from the attendant scribe a draft to cover her pay, authorizing the mansion's master smith to forge the silver hammerhead.

There was a deep silence for some while following her departure. The handle of that hammer was of a discomfortable nature; it *had* to be gristly, and some, particularly men, would call it grisly.

But to have purchased the best-quality vantcheen, and parted with mere silver in exchange . . . !

Thus they were poised, very well pleased, to adjourn for the day, the only other supplicants for audience being of the common run—disputants over boundary fences, or prospective parents-in-law come to determine the proper size of a marriage portion—when there was a furious stamping and considerable shouting beyond the door, and at the head of a gaggle of stewards, secretaries and waiting-maids their master himself came blasting into the room.

Rising to their feet, the three counsellors beheld with amazement his expression of blind rage.

"I have been cheated and deceived!" roared Garch.

By ordinary he was pretty much a fop, this lord of improbably rich estates, but now his long brown hair and beard were tousled, the laces hung down from his dark red shirt, and his fine worsted stockings slopped over the tops of his boots. To emphasize his outburst, he hammered on the table, and came near to scattering the spice.

"Search me this mansion, every nook and cranny!" he shouted. "Moreover, all the lands about! And if it be not found within the hour, send to the deceiver Buldebrime and drag him here!"

"If *what* be not found?" countered Scail, who as his sister might most freely of the three ask that simple necessary question without inflaming him to further rage.

Garch mastered himself with vast effort, drew close, and whispered in her ear. By watching the change in her face, base attendants from whom he meant to keep the detailed truth deduced at once it was a matter of grave import. Some among the best-informed put two and two together, and when a moment later they received their orders—from Scail—to bring hither all the lamps and candles that could be found, concluded it would be politic to leave in search of service with some other lord. It was, after all, a mere day and a half short of the full moon.

And many would have done so right away, had it not been for the dense dark outside . . . and, maybe, the unexpected smile that spread over Garch's face when his sister pressed the new-bought spice into his hand.

By contrast with the thegn, Master Buldebrime was in a high good humor. Walking through the back rooms of his home, that served as shop, factory and warehouse, with his own personal bright-shining lamp in hand, he no more than cuffed any of his apprentices tonight, not once employing the tawse that hung at his belt.

"Here are eleven candles almost the weight of twelve!" he

barked at one child, charged with bearing finished work from the ranked pottery molds to be checked on the steelyard—but even she and the boy who had overfilled the molds escaped with mere openhanded slaps. Satisfied that they were dutifully trimming the surplus wax to be re-melted, he continued.

"Not so lavish with that essence!" he growled at a boy engaged in adding perfumes, drop by drop, to a mix of oils for the most expensive lamps. "Don't you know it comes from Alpraphand? Hah! I've half a mind to make you walk such a distance on this floor, to brand in your memory knowledge of how far that is! Still, that would take weeks, and I'll neither feed nor clothe you 'less you're working hard enough to pay me back!"

Accordingly that apprentice too got off with a smacking.

Persuaded at length that all was well below, as much as touched the making, storing and vending of his wares, he proceeded to the upper floor. This was partitioned into three large chambers. First he came into his own, luxurious, where stood a couch upholstered in deep warm bearhide and a little girl of ten or so was industriously polishing a pier-glass.

To her, he said nothing; to himself he murmured that it was a pity she was destined for the eventual enjoyment of Lord Garch. Otherwise . . .

But the woman from Rotten Tor, who had called here this evening with her daughter, had reminded him what a miasma of scandal had already attached itself to his business. There must never be any shred of proof to back it up! If there were, respectable folk would cease to apprentice their brats with him, who kept no wife nor even serving-maid. For that reason, the two other rooms on this story could be locked at night, and the keys remained always under his hand or pillow. One room for girls, the other for boys, they were in most regards identical, each containing heaps of rags soiled by long use and troughs into which at dawn and sunset he poured bucketsful of gruel for the apprentices to lap. Now and then he also accorded them scraps of bacon and the outer leaves of cabbages: experience having shown that without a morsel of meat and a nibble of greenstuff the children grew sickly—hence, unprofitable. He tolerated the extra expense, though he did begrudge it.

The chief source of his resentment, however, so far as baseless scandal was concerned, was that he would never dare admit the real reason why he did not abuse his youthful charges. In the lands ruled by Garch, claims of unalloyed morality rang false; on the other hand, the exercise of magic was a jealously-guarded monopoly, so were he to admit the truth he would most likely be haled forth and hung from a gibbet for the crows to pluck.

One further door remained at this level, and beyond it lay his secret. He opened it with the smallest of his many keys. Revealed was a steep flight of steps, hardly more than a slanted ladder, which he climbed. Despite the effort it required to haul his bulk to the top without dropping his lamp, he was humming a cheery strain when he emerged into the attic that it led to: a large open space lighted by two dusty dormers, lately refloored with well-planed boards that did not creak.

Below, although they applied themselves to their work, the apprentices found time—as usual—to whisper and make gestures with offensive import. One boy of fourteen, bolder than the rest, well inured to being beaten for his obduracy, filched a finger-sized piece of wax and began to shape it into human form. Pausing beside him, a girl offered criticism and comment; she had been pretty before a spill of boiling tallow seared a puckered scar down her left cheek. Others gathered to see what was happening, and suggested improvements. In a little while the likeness to their master was unmistakable, and they chuckled and clutched at one another in delight.

When the doll was perfected, they hid it in a chink between the planks of the wall, to furnish more amusement at some future time.

Overhead, unaware of this, Buldebrime approached the center of his attic room. There stood a stool adjacent to a table bearing five thick books, bound in leather from unconventional sources. Also there was a brazier, and a locked aumbry with carven doors hung from a mainpost of the roof. This last the lamp-seller opened, and removed from it a number of small articles: a bunch of feathers, a bag of herbs, and some vials of powder.

Watching from deep shadow, the traveller in black repressed a sigh. He hated these hole-in-corner enchanters, not merely because they were victims of the same paradox that had misled their more distinguished predecessors—desiring to control chaos for the sake of the power to be had from it, yet anxious not to destroy it by exerting overmuch control—but also because he'd found them mostly ignorant, discourteous and braggardly. Buldebrime seemed all too typical: having learned how to make his lamps burn bright against unusual dark, he thought himself a master of all magic arts, and was restrained from boasting solely by fear of a scandal that might deprive him of apprentices.

He did not attempt to make himself known. Had Buldebrime been half the adept that he liked to think he was, he would not have needed to be told there was a Presence in the room.

The lampmaker set out what was requisite for the sorcery he intended, bar one crucial item: a candle. . . .

And then, in the instant before he discovered that that candle was not where he thought it was, there came a thunderous hammering from the entrance to the shop, followed by a shouted order.

"Buldebrime! *Buldebrime!* Open in the name of Garch, the thegn of Cleftor Heights!"

So far, so good. The traveller gave a nod and took his secret leave.

V

THERE WAS A CERTAIN SPOT, a fair sward set with rocks flat-topped as though designed expressly to be sat upon, commanding a fine view of the thegn's mansion and within lazy strolling distance of the villages nearest thereto. In any other community it might safely have been predicted that on the evening of a fine clear day, such as today had proved, local folk would tend to congregate here, bringing provender and beer and possibly a tabor and some fifes, to enjoy the pleasant outlook and reflect on their luck in serving so notably able a ruler.

Here, however, the safe prediction was that by late afternoon all who did not have utterly unavoidable business out of doors would have retreated to their homes, bolting and shuttering them against the onset of that unnatural dark which soaked up star- and firelight and bit into the bones with vicious teeth.

So indeed the case eventuated. The last herds were driven to their byres, the last flocks were folded, long before the sun touched the divided peaks of the Cleft Tor. As the shadows lengthened, the air grew thick, and a distasteful aura which had infected even the sunniest hours of the day curdled into a foretaste of the night to come.

Seated alongside a curving track, his staff across his knees, the traveller gazed towards Garch's residence. It was a handsome edifice, if uninspired. Girdling it in the place of a curteyn wall there were low-roofed outbuildings perhaps two hundred paces by a hundred, constructed of grey stone, interrupted by a gate and speckled with windows. These enclosed a courtyard above ground level, whose cobbled surface concealed dungeons and other subterranean chambers, and from the center of this yard upreared a tower, or rather frustum, its sloping sides approximating the base of a cone. There were the private quarters of the thegn. Terminating its truncated top, there was a wooden winch-house, where by shifts a score or so of muscular deaf-mutes waited the signal to save Garch the effort of climbing stairs, by hauling on ropes to hoist a kind of palanquin steadied by greased poles and capable of being halted at any floor of the tower.

As the traveller studied the mansion, he saw servants emerge to set torches by the gate, though considerable time remained before sundown.

Eventually there came in sight around the bend of the road a sort of small procession. It began with a striding man-at-arms, staring suspiciously this way and that. It continued with a personage in the garb of a Shebya: blue cap, green coat and hose, black boots and silver spurs. He rode astride a palfrey. Then came a girl on foot, attired in pink as a page, but bosomed too conspicuously for there to be much chance of mistaking her sex, leading the first of a pair of pack mules whose wooden saddles were half empty, and lastly another man-at-arms leading the second mule. Such was a common spectacle in any well-governed realm; the Shebyas were the greatest traders of the age, and even the poorest among them possessed at least a couple of beasts and an attendant.

The leader of this party, however, was clearly not overjoyed with whatever business he had most recently transacted. He frowned as he rode, and uttered not-infrequent objurgations.

Which he redoubled for fluency and loudness when, on spotting the black-clad figure by the track, the leading man-at-arms dropped his spear to an attack position and cried, "Halt!" The palfrey obeyed with extraordinary promptness, and thereby almost spilled his rider to the ground.

"Good morrow," said the traveller mildly. "Sir, would you instruct your man to put up that overeager point? It's aligned upon a portion of my carcass that I am anxious to preserve intact."

"Do so," the Shebya commanded, and pulled a face. "Forgive him," he continued, doffing his cap. "But we're collectively upset, I'd have you know, and extremely edgy, as it were. We've done so poorly on our errand to this famous thegn—of which we had, admittedly, high hopes."

"The saddles of your mules seem light enough," the traveller observed.

"Oh, ordinary pack-goods one can dispose of anywhere," the Shebya said. His keen eyes were fixed on the traveller's curious staff, and one could almost hear the logical, though erroneous, deductions he was making. "But . . . Well, sir, might I hazard a guess that you too are bound to call on Garch?"

"That possibility," the traveller conceded, "should not be totally ruled out."

"I thought so!" the other exclaimed, leaning forward on his palfrey's withers. "Might I further suggest that you would welcome information concerning the thegn's alleged willing-ness to purchase—ah—intangibles and other rare items at a respectable price?"

"It would be rash to deny that I have heard reference to some such habit of his."

"Then, sir, save your trouble. Turn about, and evade the oncoming night—for, truly, the nights they have hereabout are not of the common cozy kind. The tales you've likely heard are arrant nonsense."

"Nonsense, you say?"

"Yes indeed!" The Shebya grew confidential, lowering his voice. "Why, did I not bring him an object virtually *beyond* price? And did I not in the upshot have to peddle it door to door, for use in some lousy household enchantment instead of the grand ceremonials of an adept? That it should keep company with pollywogs and chicken-blood—faugh! I ask you! Would not dragon-spawn have been meeter?"

"And was the article efficacious?" the traveller asked, hiding a smile.

The Shebya spread his hands. "Sir, that is not for me to determine. Suffice it to say that tomorrow will tell. For the sake of insurance, as it were, against the risk that the purchaser may prove inadequately skilled in conjuration to derive maximum benefit from her acquisition, I purpose to be some distance hence." His mask of annoyance, willy-nilly, gave place to a grin; it was granted by everyone that, rogues though the Shebyas might be, they were at least engaging rogues.

"Howbeit," he appended, "do take my advice. Don't go to Garch expecting to sell him remarkable and unique artifacts or data at such price as will ensure comfort to your old age. Apart from all else, the mansion is in a turmoil. Someone, so to speak, would appear to have laden the thegn's codpiece with live ants, and he gibbers like a man distraught, ordering all who displease him to be shortened by the head without appeal. Another excellent reason for departure—which, sir, if you will forgive the briefness of this conversation, inclines me forthwith to resume my journey."

After the Shebya and his companions had gone, the traveller remained. The air thickened still further. It grew resistant to the limbs, like milk on its way to becoming cheese. Lost on a high outcrop, a kid bleated hopelessly after its nanny. Chill that one might have mistaken for agonizing frost laid a tight hold on the land, yet no pools crisped with ice. The traveller frowned and waited longer still.

At last, over the high tower of the mansion, the coffin black of night started to appear: solid-seeming blotches on the sky. At roughly the same time, there were noises to be heard along the road again, coming from the direction which the Shebya and his troupe had taken. Into sight came a party of hurrying horsemen, full-armed, glancing apprehensively at the gathering dark. Some had equipped themselves with torches, and kept making motions toward their flint and steel.

In their midst, tied face to tail on a dirty donkey, was Buldebrime moaning and crying out, hands lashed at his back and his grease-bespattered smock in rags.

Some distance behind, unable to keep pace, a furious driver cursed a pair of shaggy-fetlocked horses drawing a cart loaded until the springs sagged with candles, lamps, and articles in bags whose nature could not clearly be discerned.

Of itself, the parade might have been amusing. Given the circumstances which had led to it, the traveller could not find it other than appalling.

The darkness spread, and yet it did not move. Rather, it occurred, moment by moment, at places further from its source.

VI

"BE CALM!" Lady Scail adjured her brother, for the latest of countless times.

"Be calm?" he echoed, mocking her. "How can I? Are they not deserting us, the traitors, deserting *me* who won them prosperity from this lean harsh country and made them the envy of folk in richer lands?"

It was true: news was arriving every few minutes of some trusted serving-man, soldier or steward who had surreptitiously crept away from the household.

"Is it not, moreover," Garch pursued, "the night before full moon? At midnight must I not go into the prescribed retreat? And how can we tell as yet how greatly we've been deceived by Buldebrime? Perhaps he miscalibrated our time-candles, so we'll have no means to judge the proper hour!"

Admittedly, it was impossible to make astronomic observations under such dark as this.

Nonetheless, Scail blasted the same injunction at him, saying, "You fool, you have to keep your head at any cost! Countless enchanters, so they say, have met their doom because an elemental took advantage of just that weakness in their character!"

Sweating, gulping draft after draft of wine to lend him courage, he did his best to comply, since reason was on her side. However, self-mastery was hard. The mansion—and not only it but the entire surrounding countryside—was aquiver. The jagged range of Cleftor Heights was thrumming to a soundless vibration of menace, as though some being incarcerated in a restless star had found the means to transmit terror down a shaft of light and struck the bedrock into resonating the keynote of a symphony of disaster, against the advent of the instrumentalists.

Moreover, it is not good for one who invokes the forces of chaos to pay any attention whatsoever to reason. . . .

"Where's Roiga?" Garch demanded of a sudden.

"Where she should be: making ready in your room."

"And Runch?"

"They called him to the gate a while ago. They've sighted the party bringing Buldebrime."

"Then I'll go down to the dungeons," Garch declared, and drained his goblet. "I must be first to learn what that traitor's done!"

There was routine in this mansion, as in the household of any great lord, and to outward appearance it was being maintained. At the intersection of two echoing corridors the traveller in black saw proof of this. Thump-thump down the passages to the beat of drums came provisions for the nightly company at dinner: pies stuffed with game, so heavy two men staggered under the load, and the whole roasted haunches of oxen and sheep; then trays of loaves; then serving-girls with jugs of wine and beer, and butlers carrying fine white linen napkins on their arms, and boys with ewers and basins that the diners might wash their hands in scented water, and harpists, and flautists, and a female dwarf. This last hobbled awkwardly in a floor-length gown, designed to make her trip often on its hem for the amusement of the gathering.

One could not reasonably foresee there being much laughter in the banquet-hall tonight. The stones from which the building was constructed shared the incipient convulsions of the landscape, and overmuch dust danced in the light of the torches.

Intermittently, from beneath the floor, issued screams.

Orderly, with professional niceness, the least spoken-of among Garch's retainers—Tradesman Humblenode, the torturer—had set out the various equipment of his calling: here whips and fetters, thumbscrews there; tongs, knives and nooses at another place; and in the center of all a brazier, at which a little dirty boy worked a blacksmith's bellows in a vain attempt to make the fuel burn as bright as was required. Even here beneath the courtyard, where the walls oozed continual damp, the pervasive obliterating light-absorption of the strange night might be perceived.

At the mere sight of Humblenode's instruments Buldebrime had collapsed into snivelling, and it was long after the thegn's intrusion into the dungeon that they contrived to make him utter coherent words.

"No, I did not filch any such candle! I have no knowledge of enchantment—none!"

"Try him with a little red iron," Garch proposed, and Tradesman Humblenode set a suitable tool to the fire.

"Have pity, have pity!" Buldebrime whimpered. "I swear by Orgimos and Phorophos, by Aldegund and Patrapaz and Dencycon—!"

"I thought you had no knowledge of enchantment?" murmured Garch, and gestured for Humblenode's assistants to stretch the lamp-seller on a rack.

But in a short space from the application of the first iron he escaped into unconsciousness, and not all Humblenode's art sufficed to waken him.

"Is Runch meantime testing all the lamps and candles that were brought from his shop?" Garch remembered to ask, somewhat belatedly. He had given that instruction, and not checked that it was carried out—though Runch and Roiga, of all his retinue, had most to lose by neglecting his requirements.

"I come from him, sir," a nervous waiting-maid reported, who was trying not to look at the limp body of Buldebrime, or anything else present in the cell. "He assures you he has tested every one, and whatever you are seeking isn't there."

Garch drew himself up to his full height. "So the treacherous lamp-maker has tricked me," he muttered. "Can he not be forced awake by midnight?"

"By no art known to me," said Humblenode apologetically. It was the first time he had failed his master. He braced himself as though to endure treatment after his own style in consequences.

But Garch spun on his heel and strode away.

He came upon Runch, together with his sister and attendants, at the head of the dank noisome stairway to the dungeons; his private means of vertical transportation did not, for logical reasons, descend to that level.

"Have you succeeded?" Scail demanded.

"Failed!"

"And time is fast a-wasting," muttered Runch.

"What must be done, must be done," Garch answered. "Prepare me for my watch alone."

"But surely tonight it was imperative to conjure Wolpec, and ask his earnest of your ultimate success!" Under her face-mantling layers of rouge and powder, the Lady Scail turned pale.

"What's to be done will be done now!" Garch snapped. "Like it or not! You have tomorrow's daylight to run away by, if that's your plan. For the moment, leave me be!"

Without so much as a brotherly embrace, let alone that other kind which had in the past lent crucial potency to his doings, he pushed by them both and was gone.

Under the supervision of the crone Roiga, servants had toiled to bring necessary articles into the cabinet she was making ready. It lacked windows, naturally; what air there was must seep through tiny crevices, and about each had been carefully inscribed a line of minuscule writing in an obsolete syllabary. It lacked furniture, too; in place of which it was hung with curtains of goat-hide, woven marshgrass and the plaited hair of murdered girls. There was a mirror in the center of its floor, which was as true a circle as the mason's art could contrive, but that mirror was cracked across, and the traveller knew with what the blow would have been struck: a human thighbone. He had been aware that enchantments of this caliber were still conducted, but in this case at least one unqualifiedly essential preliminary had been totally neglected.

Patience.

Rat's-bane and wolf-hemp; powder of dragon-bone and mullet-roe; candied mallow and murex pigment; vantcheen spice . . . Yes, all the ancient indispensables were here. Bar one. Bar the one that mattered more than anything.

The traveller withdrew into dismal contemplation.

Then, finally, Garch came, pale and trembling but determined not to let his companions recognize the full depth of his terror, to perform the rites required of him as lord of this land which yielded more than its proper share of good things. He was correctly robed in a chasuble the hue of blood; he correctly wore one shoe of hide and one of cloth; he correctly bore the wand, the orb and the sash; and the proper symbols, although awkwardly, had been inscribed on his right palm with indigo and henna.

He entered by the door of ashwood clamped with brass, and it was closed behind him with the traditional braided withes: at the height of his eyes, at the height of his heart, and at the height of his genitals. That done, Runch and Roiga and Scail perforce withdrew. Unless they chose to run away, indeed, by tomorrow's daylight, the process was in train and they were to be dragged with it.

Even running away might not help.

As for the traveller in black, he had no choice. This was intrinsically a part of that which bound him. From this moment forward, he was compelled to remain. Here was no petty hearthside conjuration, to be laughed at when it failed and neglected thereafter; here was no witty tampering with the course of natural events, such as certain happy enchanters had counted a fair reward for the relief of boredom; here was no ritual from which profit to others might ensue, such as the merchant-enchanters of a bygone age had employed to make their cities prosperous.

No, those trivialities could be ignored. Here, though, was a ceremony so elaborate, so pregnant with possibility, and so absolutely devoid of *probability* that its very name, regardless of what language it was uttered in, sent shivers down the spines of uncomprehending listeners. Here, set on foot in a selfish lordling's mansion, was such a pattern as had not been undertaken since the epoch of the Grand Five Weavers and the Notorious Magisters of Alken Cromlech: the most ancient, the most arcane, the most honorable appellation of the Ones Who—

The traveller froze the progress of his mind. Almost, he had recited the full title to himself. And were *he* to do so, all—all—everything would be eternally lost.

If it were not already lost. He feared it was.

VII

THE LADY SCAIL slept but ill that night, and when her shoulder was gently touched at last by the maid who attended her in her chamber, she rolled her face fretfully back into her satin pillows.

"Fool!" she snapped. "I said to waken me at dawn! I'll have your head for disturbing me when it's still dark!"

Indeed, across the windows a pall of utter lightlessness was spread.

"But, madam," whispered the poor girl, "according to our time-candles dawn should have befallen an hour ago. Yet the sky remains like pitch!"

Lady Scail sat up on the instant. Through the opened shutters she saw the truth of the maid's assertion. Rising from her night-couch, she exclaimed in wonder.

"Why—why, that bodes success in spite of all! Go rout out Runch and Roiga, and bid them meet with me at once!"

Unprecedentedly, not waiting to be handed her daytime garments, she threw aside her sleeping-gown and struggled by herself into a creased chemise.

On being awoken, Roiga trembled with delight and expectation. She had spent weary decades in a worn-out body, with her knees cracking from the rheumatism and her eyes returning blurred images of the world. Now within her shrivelled bosom her heart beat hammerwise at the impending prospect of repurchased youth. She hungered—no! She lusted after what she could recall but not repeat!

It was the same for one-eyed Runch: still a mighty man to outward view, scorning the luxury that his companions loved and affecting the disciplined, hardy habits of a soldier accustomed to camping in a field after marching all day through sleet and hail. Therefore he reposed at night on a simple bed of planks, with but one blanket over him.

But during the past few years he had more and more often failed to pleasure the girls he summoned to his spartan couch, until at last he had been unable to endure further humiliation and took to sleeping alone.

The promise of being able to rectify that . . . !

These three, however—and perhaps Garch himself, but none could certify what was transpiring in his secret room— were the only persons in the whole of the Cleftor lands who found any semblance of joy wherewith to greet the advent of this amazing and unprecedented . . . day? Well, "day" it should indeed have been by rights, and everywhere there should have been the normal daily bustle: the younger children playing by the doorway, the older dispatched to the dame-school with their slates and pencils; the farmers bound to market hauling their travoises laden with cheese and bacon, their wives plucking geese or hunting eggs . . .

But over all the country from Deldale to Herman's Wynd, and back again from Contrescarp clear to the Ten Leagues' Stone, at Poultry Rock and Brown Hamlet and Legge, at Yammerdale and Gallowtree and Chade, at Swansbroom and Swingthrimble and Slowge, it was dark until what should have been high noon.

And when the light eventually came, it was the wrong sort of light.

It was the sickly greyish glow of chaos, that bleached all color into the dullness of ash.

Now the mountains showed deformed, like mutant fungi; now the trees, still vaguely visible, stood rigid as parodies in a picture, and the random disposition of their branches seemed to summate the entire gestural vocabulary of obscene signs such as might be made with upraised fingers. Watching the changing sky in high delight from the vantage point of the tower's solar, Roiga and Runch and Scail shouted in succession for the best wine, the richest mead, the finest delicacies that the stores could offer, by way of pre-celebrating their anticipated triumph. The obscurity of night and morning had retreated to the fringes of the Cleftor domain, and now it was as though a tunnel had been opened, vertically to the frontiers of the sky, for the beings from beyond to make a grand re-entry to their former state.

But the servant-maids gawped and gaped and rubbed their ears as they came and went, for there was a dullness to their hearing that occasionally attained an ache, and there was a stale taste in all mouths which twice made Runch accuse a waiting-wench of giving him vinegar, not wine, and a dragging heaviness oppressed all bodies. Yet for the most part those three frenetic counsellors—if no one else—were able to ignore it, and drank toast after toast to the wonderful skills of Garch their thegn.

It was not until they were three parts drunken that they realized there was another in the solar apart from the servants they had bidden to attend them.

"Who's that?" cried Scail, and slopped wine down her dress in haste to look over her shoulder.

"Oh—oh!" Roiga moaned, and would have shrunk into hiding like a mouse scuttling to its hole.

"Declare yourself!" shouted Runch, rising and drawing the sword he always wore.

"Here I am," the intruder said, black cloak swishing as he strode forward to the tap-tap measure of his staff. "Put up that blade, for it's no protection against the doom that's coming on you."

Runch hesitated, and the swordpoint he had presented to the traveller's chest wavered back and forth. He said, "Who . . . ?"

"One who has many names and yet a single nature!"

They were thunderstruck on the instant. Dropping her wine-mug, Scail whimpered, "But I thought—"

"Did you?" the traveller snapped. "Yes, I can believe that you must have regarded my existence as so much superstition, and your brother likewise. Else you'd have buckled to like ordinary sensible folk, and taken what was to hand and made the most of it. Instead of which . . . Do you not know who wait admission to this place?"

Uncertain, but feigning bravado out of shame at her fit of cowardice, Roiga said bluffly, "Why, of course. Have we not agreed to call on Tuprid?"

"Tuprid who takes pleasure only in destruction, whom I saw snuff a star as men would snuff a candle, that he might witness the dying agony of the creatures on its planets as they froze into everlasting ice! And who else?"

"Why, Caschalanva, naturally!" Runch exclaimed.

"He who prefers fire to Tuprid's cold! They're ancient rivals. Each struggles to outdo the other in causing pain. And with them?"

"Quorril," muttered Scail, and began to sound a fraction nervous, which though well justified was a belated sign.

"Whose diet is souls," said the traveller. "And Lry as well?"

They all three nodded.

"To whom," he concluded, "love is hate—who breeds discord and warfare like the plague. And you believe these to be the only ones your brother has invoked?"

There was a heartbeat's worth of silence.

"It was all that we agreed he should invoke," Scail said at length. "It's with those four that we struck our formal bargain."

"Bargain!" The traveller gave a sad laugh.

"Why, certainly! Do they not owe us toll, for opening the road back to where they once ruled?" She was on her feet, facing him defiantly. "Should they not be grateful?"

"Yes! Is it not a trifle, in view of such grand service, that they should restore my manhood?" Runch demanded. And—

"Will they not give me back my youth?" shouted Roiga.

At the same moment there was a shifting underfoot, as though the land had taken on colossal weight, and their converse with the traveller in black was instantly forgotten. They rushed to the windows and peered out, this way and that, striving to catch a glimpse of whatever had descended to the earth.

"Oh, my wonderful brother!" Scail cried. "Had I but the *half* of his skills!"

"Well, well!" said the traveller, and then again: "Well, *well!* As you wish, so be it!"

None of them heard him. Nor did they hear the later whisper that echoed from the stone walls following his departure, which sounded a little like:

"Now why did I not think of that before?"

IX

THIS THEREFORE WAS THE MANNER of the coming back of the former Great Ones to the world. And it was not entirely to their liking.

* * *

Left alone in the stock-depleted house of Buldebrime, the gaggle of apprentices had at first been worried and afraid; then the boy of fourteen who had conceived that mocking doll sought to calm the youngest of his companions by producing it again, and they dissolved into laughter as he forced it through absurd motions by heating it so the limbs could be deformed without breaking. As well as making them bolder, laughter recalled them to routine. They fed themselves, and then, since no master was present to forbid them, they made free of the house, tumbling together in many enjoyable games until sleep overtook them.

On the morrow, however, they were frightened anew by the curious unprecedented length of the darkness that enveloped the neighborhood, and moreover they were hungry, because last night they had eaten their fill from the supplies in the pantry. For most of them it was the first time in months that they had had a square meal; so nothing was left but crumbs.

They hunted high and low by the wan light of such candles as they had managed to make for themselves after Buldebrime's stock had been confiscated by Garch's men, and ultimately found a way to prize off the padlock blocking access to the attic room. In company of the girl with the scarred face, the leading boy braved the ladderlike steps and looked around the shadowed books and mystic articles with frank amazement.

"Would that I knew what all these things are for, and could employ them!" said the girl.

The traveller spoke soft words, unnoticed, in a corner.

In the increasing chill of their hut by Rotten Tor, little Nelva and her mother listened in agony to the racking coughs the cold inflicted upon Yarn.

"Oh, Mother!" cried the bairn, seeing how the fire faded and gave off no heat. "Would I knew what the nice man with the black cloak did, to make the lamp burn brightly! Then would I do it to the logs, and we would all be warm!"

The traveller again spoke unheard words, and went his way.

*   *   *

Trapped by the incredible darkness in a very bad inn, the Shebya trader scratched his flea-bites and wrangled with the landlord, claiming that anyone who offered such hard beds and such foul beer had no right to the regular score from his clients. At length, losing temper, he shouted out aloud.

"Ho, that I knew a way to rid the world of greed like yours, that turns one's belly sour with rage! Ho, that I dealt only with folk as honest as myself, having codes and principles that require strict adherence to a contract!"

He was exaggerating just a smidgin; nonetheless, as all agreed, the Shebyas were on the square, though a hint of sleight-of-mind might sometimes afford them the better of a trade with anyone less subtle.

Chuckling, the traveller tapped his staff against the wall.

He wondered how it was faring with Garch Thegn of Cleftor Heights.

And the answer, framed in brief, was—not so well.

Down to him came the powers to which he'd bowed, weary of long conjurations, but content inasmuch as all had said to him, "We'll go see first that you have kept your word, and then we'll talk of settling our bargain!"

Which, according to the books wherein Garch reposed most trust, was as fair an answer as they'd ever given anyone.

So into the nervous night he waited on their presence, and ultimately at the moment which—said a well-measured time-candle, if no visible stars—corresponded with the hour of the full moon, he rose expectantly from his discomfortable position in the middle of his cracked mirror.

One came of the Four, and only one, and in such rage as made the walls shake and the tower tremble. And reached out for Garch with impalpable but cruel claws.

Because . . .

That elemental, Tuprid, who had snuffed stars, had gone to see first of the places in his allegedly restored domain the nearest to a star, a place of light: to wit, a lamp-maker's shop. And there had found awaiting him a little girl, scar-faced,

beside whom a boy clutched her hand to loan her courage,
chanting at a candle they had brought, somewhat after the
shape of a human being, and compelling it to burn against the
fiercest orders of the visitor. Below, the other children cried,
and she thought of them, and made her efforts double, and
in the upshot melted a maker of great darkness into shapeless
wax dribbling across a book bound in human skin.

After that, very suddenly, the moon could be viewed
through the skylight.

Also the elemental Caschalanva, who preferred the taste of
fire to that of ice, had gone down by the bitter vales under
Rotten Tor, and a little girl who wished desperately to make
the logs burn brighter had sensed in a bout of inspiration precisely what was needful to be done. . . .

And in an inn where fleas plagued the customers, the being
Lry who fostered dissension found a predilection towards
greed that was emanating from the spot with such force as
gales have that choose a mountain-range for organpipes. Greed
being among the chiefest of his tools, he snatched at it—and
when it dissipated fractionally after, upon the granting of the
Shebya's wish, he was swept along with it into nowhere.

Whereupon, learning of the fate of his companions that were
a good deal more than merely companions, Quorril returned
to cry that they were cheated, and—souls being his diet—seized
Garch's with a snatch of an immaterial claw that laid wide open
the wall of his secret room, releasing potent fumes. The high
tower of the mansion tumbled down, its foundations changed
to mud and sand.

Among the ruins, with her dying breath, the lady Scail called
down a doom on Quorril for what he had done to her brother,
and—she being now dowered, as she had desired, with the
half of Garch's skills, and in particular that half which concerned the binding, rather than the releasing, of elementals—
that being ceased his flight towards the sky, and perforce joined
her, and Runch, and Roiga, buried forever beneath that stack
of masonry.

* * *

"Where let them rest," the traveller said contentedly, having viewed all this from the vantage of the same sward where he had conversed with the Shebya.

"And Buldebrime, and Tradesman Humblenode," said a quiet voice beside him. He had not expected to be alone at such a moment; he did not look round. "And many more!"

"And many less guilty, Highness," he appended. "Inasmuch as 'guilt' has any meaning to Yourself. Yet none of them entirely innocent. Willing, at least, to serve a lord whose power was drawn from chaos, it being apparent to any commonsensical mind that no mortal force could make his barren land so wealthy. Equally, prepared to apprentice children to masters who starved and beat them, for the sake of having them put to a supposedly profitable trade. . . ."

He shrugged, both hands clasping his staff. "No matter, though," he concluded. "Has it not all come to a most tidy end?"

There was a silence. Also it was dark here. But it was the regular honest dark of a spring night around moonset: nothing worse.

"An end," the quiet voice said meditatively. "Yes, perhaps it is an end. It might as well be. . . . You know, my friend and brother, my child and self, there's something very curious about what has transpired!"

"Tell me," the traveller invited, who now knew in any case the most important motive that had guided his existence. Still, there were degrees of importance, and even a triviality might provoke interest.

"Of all the qualities that I endowed you with," the calm voice said, "the most potent has proved to be a certain witty elegance. A . . . a neatness, a sense of practical economy!"

"I've fostered it," the traveller agreed. "Having but one nature, I must needs make the most of what I had, and that aspect of me seemed most diametrically opposed to the extravagance and wastefulness of chaos. My conclusion, I submit, was the correct one." He gestured with his staff to encompass the barely-seen landscape. "Was it not that mode of thinking

which reduced the opportunities of access for the Four Great
Ones to these few should-be-barren acres?"

"Yes, it was."

"And was that not the designated purpose of my being?"

There was no answer. After a while the traveller said, "I'm
sorry. You must be feeling grievous loss."

"I?" Beside him the One Who had assigned him to his task—
She, the Genetrix and the Generatrix, come to witness this final
confrontation in the sole aspect he had left to Her, the guise
of a tall pale girl too thin to be alive and credible—shook back
long locks beneath a wide-brimmed hat. "Loss of the other
natures that were mine? Why, not at all! Is it not the goal and
purpose of the universe that all things shall ultimately have
a single nature? I know that to be true, for *I* decreed it."

This was what they had not realized at Cleftor Heights: that
Tuprid and Caschalanva, Quorril and Lry, and moreover Wolpec
and Yorbeth and Farchgrind and Fegrim and Laprivan of the
Yellow Eyes, and all the countless roster of those elementals,
were the fellow natures of the One Who had conceived them
in the Age of Chaos; then wearied of the instability of Her
creation, and ordained an age in which no being should possess
more than one nature.

And had sent forth a personage with many names as earnest
of that eventual occurrence.

Accordingly the last remaining nature of that One spoke
with the traveller and sounded weary.

"So here I stand, my friend who are myself and yet my
opposite, to link with you like the interlocking of a pair of
hands. What remains to me is what you never had; what remains to you is what I never could have. But after all these
aeons you must understand that."

The traveller nodded, and She heaved a sigh.

"Hah, yes, old friend, my age is past—past like that unnatural
night which will nevermore be seen in Cleftor's vales. Eternity at last has found its end, because the mightiest powers of

chaos have been tamed. And with what little snares were they entrapped! The wish of a child to help her mother; the distaste of apprentices for their cruel master; the annoyance of a pedlar-man; and the love of a sister for her stupid brother!"

"Then my time too is past," the traveller said, ignoring that recital of his tricks-to-triumph—which was just, for all he had was in Her gift. "And . . . and I'm not at all sorry. I was almost coming to miss the enemies I matched against in former ages. You could have undermined me by that weakness."

"I could." The answer was predictable. She *could*—everything. Now, however, it was not a question of "could" but "would," and the time for willing chaos had gone by.

More silence intervened. The traveller stretched and yawned.

"I long for rest," he said. "But—one more thing. Who is to come after us?"

"Let him decide who he is," said the pale girl, and took him by the hand that lacked the staff. Turning, they went together into absence.

ABOUT THE AUTHOR

Winner of the Hugo and Nebula awards for science fiction, John Brunner has been one of the more original and compelling voices in fantastic literature for more than three decades. His novel *Stand on Zanzibar* (1968) won the Hugo Award for Best Science Fiction Novel. Among his numerous works are such highly regarded novels as *The Whole Man*, *The Jagged Orbit*, and *The Squares of the City*. He has also won the British Science Fiction Award. His range has always been great, his ideas original, his approach to each new work something unexpected.